the Anatomy of Curiosity

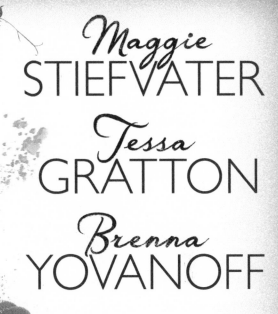

Maggie
STIEFVATER

Tessa
GRATTON

Brenna
YOVANOFF

the Anatomy of Curiosity

carolrhoda LAB
MINNEAPOLIS

Carolrhoda Lab™ is a trademark of Lerner Publishing Group, Inc.

Carolrhoda Lab™
An imprint of Carolrhoda Books
A division of Lerner Publishing Group, Inc.
241 First Avenue North
Minneapolis, MN 55401 USA

For reading levels and more information, look up this title at www.lernerbooks.com.

The images in this book are used with the permission of: © Olena Chernenko/E+/Getty
Images (flower explosion); © Katie Edwards/Getty Images (birds); © iStockphoto.com/
HiBlack (floral design); © iStockphoto.com/_zak 9 (frame); © iStockphoto.com/IADA
(octopus).

Main body text set in Janson Text LT Std 11/16.5.
Typeface provided by Linotype AG.

Library of Congress Cataloging-in-Publication Data

The anatomy of curiosity / by Tessa Gratton, Maggie Stiefvater, Brenna Yovanoff.
    pages cm
   ISBN 978-1-4677-2398-5 (lb : alk. paper) — ISBN 978-1-4677-8812-0 (eb pdf)
   1. Fiction—Authorship. 2. Young adult fiction, American. 3. Creation (Literary, artistic,
etc.) 4. Young adult fiction—Authorship. 5. American fiction—21st century. I. Gratton,
Tessa, author. II. Stiefvater, Maggie, 1981– author. III. Yovanoff, Brenna, author.
PN3355.A67 2015
808.3—dc23   2014046862

Manufactured in the United States of America
1 – BP – 7/15/15

to Andrew Rarre

INTRODUCTION

There are two ways to read this book. You can read it merely as three pieces of fiction from three different authors, or you can read it as a book about three different approaches to writing fiction.

If it's the first, you can skip this introduction. We'll see you on the other side!

If it's the second, read on. (We tried to be as spoiler-free as possible in our discussions of *how* and *why* we wrote these stories, but if you dread the slightest spoiler, we recommend you read the stories themselves before the commentary!)

Although this is a book on methods of writing fiction, it is not a book on *the* method of writing fiction. We—Tessa, Brenna, Maggie—are each professional novelists, but we approach writing in different ways. This book is meant to illuminate just three of the infinite ways to get to *The End*.

We meant for this book to answer the most common writing questions we are asked:

1) Where do you get your ideas?
2) Why do you pick one idea over another?
3) How do you go from idea to book?
4) How much do you plan before you begin?
5) Where do you start?
6) How do you come up with characters?
7) How do you write description?
8) How do you invent a new world?
9) How do you know when the draft is done?
10) How do you deal with writer's block?
11) Do you revise while you write?
12) How do you know what to edit?
13) How do you deal with doubt?

We didn't want to write a book that told writers our answers to these questions. We wanted to write a book that *showed* the answers to the questions. Instead of making the answers theoretical, we wanted a book that would demonstrate how we made our creative decisions, solved problems, and brought an idea from spark to bonfire.

In order to show our process, we each wrote a story for the book, keeping notes on the idea forming, character building, and world creation as we did. Then we critiqued each other's stories—just as we do with our novels—and incorporated those revisions into our stories. We're presenting all of that here as thoroughly as we can manage.

Because we're three very different writers, with very different work methods and, equally importantly, very different priorities for what we want out of fiction, both the stories and the processes are strikingly different.

Maggie's story, "Ladylike," is a reflection of the place her stories begin and end: character.

Tessa's story, "Desert Canticle," shows how important world building is in both her process and end result.

Brenna's story, "Drowning Variations," demonstrates how her priority remains with the idea.

IDEAS

Brenna

I'm kind of like some hypothetical structure made entirely of ideas—like a tiny candy pig made of marzipan. Except shaped liked me. Made of ideas.

Maggie

When writers reply, "You can find ideas anywhere," I reckon they really mean "prompt," not "idea." Anything can prompt a story. But ideas—viable ideas, ideas you can really run with for an extended piece of fiction—have to mean something to you personally. They're a question that's been resonating inside you, a fight with a friend you need to understand, a fairy tale you've loved since you were little. A story doesn't need to contain all of you but it has to hold some of you, or it's not going to be a very good story.

Tessa

Idea for me nearly always arrives in the form of world—ideas are what-if questions: What if roadside bombs were magical? What would that world look like? Wow, Viking culture and modern American warrior culture are so similar! What if Viking gods were real and founded the USA? What would that world look like?

I love world building and the process of exploring those kinds of questions in experimental ways so much that I could make any world idea viable if I chose to. So what makes me choose? The transformation of an idea from a *world idea* into an *idea of change*. The vehicle for that is always me creating a character who will/can directly affect and change that world. It sounds grandiose and epic, and it can be depending on the scope of the story, but it doesn't have to be. The idea of change can be small and metaphorical, and it should be both internal to the character and reflected in external world changes.

I know I have moved on from a world idea to an actual, viable story idea when I can say, "Here is this world, and here is how this character will change it."

CHARACTERS

Maggie

Characters are people. Real people have complex motivations for their actions—motivations that are neither good nor bad until shoved up against someone else's motivations and actions. They have complex and contradictory hopes and fears. They have pimples and tics, words they always say and words they would never say. And these specific attributes must follow each other naturally—there's no point saying a character always wears blue shoes and enjoys tennis unless the reader also understands how those facts are intrinsic to their personality and upbringing. A character plays a role in the story, yes, but the character should also be *more* than that role: a real person.

Tessa

Characters are born out of their specific world and circumstances. Characters must want something. What makes a character a hero or protagonist is that their needs and desires create the conflict that will drive the story. And they change by the end.

Brenna

If you ask Tessa and Maggie what a typical Brenna character looks like, they would probably say, "Weird, misanthropic weirdos who are dysfunctional and strange. Also, weird." This is approximately true. My first-draft people are prickly and hard to like. Sometimes they swear a lot. They would not make good social workers or class presidents. Later, I take them apart in little revision-pieces, looking for something lovable. My goal is always figuring out how to make them into the truest, most interesting versions of themselves. Only, in a way that makes other people want to be in the same room with them.

WORLD

Tessa

The world is everything. Literally. It is the ground
your character walks on, the air she breathes; it is
her name and her parents' names, religious beliefs,
political situation, school system, how she buys cable
TV, the Internet, architecture and plumbing and types
of flowers, if the roads are made of asphalt or gravel
or dirt or if there are no roads at all. World is dialect
and dialogue; it's race and creed and nationalism and
ethnicity; and it is *how all those things affect everything
else.* It is sexuality and gender and, more importantly,
how different sexualities are treated or seen (or
unseen); it is whether gender is recognized apart from
biology and how. World is dancing and rules about
dancing. It is magic or technology or science and the
interaction between all these things. World is culture.

World is nature versus nurture. World is do they teach history in school and what kind of history? World is do you have high school or do you have tutors or do only the elite read at all or does writing even exist?

World is everything. The trick for the writer is discovering and choosing which details, which pieces of the world, will communicate to readers as much as possible about the characters and the characters' desires.

Maggie

I think of world building in painting terms. In real life, all details scream for attention, existing without priority. A painting can not only eliminate details but also shift colors, shapes, and sizes in impossible ways. A landscape can be painted all in blue, a mouse can be exaggerated in size, a man drawn impossibly thin or fat.

I begin every novel with an idea of what I want my book to look and feel like. When I revise, I go through every scene to make sure every description and setting reinforces it. It means that I omit—or cut—some details (like in the painting, when every color but blue hues is removed), exaggerate some details (like calling repeated attention to loud noises or claustrophobic landscape elements), and stylize still others (like only describing the people at a party who match the mood I desire). I'll cut entire scenes in revision if they jar the overall mood I want.

Brenna

My favorite worlds are weird ones. I like pretty things
and frilly dresses, and teeth and bones and science,
and knowing all the little secrets about a place, and
the cruelest, pointiest monsters. That's a lot of stuff
to figure out, and so my first foray into a story always
means exploring, looking at all kinds of details in
isolation. Early drafts involve a lot of wandering into
various scenes and settings, looking into closets and
random cupboards, then wandering out again.

Part One

Characterization and "Ladylike"

by

Maggie Stiefvater

INTRODUCTION

One of the questions I'm often asked by aspiring
writers is "How do you make an idea into a novel?" I
used to think it was a spreading, borderless question:
How do I write a book? But I understand now that the
question is asking about that nebulous time that exists
after a compelling idea springs into your head but
before you actually begin putting words on paper.
Or possibly extends to even *after* you begin writing.
Maybe all the way up to when you've put down a few
tentative scratches and then realize that, at this rate, it
will never be novel-length, and you might as well take
up needlepoint or big-game hunting instead.

    This was a state I lived in for much of my teen
years. My head was full of ideas, partial stories, and
sort-of characters, but they all turned clumsy or
insubstantial when I tried to write them out. Often
I'd throw out the ideas during that stage because I
figured if I couldn't figure out how to write it, it wasn't

a good enough idea. I know better now: any idea can be a good one—you'll see Tessa and Brenna say that as well. But an idea isn't enough. It's the execution that you get gold stars for.

I know now that when I want to get an idea out of my head and onto paper, I have some questions to ask myself. Idea-to-novel is really a process of elimination. Every question I answer and every decision I make— the narrator's age, the story's location, the time of year—narrows down the possibilities. I figure out the story I want to tell by establishing the stories I *don't* want to tell. Eventually I've ruled out everything, and the infinite possible versions of an idea become the one I'm putting on paper.

I'm going to try to show you that process for "Ladylike." It's a process that is pretty much defined by *not* making sense when it is written down, but I'm going to do my best. The thing to watch for is how important character is to me throughout. Even creative decisions that look, on the surface, as if they may be about other things are really character decisions once you dig down deep enough. My thinking goes like this: Idea! Character! Setting! World! Now back to character to clean up any drool!

Well, you'll see.

The original concept of "Ladylike" was not specific or revelatory in any way: I simply thought it would be interesting to write a story about a caretaker hired to tend a genteel but deadly woman who hadn't left her home in years.

At this point, the idea could have turned into any

kind of story: a tragedy, horror, a sweet love story. The staggering weight of all those possibilities is what used to hold me in stasis for so long. *How do you make an idea into a novel?* ("I have no idea!" says PastMaggie. "Let's run away!")

Here's another question writers ask me a lot: How much planning do you do before you begin writing? I do a lot of work before I allow myself to start, but I'm not certain I'd call it "planning." A better term would probably be "ruling things out."

The first thing I ruled out was vampires.

My first question: Why is the woman deadly? I needed someone who would eat people, and vampires ate people, right? *Vampire* was the first answer that came to mind. It was also the easy answer, so I threw it out. Chucking the answers anyone might give is a simple way of avoiding clichés or stereotypes. I want the most Maggie-specific answers in order to get to the story that only I can tell.

Here's another thing about vampires. I love mythology, and using an existing, familiar myth can add wordless, efficient depth to your fiction. But the same familiarity means that the myth arrives with a lot of baggage that my story will have to either accept or refute. I considered all of the elements of the vampire myth I'd have to throw out or change before I got to the story I wanted and realized it was all of it. Same with fairy mythology—an aging fairy queen would be interesting, but not the story I wanted to tell. I quickly eliminated a list of existing mythology and realized all that was left was an unknown, invented magical creature. She would have only the magic rules that I wanted. My old lady would not be a lady at all, I decided: she would be merely an elegant creature in womanly form. Lady*like.*

Geraldine.

There it was, her name. It sounded fussy and old and lovely, just what I wanted.

That left my other major character: the caretaker. Because I had Geraldine—genteel, polite Geraldine—in place, I knew that the caretaker had to act as a foil. Their character arcs would need to be complementary.

The more questions I answer about my fiction, the more decisions I make, the more my subconscious begins to shift into a higher gear in the background. For instance, as I shuffled through questions about this caretaker (Ada? Petra? Petra.), a small voice in my head said,

—*Are you sure you meant "caretaker"?*

No, I wasn't sure. What are you trying to say, subconscious?

—*Just that you know Petra's a teen, and teens aren't often caretakers, and is that really what you're trying to tell a story about anyway?*

Spit it out, subconscious.

—*Possibly consider the word "companion" instead?*

Of course. Of course I had meant companion. I didn't need Geraldine to be frail, only lonesome. Good catch, subconscious.

—*Anytime. Except when you're tired, or when you try to write too much in one day, or when you ignore me for so long that you take a wrong turn in the manuscript and you head down ridiculous literary corridors without me.*

Perhaps, I thought, Petra—the companion—could be a musician. Geraldine's daughters could have heard her busking on the street and decided to pay her to entertain Geraldine for a few hours each week. Oh, yes, I thought, I love writing musicians!

But I always default to writing musicians, since I am one. Like "vampire," it was an easy answer. Throw it out. I cast about for other possibilities, rejecting them each in turn. Too simple, too convoluted, too complicated when placed up against the already fidgety concept of a deadly old lady. Then I got a letter from a reader that was less about my books and more about her. She confessed that the tiniest of insults at school would make her blush furiously. She felt like a lump. She didn't know what to do with her hands. She was always messy. She was worse than invisible, because she was lumbering and awkward and going red every other minute.

Oh, hello, Petra, I thought.

A self-conscious, uncoordinated teen would contrast beautifully with my poised and deadly old lady. But then how had Petra had caught the eye of Geraldine's family? Geraldine loved beautiful and elegant things, and Petra was now defined by being *not* beautiful or elegant. I brainstormed for options that would appeal to the rather old-fashioned Geraldine. There had to be some way for this awkward teen and this centuries-old creature to make a connection.

A few days after I'd discovered my Petra, I was

typing an epigraph into the beginning of one of my other novels. As I misspelled the archaic language, backspaced, and tried again, I realized I was looking at the solution. Poetry was a language that would easily translate over generations.

Ah! Now I was nearly there. Time for setting and atmosphere and world questions. All of these would be easier, though, because I had already figured Geraldine and Petra out already. Recall how I said everything always came back to character. The more I knew about them, the more obvious the answers to every other question became, like doing the edge pieces on the puzzle first.

Because I'm a very visual person, my first setting question is nearly always the same: What kind of movie or painting would this story look like? Every setting question after that is really still a question about character: What sort of lodging will best showcase Geraldine's fussy love of manmade things? Which time of year will make the outside world contrast the most with Geraldine's lush oasis of an apartment? What can I do with the setting to show how removed it is from Petra's ordinary life?

I wish there was a better word than "brainstorming" for this process. It's more like "brain-drizzling." It can go on for a furious week of drenched activity, or it can dribble in fitful cloudbursts for years. I know this about myself now, so I always have several stories gestating. I can leave the ones that need more time sitting in my head while I pluck out the developed ones for actual writing.

This process used to madden and bemuse me. I thought it was something wrong with my skill set, not just an inherent part of my story-making process. I thought I was failing, that I was stuck, that I had run out to the end of an idea and needed to throw it out and find a better one. Now I know that that feeling really means I have only just found the *beginning* of an idea. Yes, I must put words on paper eventually. But I have to know *why* I'm telling the story before I do.

The most important thing is to tell a story that you want to hear.

—*Maggie*

LADYLIKE

Petra would never forget the stairwell to Geraldine's
loft. Calling it a stairwell was about as appropriate
as referring to Geraldine's living space as a "loft,"
actually. The vertical concrete tunnel was far more
than a stairwell. It was an undertaking. A career. A
journey marked by frequent pauses to massage knees
and suck in a deep breath and press hand to side like
the statue of the Wounded Gaul.

The first time Petra climbed the stairs, she was too
consumed by physical anguish to think of the five floors
she was passing; it was like being lost—blocks stretched
endlessly until a familiar waypoint appeared to shrink
them back to size again. She would never reach the
sixth floor, she thought. She would die, unmourned,
on this landing, under buzzing fluorescents. She would
not even have the dignity of rotting: it was so dry and
sunless that her corpse would desiccate, like cat shit
hidden in the back of the cedar closet at home.

That first time that she successfully ascended, she took thirty seconds before the door to grip her knees and catch her breath, even though she was already late (delay courtesy of the unfamiliar bus route and the converted Greenpoint warehouse's confusing main doors). Her mother was ever and always telling Petra that if she would just take thirty seconds to breathe, life would stop attacking her with such gusto.

"Time gives you perspective," her mother was fond of saying.

Petra breathed in for fifteen seconds. Petra breathed out for fifteen seconds.

She felt sweaty and wobbly and lacking in perspective on the other side of the thirty seconds. She resented her mother, for giving advice that clearly didn't work, and herself, for continuing to try it.

Petra rang the bell. Already she was going red. The worst part about her blushing was that she could feel the moment it began and yet was powerless to do anything to stop it. It started with the scalp under her hair, nearly discreet, and ended with her ears, dreadfully exposed, flaming stop signs on the side of a messy school bus. In the face of adversity, Petra was a reluctant chameleon perfectly evolved to hide in poppies, in front of crimson wallpaper, or submerged in baths of blood. The door opened. She was messy. She was

Line editing is the very last step of my writer's process. (What is line editing? you ask. It means improving the nitty-gritties of a story—grammar and word choice—rather than big-picture elements like plot, pacing, and character development.) It's easy to get caught up in line edits too early in the writing process, but the reality is that it's generally a waste of time to fuss over the perfect dialogue tag when you might end up cutting that conversation entirely in your general edits. These days I write long and then cut back, so my line edits generally involve me making sure I'm only saying each thing once. In this paragraph, for instance, I had three more sentences describing Petra's blushing—all of them repeating the words "transformation" and "messy" and "began." Yes, Stiefvater. We get it. My line edits involved me pruning the paragraph back to the most specific and vivid description: in this case, the school bus line.

flushed. She was late. This is what it was to be her. *Say something, Petra*, she thought.

"I'm here," she said.

"Yes, you are," said Geraldine.

. . .

Geraldine was not what Petra had been expecting. Before the door opened, Petra hadn't been aware that she *had* expectations, but the surprise of Geraldine's person assured her that she had. Because Petra had been told that Geraldine had not left her apartment for years and years, it did *seem* as if she should have been frail. Musty. One of those folded-over elderly women clearly on the verge of extinction. But instead Petra found herself facing a genteel old lady formed like a department-store mannequin. Not like a long-legged modern model, but rather like an old-fashioned dress form, something elegant and restrained from long ago. Something with very pointed breasts.

Geraldine stood straight. Her hair was a bobby-pinned vintage piece of silver-gray. Her hands clasped each other in such a way that her large rings did not touch. Pride lifted a sharp chin.

Petra felt messier than she had before the door opened.

"Geraldine," said Geraldine. She clasped Petra's hand in both of hers, her rings cold in

First appearances matter. You know how when you meet someone, you make an immediate snap judgment about them? Later, of course, you can revise that impression based upon real knowledge of the person's character, but that first impression sets the tone for a long time. The first time you describe a character, that's the moment you're giving the reader. As a writer, I'm not particularly interested in using this space to list specifics because when we meet a person in real life, we don't catalog stats (five-foot-four, gray hair, blue eyes). Instead we form an emotional impression, which is why it's sometimes hard to remember if a new acquaintance wears glasses, or whether they have a mustache. That emotional reaction is what I try to convey.

Petra's palm. Then she smiled, entirely around the eyes. Petra felt more at ease at once. Her ears cooled.

What magic is this!?

"Petra," Petra said, copying Geraldine's method of greeting. Then more clearly, because she'd mumbled—she was always mumbling, her mother said, her teachers said, her stepfather said, her grandparents said—"I'm Petra."

"And you're the reader!" Geraldine said with delight. She had an accent, or perhaps merely a very careful way of pronouncing her words. Like Petra did when she was reading out loud, only all the time. She patted Petra's hand and released it. "How wonderful. Do come in from that concrete tomb."

She meant the stairs. That was the first moment Petra thought she might become friends with this creature.

. . .

Geraldine's apartment was not an apartment: it was a world. *A habitat*, Petra thought the first time she entered, not realizing at the time how true that was. Petra's rudimentary investigations into the address revealed that it belonged to a nineteenth-century commercial laundry converted to apartments. Because Petra knew Brooklyn, she had expected to find something chic and large-ish. She had also expected a retroactively installed elevator.

Teen readers often ask me if I am trying to secretly embed meanings in my novels. "When you make the curtains red," they ask cunningly, "do you actually mean that the main character is angry?" They are certain that this is a trick their teachers are playing on them to make boring homework. But the truth is that I *do* sometimes mean that the characters are angry when I make the curtains red. I want to embed clues in the reader's subconscious so that the reader *feels* the truth as well as knows it. So I am trying to tell the reader something about Geraldine's life with my word choice—without saying it outright just yet. I want it to play in the background until I turn up the volume later. "Oh," thinks the reader, "this song was actually playing all along."

Just like the first description of a character, the first description of a setting needs to pack an immediate punch on a nearly instinctual level. Too many words will slow down the story and remind us that we're reading description. Too few and the action will take place in a floating, empty room. Ideally, I strike a balance that lets the reader *feel* they know precisely what the space looks like. Oh, and another thing: if we're in close third person or in first person, the description can't know more than our point-of-view character. So if Petra wouldn't know the specific names of the plants, I can't list them. She's the camera I've chosen for the story, and I have to accept the limitations of her knowledge.

Wrong, wrong.

She'd already encountered the concrete pilgrimage in the place of an elevator, of course, and now she discovered that there was no *ish* in large-ish. Geraldine's living space occupied as much space as Petra's high school gymnasium, perhaps more. And *chic* was utterly the wrong word. Because of its past as a laundry, the floor was the same concrete as the stairs, but it was covered here and there with Persian rugs and grass rugs and yet more Persian rugs, all of them sumptuously shaggy and colored in the blue of blood and the red of lips. There were more plants than anything else. Palms taller than Petra, potted trees that seemed like they might grow bananas, fairy-tale vines trailing from stands like coatracks. Hundreds of tropical plants unfolded and strove and pushed out blooms only slightly more exotic than the leaves around them. There were nearly as many lamps, old and curled, and all of the light through the plants was beautiful and alien and unexpected. The furniture—antique desks and foreign-looking screens, old-fashioned chaises and filigreed settees—formed carefully distinct chambers. It was one room, but it felt like a place to explore. A maze of secrets.

"This is really cool," Petra said, and felt stupid immediately after she spoke. She could tell already that *cool* was not a Geraldine

One of the French translators of my novels once told me that, in France, it was widely considered a terrible flaw to use the same word twice in a paragraph. She said that translating my novels was a challenge because I would often use words with very similar definitions in my descriptions (i.e., "enchanting, magical") and she would have to struggle to find two different French words with the same meaning and rhythm and then hope I didn't use a third similar word later in the paragraph, because she could not repeat one she had just used. Ever since that conversation I've been far more attentive to redundant word choices and repeated words in my writing. It might not be a terminal flaw in American writing to use "nineteenth century" twice in as many paragraphs, but I do think it's more interesting writing if I don't. Much of my line editing for "Ladylike" involved murdering repeats, especially in this section. How many times, Stiefvater, can you say that everything looks "old-fashioned"? A lot, apparently.

word. She mumbled, "Beautiful, I mean. It's like a conservatory."

"You're very kind," Geraldine said. "Please make yourself at home."

Petra's actual home was covered with framed inspirational sayings and wedding photos and sports team logos. Less *distinguished* and more *peppy*. She wouldn't know the first thing about acting as if this place were her home.

"Thanks. Uh—" *Be cool, Petra!* "I didn't know what you wanted me to read, so I brought a lot of things."

"Very clever," Geraldine said, without a trace of sarcasm. "Shall I make us some tea before we begin?"

Petra didn't drink tea, but she didn't want to be rude. "Oh, thanks."

"Would you like honey or sugar? Honey, I suppose? It's supposed to be good for that lovely voice of yours."

Lovely voice. Petra's ears burned anew. They would never stop; there would be waves of redness like a constant heaving shoreline of humiliation. Geraldine was getting the full Petra show in no time at all. "Uh, thanks—" *Stop saying thanks, Petra.* "Honey would be great."

Petra's voice was what had gotten her this job, after all. There was one blushing Petra who hunched like a lump in her school desk, who possessed hair that frizzed in the humidity and a face that pimpled at the suggestion of sugar and lips that mumbled every answer to every question. But there was another Petra who was a member of the Two-Three Oratory Club, who stood at a lectern and recited Yeats, Hopkins, and

Swinburne with perfect, ringing clarity. Both Petras had pimples, but the zits didn't matter as much to that second one.

Supposedly, Geraldine's relatives had heard Petra reciting "The Song of Hiawatha" at the Two-Three open mic and had at once made inquiries to see if Petra could be secured as a companion and reader for Geraldine.

"See, boldness makes opportunity!" Petra's mother had said. "That would be a good cross-stitch. It will be good for you to not sulk around here with the babies." By "babies" she meant Nikki and Mae, Petra's sisters (who had not been babies for eleven and thirteen years respectively), and by "sulk around" she meant "avoid public humiliation."

Now, Geraldine handed Petra a gilt-edged teacup nested on a gilt-edged saucer and sat elegantly on one of the sofas. She asked Petra how she had come to be in the Oratory Club. Petra muttered something about her mother's ideas about facing fears head-on before petering out. She didn't know how to talk about herself—she wasn't sure how she was supposed to tell if Geraldine was merely being polite, in which case Petra needed to answer in the briefest way possible, or if she wanted to be informed, in which case Petra's shortness would appear rude. In any case, when Petra's reply occupied only twelve seconds, Geraldine smoothly leaped from that topic to a discussion

I used to always forget siblings in my writing, even though I have a ton of them in real life. When I was starting out, I knew that I needed a main character, some conflict, a fleshed-out setting, character arcs. Juggling just these elements occupied all of my brain; I had no more neurons left to consider something like siblings, pets, grandparents. It wasn't until I began thinking of my characters as portraits of real, living people that I began to more naturally populate my world with dynamic, nuanced characters. My life was full of people influenced by sibling relationships, and it was my job to see if I could mirror those relationships in my writing. I did have to learn to add them in organically, however—I can't just throw in siblings willy-nilly. Every person I add to my narrator's family must have an influence on the narrator in some way. Yes, writer-brain, another thing for you to juggle. It's worth it, though. Even if the siblings or grandparents don't appear on screen, a mention of them can make the world feel fuller.

of tea. Did Petra like it, she asked with her curious and distinct accent. Petra did, in fact, like it, though she wasn't sure whether she was actually tasting it or merely smelling it. She was experiencing roses. That was what it came down to.

Geraldine and Petra burned nearly a third of their time in this manner. Possibly, Petra thought, her services had been engaged out of pity, and Geraldine was merely stalling.

But finally Geraldine said, "Well, this is splendid. Shall I take that?"

With relief, Petra offered up her teacup—it had an old red-brown stain on the rim, she noticed—and asked, "Do you know what you'd like to . . . uh . . ."

Geraldine swirled away with the cups in hand. Over her shoulder, her voice rang out crisply. "Perhaps something short to warm up?"

Petra fumbled through her bag for the book and fumbled to double-check that it held the poem she meant it to and then, as Geraldine returned from behind one of the decorative screens, she gracefully stood in a patch of sunlight. There was no lectern or stage, but the light seemed dramatic enough to act as a focal point. Petra stood up straight and didn't feel foolish about it. She swept her hair out of her eyes and did not find the motion clumsy.

Poetry was magic. The words in this book were the magic spells necessary to conjure the Petra that Petra was good at. Her own words she fumbled and her own gestures she smeared, but someone else's words—yes. Magic.

In a clear voice she said, "I will be reading 'Dead Love' by Algernon Charles Swinburne."

"Oh, Swinburne," Geraldine said, as if she knew him personally. "Why did he write this one?"

"Oh." The inferior Petra was back, unable to form sentences. "I don't know. I, uh, will look it up. Do you want me to look it up now?" The unexpected question was already burning her ears again.

Geraldine waved away Petra's phone. "No, later, later, don't trouble yourself, Petra. The context is part of the poem, though, so I always enjoy knowing it. Please carry on!"

Petra carefully folded a yellow Post-it note out of the way; she'd marked each poem for performance with a different colored sticky. The book's edge fluttered with notes the color of a marigold, the sky, a fern, a pumpkin, a furious blush. Then she swallowed the spit from her mouth—too much saliva ruined the *p*'s and *s*'s—and read:

Dead love, by treason slain, lies stark,
White as a dead stark-stricken dove:
None that pass by him pause to mark
    Dead love.

His heart, that strained and yearned and strove
As toward the sundawn strives the lark,
Is cold as all the old joy thereof.

Dead men, re-arisen from dust, may hark
When rings the trumpet blown above:
It will not raise from out the dark
    Dead love.

Not every main character has to be likeable or sympathetic—really, all you need to hold a reader's attention is *relatable* or *interesting*—but likeable is the most straightforward version of relatable. I very much wanted readers to like Geraldine: first of all because I wanted them to see what Petra saw in her, and secondly because the conflict later in the story means nothing if the reader finds her unsympathetic. I looked for ways to make the reader approve of her, and here is one of them—Geraldine as the perfect audience, appreciating the thing Petra appreciates most herself. Tiny acts of casual kindness go a long way toward likability, just as tiny acts of selfishness or casual cruelty go a long way toward unlikability. A good character is a combination of both . . . just like a real person.

I believe every writer in the world has heard the advice "Show, don't tell." It's fine advice, and certainly the secret to tricking a reader into feeling and seeing things your way. But it's also oversimplified advice, and my early attempts to slavishly follow it resulted in some very oddly paced stories. I couldn't figure out how to *show* passing of time in an abbreviated way, and so I ended up with stories that only took place over one day, every minute laboriously chronicled, because I didn't know how to *not* write every moment awake. The answer is telling, not showing. Sometimes you have to say "Time passed," and sometimes that is not wrong. If nothing is happening in a space of time—or, more importantly, if nothing *new* is happening in a space of time—skip it. Tell how much time we lost if you must. The advice should really be "Show (a lot), tell (a little)."

Geraldine listened with her eyes cast up, hands folded in her lap, a demure smile on her lips. A portrait of quiet enjoyment. She was, in fact, the perfect audience. Not so diffident as to make Petra doubt her performance, and not so effusive as to make Petra doubt Geraldine's sincerity.

"You read beautifully," Geraldine said. "You are just as Marla described."

"Uh, thank you." Petra was clumsy again. One of her favorite aspects of the Two-Three was that speakers escaped behind the stage as soon as their reading was over. She didn't know how to accept compliments. A lot of Petra's problems would dissolve if every interaction ended with either applause or bored silence from twenty feet away or more.

"Do you need a break?" Geraldine asked. "I need to water some of my plants, so you could rest while I do that."

Petra did not need to rest—it took more than three stanzas of iambic octameter to wear her out—but she didn't want to be rude. There were so many plants that it took nearly the rest of Petra's scheduled time; she only had time to read two more poems (Geraldine asked for the context for both, although Petra had context for neither).

Then Geraldine clasped Petra's hand in farewell, as straight and energetic as when Petra had arrived. "I do so hope that you enjoyed this wonderful afternoon as much as I, and that you'll come again."

"Uh, thanks," Petra replied, because that was evidently all she knew how to say when she was not performing.

Geraldine held onto Petra's hand for long enough that Petra wasn't sure if she was supposed to take it back or wait for it to be returned to her. Finally, Geraldine said, "Petra. The feminine form of Peter, which is, as you know, from the Greek for 'rock.'"

More like a boulder, really, Petra thought. Her ears were at the ready for another blush.

But Geraldine seemed to anticipate the wave and then part it. "A unique, beautiful name. A *foundation* for something, certainly."

"Oh," said Petra. "Uh, thanks."

The last things Petra saw before the door closed were the same smiling eyes that she'd been greeted with hours before.

As she descended the stairs, the hero's journey into hell, the knock-kneed decline not quite as arduous as the climb but taxing nonetheless, her phone dinged as an e-mail came in: "You've got money!" Marla had efficiently sent Petra's fee via PayPal. Whatever Petra had just done for the past two hours, it was a job.

. . .

Petra took the 32 bus home. Early holiday shoppers kept pace with them on the sidewalk. As Petra disembarked the bus, a homeless man shouted that he'd like to see her without her sweater on. She went so red that he went red too: a new personal low.

"How's my hero?" Petra's mother asked at home. "Super proud of you. All the kisses." She didn't ask: *Did anyone laugh at you when you dropped your tray in the cafeteria because the girl behind you said "excuse me"?* or *Have you worked out how to walk without feeling like Jabba the Hutt?* or *Were you able to answer a question without blushing?* She never asked for context. She just clapped as Petra ducked backstage.

"Uh, thanks," said Petra. On her phone's search engine, she typed "Algernon Charles Swinburne dead love."

.   .   .

The next time Petra climbed the stairs to Geraldine's apartment, the sounds of classical music greeted her at the top stair. The violins, somewhat faint, became louder as Petra expired on the concrete, bringing her ear closer to the crack beneath Geraldine's door. Whatever she was playing, she was playing it loudly.

Petra clawed feebly at the door; Geraldine opened it. The music swelled hugely around her silhouette.

"These stairs are terrible," Geraldine apologized to the deceased, crisp voice audible even through the violins. "I've told them I simply won't go out again until they put in an elevator, but I don't think that will ever happen so I suppose I am in here for always. Come in and have a cup of tea, poor thing. I'm so glad you've come."

Inside, Petra lowered her backpack to one of the sofas and rubbed her aching kneecaps. Geraldine handed her a cup, nursing the climber back to health.

"Uh, thanks," Petra said, and then immediately went red as she realized she had already begun with her signature statement. "Where is the music coming from?"

Geraldine seemed delighted to be asked. Gesturing for Petra to follow, she moved elegantly through a company of ferns until she came to a sizeable and apparently ancient record player. The music roared so loudly that the cabinet vibrated. As the song drew to a close, a miraculous clockwork arm descended to remove the completed record and replace it with a new one.

"Oh, coo—very interesting," Petra said as the music began again. It was loud, but tinny, like it was being piped in from another century.

Geraldine smiled approvingly, hands clasped, rings carefully not clicking together. "This next one will be Brahms's Lullaby. 'Cradle Song,' more correctly." She leaned toward Petra, and her voice lowered. "Once upon a time, Brahms had a lover who used to sing to him, and years later, long after they'd separated, he wrote this piece when she had a child with her new husband. He used her old melody as a countermelody, knowing she'd recognize it! Then he sent the finished piece to her and her husband."

Petra thought this sounded like a fairly assholey thing to do, but she couldn't think of a Geraldine sort of way to express such a sentiment out loud.

Geraldine said, "It always struck me as a singularly unpleasant impulse."

Ah.

"Singularly unpleasant," Petra repeated, feeling Geraldine's precise accent in her mouth. Geraldine smiled at her, recognizing herself. "I've heard this song a lot of times before, but I don't think I've ever heard the, uh, real version."

She watched Geraldine crouch by a screened cabinet, opening it to reveal a vast collection of charmingly tatty record sleeves. She tried to figure out how Geraldine managed to look perfectly posed even when crouching. Possibly Petra didn't have the back and neck muscles necessary to stand straight at all times. Possibly she had been born with fewer muscles. Possibly Geraldine was like a fine show horse and Petra's genes tended more toward some lumbering beast meant to haul wagons.

All the same, Petra pushed her own shoulders back and raised her chin a bit. As she did, she caught another glance of red-brown stain by the edge of the rug, the same color as the stain on the edge of the teacup. The dramatic side of Petra wanted it to be a bloodstain, but it was probably furniture polish.

Then Geraldine stood, her tidy shoe hiding the mark from view. She held an empty sleeve in her hands. "I think I'll retire this one for a bit. Would you hand me the record?"

Petra didn't know the first thing about how to remove a record from the machine. She was sure it was a quite simple process, but knowing that and still not being sure of how to tackle it made it worse. Immediately she blushed, hot and complete. *It's just a record*, she told herself, *just lift it, probably.* But another part of her whispered, *There's bits you have to move out of the way; what if you break it? Imagine her crouched there perfectly and you the mountain troll looming over her with wires and cranks in your paws.* And then the first part said, *Do it now, she's going to think you're an idiot just standing here.* Immediately followed by *She'll think you're more of an idiot when you can't work it out.*

"That one is a little tricky," Geraldine said smoothly. "You have to push that fiddly bit there to stop it spinning. And then make sure you lift the needle arm straight up or it will make a terrible creaking sound. And of course just touch the edges or the label, but you know that."

Petra removed the record, feeling unduly accomplished.

Geraldine slid the record back into its sleeve. "This piece was very popular, you know, even in Brahms's day. His publisher released many different arrangements for it to appeal to all sorts of players, from the most skilled to the least." She smiled, delighted

If I could be a floating writing godmother for all new writers, I would whisper over and over in their ears, "Be specific!" It's not enough for me to write that Petra is shy and awkward. That describes too many people in the world; the reader's no closer to knowing Petra in particular. I need to pile on the specific ways this manifests in her life, being as realistic as I can manage. Sometimes I rely on my own feelings for this, but that only goes so far—if I use only my own feelings, I'll just end up writing a character that is me. So I turn to careful observation of other people. When I meet someone new, I like to play a game called "make this person a character." I imagine how I would write them: How would I describe their appearance so that others immediately understood how it felt to meet them? How would I sum up their personality so that a reader would know them at once? Specifics.

by her beloved context. "I adore this bitter Brahms quote—he said, 'Why not make a new edition in a minor key for naughty or sick children? That would be still another way to move copies.'"

Petra laughed. "I don't think I'll ever listen to that piece the same way."

"Such is the power of context! We make our own, you know, and carry it with us." Geraldine gestured first to the ferns around her and then to her hair and clothing. "All of this makes you understand *this* in a different way." She pressed her hand over her heart.

That was a terrible lesson Petra had already learned about herself.

Geraldine touched Petra's cheek with a finger; the cold touch of her skin demonstrated Petra's blush clearly. "What have you brought to read today?"

Petra was being rescued. She was relieved.

"I tried to look up context for the Swinburne poems last night," she admitted. "I didn't find anything about, uh, 'Dead Love' or the other one. But I found some stuff about Swinburne."

"And?"

In fact, most of what Petra had found had to do with Swinburne's habit of hiring prostitutes to beat him, but she couldn't think of a Geraldine way to say *that*. So she just said, "It turns out that he was, uh . . . singularly unpleasant."

Geraldine laughed with delight. "They all are, my dear."

"I've composed an introduction," Petra said. It was the sort of sentence that the babies—her younger sisters—would have giggled over, but it seemed about right in this place. As Geraldine settled herself into a small wicker chair, Petra turned to a page marked by a sticky note the color of a robin's egg. In her orator voice, she announced, "I am going to read 'The Eve of Revolution,' which is from Algernon Charles Swinburne's *Songs before Sunrise*. I chose this one because I was reading about his life, and one of the things I thought was interesting about him was that he lived a life of drunken and gleeful debauchery"— Petra tried not to pause too long at that part, although she'd thought a lot about her introduction, and she was badly pleased with the phrase "gleeful debauchery"— "such that it seemed like he was on a track to be dead of alcoholism at a young age."

She faltered. "Dead of alcoholism" was not at all what she had planned to say, and it sounded clumsy enough that she doubted herself. It was so much easier to read someone else's words.

Geraldine asked, "Did he die of alcoholism?"

Die of alcoholism. It sounded better when Geraldine said it—was it because it was in present tense? No, it was because she sounded distinct when she said it.

Petra did her best to enunciate clearly as she continued, "He didn't die at a young age, but only because his friend and lawyer took him into his home and nursed him back to health."

"As lawyers should," Geraldine said, which was the first joke Petra had heard her make. "Edith is a lawyer. I should remind her of this. Continue!"

"Later, someone would say—" Petra forgot who the *someone* was but pressed on, just as she would if she forgot a word in a poem. The point was to sound like you had missed nothing. "—that his lawyer 'saved the man but killed the poet.' But he was very prolific those first few years he was there, and so I've chosen 'The Eve of Revolution' because it is from one of the first volumes he published there. How is that?"

Geraldine didn't answer at first—she didn't realize Petra was addressing her, and Petra had spoken very tentatively, unused to asking for feedback from her audience. "Oh! It was very good. Masterfully done. I liked 'gleeful debauchery.'"

Pleased, Petra began to read the poem: four hundred uneven lines of fiddly rhyme and lovely language. As she read the stanza that had made her choose the poem in the first place, she saw Geraldine smile again:

> Light, light, and light! to break and melt in sunder
>   All clouds and chains that in one bondage bind
> Eyes, hands, and spirits, forged by fear and wonder
>   And sleek fierce fraud with hidden knife behind;
> There goes no fire from heaven before their
>   thunder,
>   Nor are the links not malleable that wind
> Round the snared limbs and souls that ache
>   thereunder;
>   The hands are mighty, were the head not blind.
>   Priest is the staff of king,
>   And chains and clouds one thing,

And fettered flesh with devastated mind.
　　Open thy soul to see,
　　Slave, and thy feet are free;
　Thy bonds and thy beliefs are one in kind,
　　And of thy fears thine irons wrought
Hang weights upon thee fashioned out of thine
　　own thought.

When Petra was done, she added, "Here's
another thing I liked about Swinburne! He used to
walk around *declaiming*—that's what they called it.
Declaiming poetry to people like a madman, whenever
the moment hit him."

Geraldine didn't immediately respond, and Petra
couldn't recall why she had begun this confession
after her delivery. She fell hastily silent. Her ears
burned once again. Really what she liked about that
aspect of Swinburne was the idea that if Petra did
that—walked around *declaiming*—she'd never go red.
Because she could always speak clearly as long as she
was reciting.

"I always think that I am declaiming," Geraldine
replied thoughtfully. "Performing, yes? I suppose that
sounds like I'm being insincere; if I speak out loud,
it is for the benefit of other people—I want it to be
composed in such a way that they understand me. If I
don't care how other people interpret an idea, I don't
say it out loud. I don't need to hear myself to know my
thoughts."

Petra thought this over. "So you're saying that you
think before you open your mouth."

"I'm saying that I *think* all the time," Geraldine said, "I only *speak* for other people."

"I'd like to be you when I grow up," Petra blurted.

She had said it out loud. She couldn't believe that she'd actually said it *out loud*.

Her skin figured it out before her brain did. She went red so fast that her cheeks hurt.

Geraldine spoke loudly to be heard over the color of Petra's ears, "What a lovely thing to say. I'm much nicer than I used to be. I was a savage young thing."

Petra still couldn't speak; she was blushing too hard. She couldn't meet Geraldine's eyes.

"Just give it words," Geraldine suggested. "That will help. You don't have to pretend it's not happening. Just give it words that you like. Say it in a pretty way."

There was nothing likeable about going red. Petra had no words.

"My name is Petra," Geraldine prompted. "And I wear my heart on my sleeve."

"On my ears," muttered Petra. Then, because it felt wrong to be surly to Geraldine, she repeated, "My name is Petra, and I wear my heart on my sleeve."

"Nice to meet you." Geraldine smiled gently. She had a smile directly from old paintings. "Now let's rest your voice, and you can have some tea while I work on this landscape."

Petra was being rescued. She was relieved.

She slumped on one of Geraldine's chairs with yet more rose tea, while Geraldine perched on a chair, perfectly upright, and dabbed tiny, perfect leaves onto a painting in progress.

"It's—so—neat," Petra said, haltingly. She thought of what Geraldine had said earlier and wished that she had thought the entire sentence through before she'd said it out loud. *Choose words, Petra*, she thought, *words that you like.* Thinking that and doing it were miles apart, though. "It seems so particular, I mean. So delicate."

"Thank you." Geraldine dabbed another perfectly formed leaf onto the canvas. It was magical: one moment there was nothing, the next the bristles touched down and dribbled out a precise leaf. "I am not great, but I do enjoy it immensely. Do you think I might paint you? We could do short sessions, just a bit each time you came. We could begin during your next visit! Don't feel you have to say yes just to please an old creature like myself."

Petra went red. "Oh, that'd be fine."

Don't paint me red, is all, she thought.

. . .

By the sixth day, Petra was feeling guilty about accepting money, as she was clearly performing no job at all.

She called Marla, one of Geraldine's daughters, who met her outside the apartment building. Actually, Petra wasn't entirely certain that Marla was Geraldine's daughter after all. Nothing about

their facial features looked the same. Geraldine
had a stately nose and a tiny jaw, and Marla had a
square jaw and a tiny nose. Where Geraldine was
elegantly understated, Marla was fancy, every inch of
her wardrobe brocaded and designed. Her earrings
looked like antique chandeliers. She ducked her head
against the wind scampering down the treeless road,
looking secretive, as if they were spies exchanging
information.

Marla asked if there was a problem. She really
hoped, she said, that there wasn't, as Petra was doing
such an excellent job and Geraldine was so pleased.

"Job. Right. Sure. That's the thing. I guess, uh, I
guess I don't really understand what I'm supposed to
do," Petra said. "What's my work day? Some days she
doesn't want me to read or do anything other than just
sit there. What is my *job*?"

"Your job is to make her happy," Marla said.

In that case, Geraldine might be performing that
job on Petra.

"You aren't uncomfortable with it, are you?" Marla
asked anxiously. The ear chandeliers swung. "There
haven't been any . . . problems?"

The way she said *problems* immediately caught
Petra. It was not so much *problems* as *Problems*.
Geraldine? Problematic? Trying to imagine her even
raising her voice was impossible.

"It's nice," Petra admitted, and this made her
flush. *Damn* her skin. She could imagine a life
avoiding humiliation, but must she avoid sincerity too?
"I like her a lot."

Marla's face relaxed. "Oh, good. Are you headed up now?"

"Yeah. Yes. Are you?"

"Oh, no. No, no. I mean, I have an appointment. Tell her I said hello and to give me a call!" Marla rummaged demonstratively in her purse and presented car keys for Petra's approval.

Then Marla headed down the street, toward her car, and Petra ascended the eternal staircase, thinking about Problems. Capital *P*.

. . .

When Petra got home, the babies were there, sitting at the table, screaming with laughter. They grinned at her as she slid her shoes off by the door.

"Is that lipstick around your eyes?" Petra asked Nikki.

Both of them shrilled with laughter again, and then Nikki turned around the magazine they were looking at so that Petra could share their humor. It was a glossy thing off a grocery store cashier rack. The page in question featured a collection of photos of starlets caught in situ on the street. There were a lot of tall boots and tank tops. Petra couldn't see the joke.

"Oh, Petra," Mae said. "*Look at him.*"

Petra pretended to suddenly see the joke and laughed as convincingly as she could manage. She wondered if the eggs Mae and Nikki had hatched out of had been more colorful than Petra's. Did their mother know right away, she wondered, that Petra was a different species than the rest of the family?

. . .

Geraldine liked beautiful, impossible things. At first
Petra couldn't find words to express what tied them all
together, even though it was obvious when something
was a Geraldine-thing. She liked fussy, deliberate
creations: nature seen through the lens of man, glass
worked by skilled hands, paper manipulated into
specific and particular shapes. Even her living things
were delicate and strange: curled ferns, combed palms,
tender-throated lilies, fine-edged orchids. Heavy
flowers somehow held aloft on spindly stems.

Geraldine's paintings were beautiful and
impossible too, and it seemed unlikely that a painting
of Petra would belong among them. That first
session, when Geraldine had showed Petra her initial
sketches, Petra had gone red. Not because they
were poorly done, but the opposite. Geraldine had
captured the essence of Petra perfectly in just a few
spidery charcoal lines. That lump was her, seen truly.
Shoulders curled in. Chin ducked to make a lump of
a second chin. Hands balled in lap, eyes heavy-lidded,
legs shapeless as if carelessly affixed to the chunk of
Petra's body.

"Oh, no," Petra said before she could help herself.
She went redder. "Never mind the painting!"

"Whatever is the matter?" Geraldine asked.
In the background, the Emperor Waltz played.
Geraldine had told her a few minutes earlier that it
had originally been called "Hand in Hand" and had
been written to commemorate the meetings of Kaiser
Wilhelm II and Emperor Franz Josef. The name had

been changed by Strauss's publisher in an effort to not offend the delicate egos of the powerful men involved, Geraldine had added, concluding with, "which is a shame, as 'Hand in Hand' is a far more emotive title, don't you think?"

"I just, uh, think—" Petra stopped. Think before you speak. Speech is an act for other people! Geraldine waited as Petra got herself together—she never rushed to fill in a silence. Finally, Petra said, very distinctly and formally, declaiming, "You're very good. But it's disappointing to think that's how I look on the outside. I don't think I'd like to have a painting to commemorate that."

Commemorate was a word that had been on Petra's mind since Geraldine had explained the Emperor Waltz. A wonderful word, too grand for everyday conversation. Petra had always been annoyed by how so much of the beautiful language she recited didn't seem to be . . . right . . . in normal life. Sometimes one of those words would sneak out in school, and the back of the classroom would laugh, and Petra would go red. Of course, with Geraldine, nothing seemed quite like normal life. It seemed correct to ask to not have Petra's hideous teen years *commemorated*.

"Very succinctly put," Geraldine allowed. "But this is not how you look all the time. It's

I like to have an idea of what the character is like before I begin, and where I'd like the character to end when I stop, but not a tremendously precise map of how to get from one to the other. As long as I have that big-picture arc in the back of my head as I'm drafting scenes, I can be open to opportunities to show lurching steps forward. This moment is one of those that I didn't have planned but fell into the manuscript quite naturally as I was writing. Petra has not embraced herself, but she's found a way, at least, to trick herself into speaking her own words with some confidence for once.

One of the themes I wanted to highlight in this story was the idea of teens feeling miserably born into a wrong era. I was one of those teens, and I have since met many, many more—possibly it's a common thing. Certainly feeling like an outsider is common enough. Anyway, growing up, for me, meant learning that there was a bigger world than the one I currently occupied, and that if I wanted to live in a world that I liked, it was perfectly possible that it already existed somewhere if I went looking. It was important to me that Petra find other people who also loved language like she did. I reckon it's possible to write a story that doesn't have a seed of personal importance to it, but I don't suppose I want to find out.

merely how you looked when you were sitting in that moment. How about you pose again, and this time you sit as you'd like to look in the painting? If you still don't like it, we can always call it off then."

Petra hesitated.

"I don't want to make you uncomfortable."

"It's just that I don't think it will make a difference. I'm—I'm a lump," Petra confessed.

"You are *sitting* lumpily," Geraldine insisted. "No one *is* a lump."

They held eyes for a moment. Finally, Petra let out a breath. "All right, I'll try."

So she sat on the couch again, and this time she looked at Geraldine's posture. Shoulders back and chin up, of course. But there was more, too. Knees together? A slight tilt to the head? It all felt ridiculous and undefinable. Her ears wouldn't stop burning.

"I feel stupid," she confessed, even though *stupid* wasn't a Geraldine word. "Foolish. I feel like I'm playing a part."

Geraldine inclined her head gently. She was still sitting perfectly straight, and that tilt of her chin was entirely natural and beautiful and ageless. Petra, still a ramrod, felt she couldn't move any of her body or she'd immediately turn back into the lump she'd just seen drawn on Geraldine's paper.

"Just recite," Geraldine said. "Fetch one of your books and read me something. You have beautiful posture when you perform."

Which was how Petra ended up reading the entirety of Ezra Pound's "First Canto" (he was also a singularly unpleasant man) while Geraldine sketched her with charcoal.

Geraldine turned the paper for inspection. Both of them smiled at it.

"I look like someone out of the nineteenth century," Petra said.

"You look," Geraldine said, "ladylike."

. . .

There were only three shallow steps into Petra's family's home. It took no effort at all to climb them. She could, in fact, stretch and take all three stairs at once without falling. They were nothing like the stairs into Geraldine's apartment. They were a real-life sort of word—"consider"—versus a Geraldine sort of word—"prevaricate."

. . .

"I believe the underpainting is finally done," Geraldine said. She had spent several sessions painting a blocky version of Petra in improbable colors. "I don't like underpainting. It's so very messy. Do you have any Dickinson? She's pleasant."

Petra was getting good at sitting for her portrait; ever since the day of the sketches, they'd spent half an hour of their time together with Petra frozen like a statue and Geraldine squinting at her to do something she called "establishing values." Now, in response to Geraldine's question, Petra moved only her mouth, not her body. "Do you think she's pleasant? She seems so dire to me."

"I like her," Geraldine said. "She was a shut-in and never left her house. Do you have 'A great Hope fell'? I like that one quite a bit."

She plunged her brush into turpentine; Petra took this as a cue that she could move.

"I don't think so," Petra replied, admitting, "I don't know if I'd even know, because my index isn't great on this book. Is that the first line of the poem? She didn't use titles, did she?"

"No, sometimes, if you can't find a prettier way to say something, it's better to just not name it at all." Geraldine had been gesturing to herself, but now she pointed to a ferny area. "If you take a look in that room, there's a small green shelf with a small green book on it, and the book is a volume of Dickinson. If you're of the mind, you could fetch it back while I clean these brushes."

Part of Petra thrilled; she was intensely curious about what the rest of the apartment contained. So much of it remained hidden to her still, coyly peeking from behind screens or shrinking back behind man-sized palm trees. To be granted permission to pry seemed like a gift, and who didn't like presents?

Following Geraldine's directions, she found herself in an area so convincingly walled by great leafy plants that it was hard to believe there really weren't walls behind them. The furniture struck Petra as . . . *colonial*. Not in the American sense, but in the British sense. Fancy

I often get asked if I intentionally place morals into my stories. Not really. I don't think anyone wants to be preached at. But still, I know that I'm saying things with my stories: broad concepts, broad themes, broad assumptions. For instance, I know that with this story I'm saying that I think that being painfully shy is something to be overcome, not something to embrace. I'm saying that on purpose, but sometimes I find that my rough drafts are saying something by accident: scenes or character moments are arranged in such a way that I seem to imply that ambition is evil, or that being brave means being a bad friend, etc. At the end of the day, I always try to make sure my stories are only saying things I mean. I mention it here because I had to revamp a line of Geraldine's conversation in this section. She originally said "Some things are better not named," which is in direct conflict with what she said earlier to Petra, about just acknowledging Petra's blushing with pretty words. Is that what I want to say—that Geraldine is living her life by not acknowledging what she is? No. What I want to say is that Geraldine is repurposing her identity—she knows what she is, but she embroiders and beautifies it into something more elegant than the raw truth.

old British tents set up in the jungles of a far-flung empire. It contained an old trunk with a beautiful latch that begged her to open it (she did not) and a faded teal chair that looked like it might be easily folded (she did not) and a bookshelf that only came up to her knees. Everything was either Lilliputian or collapsible, the better to be conveniently taken to the next small country to be colonized. Petra had to kneel on the Persian rug and turn her head sideways in order to find the Dickinson on the bottom shelf.

Possibly Geraldine's accent, Petra thought, was also *colonial.* It wasn't English, that was for certain. But she was hard pressed to further identify it. Perhaps it was English by way of a non-English-speaking colony.

As Petra stood, her eye was caught by a cage. It was in the next "room" over, behind the ferns, barely visible in the dying afternoon light and the shadows of plants. It was as tall as Petra and only a meter or so wide, with wrought iron bars spaced as wide as her hand. It must have been decorative, she thought, because an animal large enough to not be able to slip through those bars would have been too long to fit inside it. Petra stepped closer, craning her neck. If she didn't leave the ferned room she was in now, it wasn't trespassing; it wasn't rude. The bars were dinged and worn. This close she could see the door—thin and nearly as tall as the door to the apartment—and see that it had a newish padlock hanging open on the latch. There was something dark stained across the bars of the door.

Blood, thought Petra dramatically, since furniture polish seemed unlikely. Possibly it was paint, or rust.

But dramatic Petra preferred the idea of blood.

"Did you find it?" Geraldine called.

Petra snatched the Dickinson book closer to herself. "Yes!"

She returned to the painting area, guilty about her prying eyes, and allowed Geraldine to page to the Dickinson poem she wanted Petra to read.

It was dire, as all of Emily Dickinson's poems were.

A great Hope fell
You heard no noise
The Ruin was within
Oh cunning wreck that told no tale
And let no Witness in

The mind was built for mighty Freight
For dread occasion planned
How often foundering at Sea
Ostensibly, on Land

A not admitting of the wound
Until it grew so wide
That all my Life had entered it
And there were troughs beside

A closing of the simple lid
That opened to the sun
Until the tender Carpenter
Perpetual nail it down—

But Geraldine sat with her eyes half-closed and her mouth turned up, like a cat in the sun, listening to the words with evident enjoyment.

"Dire," Petra concluded at the end.

"Introspective," countered Geraldine.

"No," Petra argued, "it's dire because of her story. She was so shy that she stayed away in her house, and she got shyer and shyer as she went on, and so eventually she just never left her house. So this *'a not admitting of the wound until it grew so wide that all my Life had entered it'* is terrible. It's when she realizes that she's thrown herself away because she's locked herself away."

Geraldine said, "You didn't say 'uh.'"

They looked at each other. Petra thought about it. She had not said "uh." She was also still standing straight.

Petra said, "I was declaiming."

Geraldine said, "Yes, you were."

. . .

The portrait would never be done. Petra took to wearing the same coat each time so that Geraldine could spend hours just painting the reflections on buttons.

"Why didn't you like the underpainting?" Petra asked.

"It's so messy," Geraldine replied. She tapped her brush against a painted button. "I like things in their place."

Petra wondered if that cage was in its place.

. . .

"I think we should move your times up an hour, or even two," Frances said. Frances was Marla's younger sister. She was clearly composed of the same stuff as Marla—the same tiny nose, the same square jaw—only everything seemed to be fashioned on a smaller scale. Even her fancy clothing was more delicate than Marla's. Her fingers shook in the breeze, and her hair trembled when she moved. Her words were like little birds in a tree, fluttering for only a moment before they flickered off to a safer branch. "Now that it's getting later in the year and we're losing so much sunlight."

Petra tried to think of everything she wanted to say before she said it. "This timing works really well with me, though, because of school. And, uh, the bus schedule."

"One of us could drive you," Frances said. Her words darted to a higher branch as she considered the logistics. "Or we could pay for a taxi."

"I don't mind going home in the dark."

"Well, we do worry so." Frances's fingers frantically built themselves an invisible nest and then took it apart. "You've become so important to Geraldine, and we wouldn't want your discomfort to get in the way of that."

This struck Petra as ridiculous. She'd just *said* that she wasn't uncomfortable, hadn't she?

"I'm fine."

"Well. Just. Think about it?"

"Okay," Petra said. She put her hand on the handle for the door. Behind it was the eternal staircase, and at the end of it, Geraldine. "Are you headed up?"

"Oh, no," said Frances. "No, no. Those stairs! Tell her I will call. Give her my love."

What sort of love, Petra thought, wouldn't climb the stairs?

. . .

There was a third daughter-not-daughter whom Petra had not met. Edith. Lawyer Edith. Both Marla and Frances spoke of her in a hushed tone; the dramatic side of Petra who appreciated long words and the possibility of bloodstains also liked to spend time imagining why Edith might be spoken of sotto voce. Perhaps she was ill, and they feared she would die if they spoke too loudly. Perhaps she was hidden away—a very Victorian sort of thing to do—because she was insane, or perhaps she was serving prison time for a grievous crime. Perhaps they had been estranged and longed for her to return to them.

Now that Petra knew Geraldine better—well? No, not well. Did anyone know Geraldine well?—she wanted badly to ask her what her relationship was to Marla, Frances, and Edith, but it wasn't as if Petra could just ask her *directly*. After several days, she struck upon a sneaky possibility.

So it was December, and Petra climbed the stairs. Petra was growing better at the ascent, but the December stairs were far more annoying than the October stairs because in December one made the ascent in a coat. The coat was apropos for the first four hours of the climb, but by the time Petra had passed all of the tiny villages and the trees that had grown small because of the thinness of the mountain air, the exertion had coated the intrepid mountain climber's body with a thin film of sweat. One could not remove the coat, however, because the climber was using all muscle and mind-power just to place a foot on the next stair. There was none left over to imagine pulling the coat from the body and carrying it over one arm.

Petra ascended. She knocked on the door, loudly, to be heard over the aspirational sounds of the Peer Gynt Suite.

"Petra," Geraldine said warmly.

"I'm disgusting," Petra warned.

"We all are," Geraldine said, "but that's why we have manners, to make us bearable. Come in."

Geraldine made tea while Petra took off her coat and walked in circles, flapping her hands in the direction of her armpits.

"Shall we paint first?" Geraldine handed her the tea.

"Oh, uh, can we read first? I'm still sticky."

She was pleased to deliver this line with only the slightest bit of blushing, partially from discomfort at making a direct request and partly from a surfeit of strategy swelling within her. She was thrilled and guilty with anticipation.

As Geraldine settled herself on a chaise, transforming into an attentive audience, Petra collected her poem. As she got ready to throw her shoulders back into her oratory pose, she realized with a bit of surprise that they already *were* mostly back. She'd been simply standing around halfway to her oratory pose. Perhaps, she thought, she *had* been building muscles from posing for Geraldine. Somehow, a tiny rope bridge had been thrown across from ordinary Petra to oratory Petra. Rickety, but connected nonetheless.

"Tell me a story," Geraldine said grandly.

"This poem is from Ann Taylor," Petra said. "Not the clothing designer, but the sister of Jane Taylor, who wrote 'Twinkle, Twinkle, Little Star.' The two of them were frequently confused with each other, as they published works together. Jane died young, and so she was remembered more than Ann—O! To die young and live forever in the minds of the people."

Now that she'd said that line out loud, Petra suspected that was probably overwrought, even for an audience of Geraldines, but it had seemed fine when she tried it out to the mirror the night before. Oh well. O! well.

"I haven't heard any Ann Taylor," Geraldine mused. "Which piece are you reading?"

"'My Mother,'" Petra replied, feeling even more deceptive and crafty. Now her ears went red. But she pressed on, beginning with,

> Who fed me from her gentle breast,
> And hush'd me in her arms to rest,
> And on my cheek sweet kisses prest?
> My Mother.

She eyed Geraldine for signs of telltale emotion, but she was merely observing in the same way she always did: eyes half-closed, chin tilted, a sunflower turned toward the light.

Petra persisted—it was a very long poem, and exceedingly saccharine, if she was being honest, but the best she could do with only thirty minutes of allotted computer time after homework. There were far worse things on the Internet when one typed in "poetry about mothers."

> Who ran to help me when I fell,
> And would some pretty story tell,
> Or kiss the place to make it well?
> My Mother.

It was precisely what one would expect from the sister of the author of "Twinkle, Twinkle, Little Star." A few stanzas in, one of Geraldine's eyebrows lifted slightly, but it was hard to tell if it was because of the maternal content or because of the predictably easy rhyme of *gay* and *play* in one of the stanzas in the interminable middle.

Petra finally concluded:

> When thou art feeble, old, and gray,
> My healthy arm shall be thy stay,
> And I will soothe thy pains away,
> My Mother.

> And when I see thee hang thy head,
> 'Twill be my turn to watch *thy* bed.
> And tears of sweet affection shed,
> My Mother.

Geraldine said, "My."

"It's used on Mother's Day cards sometimes," Petra said.

"Shocking." Geraldine wasn't often sarcastic, and so this single word caused both of them more mirth than it otherwise might. But then her face turned more thoughtful. "Is that how you feel about your mother?"

Barbara Tantalo, Petra's mother, was the sort of woman who would be fond of this poem, which was also the reason why she and Petra didn't always see eye to eye. It wasn't that Petra didn't like melodrama (O Melodrama!), it just was a very different sort of melodrama. It was perhaps just that Petra liked fancy words, and her mother liked fancy feelings. Petra liked Geraldine's impossibly slender plants; Petra's mom liked photographs of joggers with words like STRIVE printed beneath them. An ode to Petra's love for her mother would more likely begin with *Who is scented with hair spray and toothpaste / and taught me to get takeaway with great haste?*

"Not exactly," Petra said. "I think she feels that way about me, though." Then she realized that the poem was working exactly as she'd intended. Quite casually, she asked, "Is it how you feel about your mother?"

Geraldine looked suddenly remote, just then, looking up toward the ceiling. Not at all emotional. Merely *nonpresent.* "Hm. No. No, I didn't know my mother. It wasn't our culture to know our mothers."

Petra opened her mouth with a burning and probably rude question, and then closed it, and then opened it with another less burning but probably still rude question, and then closed it again. Finally, she went with the rather ambiguous, "And what do you think about Marla?"

"Marla?" Geraldine's note of surprise alone confirmed that Marla wasn't her daughter: she didn't understand why Marla was being inserted into the maternal conversation. "She seems brisk, but she's not as ferocious as she seems. I know she still holidays with her mother every year."

In the face of Geraldine's ever-polite honesty, Petra felt suddenly foolish. Deceptive. All of this felt ridiculous. She should have just asked Geraldine all along, she realized. Geraldine was polite, not coy. Studying her feet, she admitted, "I thought Marla and Edith and Frances were your daughters."

There was no response, and Petra went redder than she had gone in weeks. She felt the blush in the curls of her guts. She had really put her foot in it now. Geraldine was possibly childless and barren and sorrowful, or was a dear aunt after her sister had died messily, or some other terrible scenario dramatic Petra had yet to concoct.

The silence went on forever, and then Petra looked up and saw that Geraldine was looking upon her in a rather . . . tender way.

"What a kind thing," Geraldine said. "What a very kind thing. No, I'm not their mother, Petra, but I'm so touched that you would draw that conclusion."

Her lip was doing the thing that Petra's mother's sometimes did as she cried over something touching, but Geraldine did not cry.

Petra went red again, but it didn't feel terrible, for once. It felt appropriate, which she had not thought was possible. She suggested, "Shall we paint?"

"Oh, yes," Geraldine replied. "Let's attack these buttons."

And they fell into companionable fussing over pigmented glints of light. After some space, the phone rang. Petra had not heard it ring before. It was a proper, old-fashioned phone, and the ring sounded like a real bell.

Geraldine excused herself to answer. Petra's guilt over finagling mother stories out of Geraldine earlier sadly did not prevent her from eavesdropping as best she could, especially when she realized that it was Edith, and that Geraldine was displeased.

"Don't be tedious, Edith, of course not. No, you insult me by suggesting that I would let my own appetite get in the way of my courtesy. Do you not think I would have let you know if it was an issue?"

Petra abruptly remembered how Frances had asked her to move her appointment time forward. Was it because she was treading clumsily, the great troll once again, over appointed dinners?

"Yes, fine. You would like to speak to Petra? Of course I sound strident, Edith; I'm terribly offended." Geraldine paused. Her voice called out from behind a peacock-painted screen, "Petra, Edith would like to speak to you."

Petra felt she had accidently invoked Edith by spending so much time obsessing over her, by bringing up mothers. She joined Geraldine in a room composed of old mirrors. A single claw-footed table held a satisfyingly old-fashioned telephone.

"Hello, this is Petra?" Then she repeated "Petra" because she had mumbled it.

"Excellent. This is Edith, Marla and Frances's sister. I wanted to make sure that Frances had spoken to you about moving your time up." Edith's voice was not brisk at all; it was rather more musical than Marla's. But there was a sense of surety to it that gave it more iron than Marla's.

"Oh, yes," Petra said, "but it wasn't, uh, necessary, because I don't mind traveling after dark." She didn't look at Geraldine. Instead she watched the streetlights out the window, yellow in the blue evening.

"It's just a question of timing and dining," Edith said smoothly. "It would really be so much better if you could come earlier. Or perhaps we can just end the sessions an hour or so earlier?"

Petra felt an unexpected pang at the thought of losing an hour.

She got herself together. Using Geraldine's precise intonation, she managed, "I don't want to impose."

She darted a glance to Geraldine in one of the mirrors. She wore a curious expression. It was remote, like before, but her eyes were narrowed. Her face was more intent than Petra had ever seen. She was a sharper, darker thing; it made her younger and less like someone Petra knew.

"It will be better this way. We'll have a taxi get you before it gets dark from now on. Wonderful. Thanks so much for understanding," Edith said.

"Do you need to speak to Geraldine again?"

"Oh, no. We're fine," Edith said. "Give her my love."

. . .

The bus that took Petra home headed down a street newly strung with Christmas lights; Petra could see the breaths of the pedestrians hurrying along the sidewalk. She considered what she might get Geraldine for Christmas. She didn't think about losing an hour with her.

As she stepped off the bus, the homeless man at her bus stop called, "Show me your tits!"

Petra started to duck her head, but stopped. Turning, she said, "That was singularly unkind."

He stared at her. Her ears were only flushing a little. She couldn't believe herself. Part of her was already reliving her words, trying to decide if she'd really had the courage to say them out loud. She had. She really had.

In that moment, Petra decided that she would do anything to keep from losing an hour with Geraldine.

When she arrived home, her mother was taping metallic wrapping paper on their front door to make it look like a holiday package. She asked Petra, "How's my fairy princess today? Did you see the carolers?"

There aren't any chapters in this story, but these section breaks are close enough for my purposes. Chapters used to perplex me (okay, fine, I'll admit it: sometimes they still do). I'd notice that I had written a massive chunk of text—usually all taking place over the course of a single day, because of my inability to figure out "show, don't tell," as previously noted—and I'd throw in some chapter breaks. This, Stiefvater, is not the way to chapter! If it helps, imagine your story or novel as a playlist or a music album. A great playlist isn't just thrown together, a dozen songs that all sound the same. Instead, it includes several songs tied together thematically, arranged in such a way as to pull the listener through without boredom. You wouldn't group all the slow songs together in a playlist; don't clump together slow chapters, either. Likewise, if you put a bunch of fast songs back to back, they stop being exciting. I frequently read back over my work in order to make sure the story is flowing well. Sort of like listening to the playlist you've just made before you send it to your editor with an e-mail that says LISTEN TO THIS IT'S LIFE-CHANGING.

"I'm quitting the Oratory Club," Petra said.

Her mother immediately lowered her arms. "Oh! Did something happen?"

Petra considered her words carefully before she said them, leaning to get a piece of tape to buy herself yet more time. She secured a drooping corner of the metallic paper, and then she said grandly, "I decided it was time to officially take my declaiming out of a club and into the world."

Her mother looked at her. The Santa on her sweatshirt looked at Petra too. Her mother blinked. The Santa did not.

Petra said, "I need that hour for something else."

"Oh, that makes sense," her mother said.

. . .

There was someone else in the apartment when Petra hiked the stairs the Thursday before Christmas. The presence of a third entity was so unexpected that at first she thought she had turned a shadow into a person, the way you scan past a shrub and think *dog* before a second look returns everything to inanimate objects.

It was a coat hung strangely, an easel moved, a shadow cast from a curtain fallen askew. But it was none of those things: it was a real, live man. Maybe a young man. Older than Petra, certainly, but also not old. Petra couldn't tell at first what he looked like, or if he was handsome, or what his facial expression was, because it was a rule of Petra's that unless a member of the opposite sex was very young or very old, she could not look at him straight on without going red, no matter how revolting he was. The only possible way to avoid her ears going red was to avoid eye contact for as long as possible.

So there was a young man sitting against the wall when she came in, knees up, but she could tell nothing more about him because she couldn't look at him just yet.

Geraldine shut the door behind her. She was already holding a paintbrush. Something about her face reminded Petra of the afternoon Edith had called; there was that sharp, shadowed look to it. "Good afternoon, Petra."

"Good afternoon," Petra replied.

Geraldine drifted back toward her easel. Petra's portrait leaned against the legs of it; a rather docile landscape sat at the work area.

"I thought perhaps we could read some John Masefield today." Geraldine dabbed an impossibly small dab of blue on the end of her brush, the motion delicate as a queen dabbing a napkin to her lips. "*'I must go down to the seas again, to the lonely sea and the sky*—' Well suited to this sort of drab day, I think."

She didn't say anything about the young man. This was so rudely unlike her that Petra doubted her own vision: perhaps he wasn't there after all. Perhaps he really was a coat or an easel or a shadow.

Petra risked another glance at him.

He sat alongside the wall, head hung down, earbuds in, brown hair combed over in a rather old-fashioned way. He was in a tweed vest and nice pants and wore very long leather shoes. He looked like a young William B. Yeats come from the past. He didn't look at Petra at all, and she suspected he was one of those lofty, handsome young men with the sorts of smiles that were mostly always directed at themselves if they bothered to smile at all. This made Petra amorphously angry at him. She wanted to ask what he was even *doing* there, but she knew Geraldine would find such a question rude, so she just swallowed her annoyance.

So instead she found herself pretending all was normal as she recited John Masefield out of one of Geraldine's faded old volumes, and as she drank tea as Geraldine dabbed dark promises on the bottom of the clouds in her landscape, and as she sat on the chaise and posed for her own portrait. All the while she was infinitely aware that the young man had not moved and that Geraldine was not making any allowances to include him in any of their activities.

It really was possible that he was not real. (O Spirit of the storm / Thy lightning sleeps in its sheath!) Petra simply couldn't think of any other explanation for Geraldine's impolite disinterest in his existence. Even dramatic Petra was having a hard time inventing imaginary histories for him.

Geraldine didn't so much as acknowledge him until the end of their time. She put down her brush and then—ever so briefly—glanced to the young man and away. It was abruptly clear that Geraldine was ignoring his presence, as sniffy and condescending as she'd ever been.

"What a lovely afternoon," Geraldine said coolly. "Thank you for coming, as always, Petra."

"I'm bringing Emerson to read tomorrow," Petra warned. She tried not to look at the young man, but she did, just in time for him to dart his eyes up at her and away. He ducked his head again.

"Excellent," Geraldine said. "That will be wonderful."

Petra left. He stayed.

. . .

Three *days*. He was there three days, and Geraldine didn't acknowledge him. He never spoke to them, either, just sat there with his earbuds in, wearing the same impeccable vest and pants.

Petra was going to break. She was going to bring in poetry about houseguests or strange men or pointy leather shoes or repressed silence and she would force an answer. She would march up to him and demand to know if he was a new piece of furniture. She would make a fuss.

Instead, she met with Marla.

"There's a problem," Marla asked, but she didn't use a question mark. The winter wind clawed at her hair, but it stayed on. "What is it?" Oh, there was the question mark.

"I don't mean to be rude, but who is that guy?"

"Guy?"

"In the apartment."

Marla's body went on high alert. There were not very many animals in the city, but once Petra had seen a cat that had been hit by a car on a side street. It remained there for several days, long enough to go completely stiff, with its limbs pointing out in a way that proved conclusively that it was no longer among the living.

Marla's posture suggested she was no longer among the living.

This prodded at the dramatic side of Petra, finally. Maybe he was . . . Geraldine's concubine. Or maybe he was a younger brother of Marla and Frances and Edith, estranged for years and now returned to Geraldine. Maybe —

"Is he—how did—tell me the situation."

"There's just a guy there, and has been, and Geraldine seems to be ignoring him. I didn't mean to be nosy, it just seemed peculiar."

Marla released an angry sigh, breath through a bull's nostrils. "Well, this is just too bad! When Edith finds out—so typical." She got herself back together. "I'm sorry for the discomfort. We'll take care of it. Are you headed up now?"

"Yes. Are you—"

"No. No, I need to talk to Edith. Tell Geraldine to expect my call."

· · ·

On the fourth day, the clouds finally burst in the apartment.

Geraldine let Petra in from the stairwell. She was getting fairly good at the journey; she only took a moment to collect herself. In that moment, her gaze fell upon the young man's long and pointy shoes. They were in precisely the same place they had been for the past three days. Perhaps, Petra thought, the young man had climbed the stairs and then been too exhausted to ever imagine moving again.

"I apologize for my rudeness," Geraldine said. "I was quite upset with someone else, and I took it out on Daniel here. Daniel, will you come join us?"

Daniel—he was still there! In the same clothing! He had a name! Geraldine was looking right at him!— lifted his head to gaze at them. Petra was able to study him long enough that she should have been able to pin his age to a decade, but she could not. He was young *looking*, with prematurely sunken cheeks and half-closed eyes that seemed biologically fashioned for expressing disinterest. His hands were enormous, with knobby joints. A styrofoam takeout box sat on the floor beside him. He was *comely* enough that Petra was proud of herself for not blushing immediately.

His eyes skipped over Geraldine to Petra. She couldn't begin to interpret his expression; she didn't know if she'd seen it before.

Then Daniel scowled and dropped his chin again, pressing one earbud more securely in place.

"Perhaps later," Geraldine said.

They tried to carry on as usual. Geraldine was nearly done with Petra's portrait. It *looked* done to Petra—she had been transformed into a faintly smiling lady holding a book of faintly fancy words— but Geraldine fussed over highlights on strands of hair and texture in the weave of Petra's collar. She seemed distracted—no, unfocused. Like Petra at school when she hadn't slept well. She barely commented on Petra's reading, even though Petra had spent rather a lot of time finding some context for Ezra Pound, who was even more singularly unkind than Petra had first imagined.

Daniel remained where he was.

When the taxi came, Geraldine sighed. "I'm terribly sorry, Petra, but could you show yourself out? I think I'll lie down now."

At first Petra thought she had heard her wrong.

Lie down? What was this madness? Geraldine was not an old woman; she did not lie down; she did not nap; she did not get so tired that she could not even walk Petra to the door.

Show yourself out.

Petra could. She could certainly show herself out. But why? *Why* was she showing herself out?

But she did. On the way out, she stopped by Daniel. She blamed him for this disruption to their schedule and for Geraldine's distraction and, at the most basic level, for Geraldine having to lie down. Standing there, with the toes of her shoes a millimeter away from his fancy shoes, she considered multiple ways to express her thoughts.

Finally, he said, "Look, I don't want to talk to you."

This was so suddenly unpleasant that Petra felt her lips part. Her surprise needed a path for escape. "Excuse me?"

"I don't want to get to know you, and you don't want to get to know me. So I don't see the point in talking."

Petra's ears burned, but only a little. She used Geraldine's crisp voice to say, "How do you know I don't want to get to know you?"

"Oh please," he muttered dismissively. "People like you don't want to know guys like me."

"What?"

"Just talk at me and try to straighten me out, or whatever. So just leave me alone. I'll be out of here soon enough."

Petra's mouth needed to open a little wider to let a bit more surprise out. *People like who?* Lump people? "You're being singularly unkind. I'm not going to fight with you. But if I find out you've done anything to upset Geraldine, *I'll* be unkind."

Now he looked surprised—his surprise escaped in the space between his eyes and his eyebrows—and didn't reply when she said, "Good *evening*!"

She left. He stayed.

. . .

On Wednesday, Edith asked Petra to not come in to Geraldine's—a therapist was coming to see Geraldine and that was the only time he had available on short notice.

What sort of therapist? asked Petra's brain. "Sure," said Petra's mouth. She had prepared a lengthy reading on war and poppies to lift Geraldine's spirits. And she had bought her a Christmas present. She didn't know if Geraldine celebrated Christmas, but she knew she'd appreciate the gesture. "Tomorrow's fine, though, right?"

"Right, of course," Edith said. "Geraldine would be so upset to lose more than a day with you."

Petra was going to leave it at that, but she had a thought, and she knew how to say it, so she asked, "Can I be of any help? As far as the therapist goes?"

Edith brightened at the question. "You are so kind! No, we've all heard good things about Mr. Goodminster. He'll perk Geraldine right up. He says he knows just how to make her regain her enthusiasm for eating. He hopes it might only take one session."

Eating! Enthusiasm! At least *this* made sense. Petra supposed Geraldine's newfound fatigue wasn't really Daniel's fault, then, but she was still annoyed with him.

"I could make her something," Petra said, even though she was only sure how to boil eggs. She could learn. Or she could find something; Brooklyn was full of delicious things. Geraldine would surely like something fiddly and beautiful.

Edith replied, "Oh, I don't think that would do any good. She's a very fussy eater."

Now that Petra thought about it, she'd never seen Geraldine eat anything at all.

. . .

To distract herself from her aching knees on the trek up to Geraldine's apartment, Petra sometimes played make-believe with herself as she climbed. One of her favorites was to imagine that it was snowing inside the stairwell. With each foot she placed on the stair, she imagined flakes gently beginning to dust the concrete and then pile in the corners and then, finally, drift over all of the stairs. By the time she got to the top of the stairs, she could imagine that she might be able to sled down after the session was over.

She knocked. Geraldine opened the door; Petra examined her for signs of feebleness.

"I'll get you tea," Geraldine said. Did she look more hollow-eyed?

As Petra sloughed her coat, she saw that Daniel was still there. His MP3 player was shunted to the side, the earbuds coiled into a tense noose beside it. Possibly the battery had died. He made a great show of not looking at Petra as she passed by him, but it was obvious that he could hear her footsteps. It was obvious, too, once Petra began reading, that he found it more difficult to ignore them. Petra could feel his attention on them as she read Yeats's "Sailing to Byzantium" and while she and Geraldine chatted about the book *The Golden Bough*. She saw his finger jittering against the floor in time with a rousing round of Rachmaninoff from the gramophone.

She felt his eyes as she gave Geraldine her Christmas present, a copper globe. Only the continents were formed of solid pieces of metal; the ocean was criss-crossed with thin metal wires holding the land aloft. It was intricate and fussy and Geraldine made an enormous show of adoring it.

"I didn't realize it was Christmas," Geraldine said. "I thought it had already gone by."

"It's the nineteenth," Petra replied, but Geraldine didn't seem interested in the date. It was hard to tell if this was because of her new vagueness, or because she had never been interested in time. If this was because Geraldine wasn't eating, Petra was eager for Geraldine to resume eating at once. She asked, "Do you like Mr. Goodminster?"

Geraldine turned her rings around and around. "He's pleasant enough."

Daniel snorted from his post by the wall. Geraldine looked in his direction, expression cool and polite. To Petra, she said, "He means well, even if he doesn't really understand me."

Petra asked the same thing she'd asked Edith. "Can I be of any help?"

"You're already a help," Geraldine said. The taxi was there; her head tilted sharply to the window. "You are a lovely gift, Petra. I'm going to go lie down. I'll see you tomorrow. Thank you for everything."

As Petra left, Daniel muttered, "This place is a madhouse."

· · ·

It took three sessions before Petra met Mr. Goodminster. They ran into each other outside the apartment building, him coming out of the stairwell, her heading in. The timing wasn't exactly coincidental; Petra had assumed that his sessions lasted an hour, and so she lurked across the road in the bus shelter, glancing from her phone to the door until she saw the door crack. She wasn't sure what she was expecting from the therapist, but it wasn't this: a slight man with a long braid down his back and a quilted jacket and moccasins. He looked like he should be selling psychic readings. He did not look like an expert. Petra was both relieved and angry.

She grabbed her bag to her and marched across the street.

"Hello," she said, "I'm Petra. You must be Mr. Goodminster." She held out her hand so that he had to shake as well. He had a noncommittal handshake; his fingers seemed to squeeze out of hers like toothpaste from a tube when she tried to get a better grip.

"Oh, I am, I am."

"I'm Geraldine's companion," Petra said, trying to sound brisk. "How did the session go?"

"I'm not at, uh, leisure, to uh, discuss patient? Confidential? Privilege?"

"I'm very committed to her health," Petra insisted. "I could help."

Mr. Goodminster peered at her. "Oh, right. Sure. Well, just keep coming. She looks forward to your visits like no other."

Petra was annoyed by this answer. She could have been having a visit with Geraldine this afternoon if not for his useless session. "Well, those aren't going to stop."

"Good, good. Good. Good."

"I thought," Petra persisted, "Edith said you might get this fixed in one session."

He blinked as if Petra had thrown acid in his face. "I thought she might respond to, ah, less persuasive methods. I've moved to the next step. Wait—wait, are you going up now?"

This was because he saw Petra's hand on the door handle. She had taken the fifteen seconds before her last sentence and the fifteen seconds during his to gain some perspective, and she'd decided she was going to go see Geraldine. Not as a job. As a friend.

"Yes," Petra said.

"Oh, that's very not—that shouldn't probably—"

Petra drew herself up into oratory Petra and eyed him. She waited for him to finish telling her why it was a bad idea, but either client confidentiality or fear of Petra stopped him. His ears went red, and Petra suddenly felt very bad for being brisk at him. She was unused to being on this side of the blushing table. Taking his hand, she clasped it with both of hers, like Geraldine had done on the first day they met.

"Don't worry," Petra said. "I won't stay long."

. . .

Stairs. Done. Petra wasn't even out of breath; she was triumphant.

Geraldine opened the door at her knock. Her face in the crack of the door was delighted and surprised. "Petra! My love. Do come in."

Petra did come in. She kissed Geraldine on the cheek. Geraldine had first done it to her the week previously, and it had been such a delightful and polite gesture that Petra had adopted it at once.

"I thought Mr. Goodminster had stolen today from us," Geraldine said.

"I won't stay long," Petra replied quickly, warmed

by Geraldine's affection. "I just wanted to visit for a moment."

"Oh, *do* stay long," Geraldine insisted. "*What* a pleasant surprise. You look so lovely today! Perhaps we should start a new portrait of you."

Petra shucked her coat. She shot Daniel a dirty look—he was already looking at them with his mouth twisted, a new takeout box beside him—and then hung her coat on the rack behind the door. "I like the one you're doing now."

"Oh, yes, but you're brighter now," Geraldine said. "Are we reading first today? I'll get you a cup of tea."

"Does *Daniel* want one too?" Petra asked.

Daniel's chin jerked up at the sound of his name. He scowled at Geraldine. "*Daniel* doesn't want a cup of tea. Daniel wants what he came for. Daniel wants this to be over with! Come on, you old beast!"

Petra's mouth hung open.

Geraldine's face was stricken. In a breath she had reassembled and composed it, but the previous expression was still branded in Petra's mind.

Daniel leaped to his feet. Petra had not realized the full extent of his immobility until he was mobile, because the tallness of him seemed like the most incredible thing, like watching a sapling grow in fast-forward. He was much older than Petra had remembered, too, and suddenly utterly unfamiliar. Somehow her mind had rendered him harmless, but now that he was standing, towering over them both, she realized suddenly that he was a stranger. He was brandishing something, too—it took Petra a long moment to realize that it was a small, unmarked spray bottle.

"Don't be unpleasant," Geraldine said, her eyes on Daniel, not the bottle.

"What is that?" Petra asked. Her voice came out thinner than she meant it to.

"Yes, what is this?" Daniel shook it in front of Geraldine. "Will it work? Mr. Goodminster seemed excited for us to try it."

Geraldine lifted her chin, looking defiant rather than afraid. Daniel sprayed a puff into the air, and then, oddly enough, onto himself. He pumped it a few more times in his direction, and then hers. Geraldine held an elegant hand in front of her, mouth pursed in distaste, as spray misted the air. She turned her face away as the drops shone around her head.

"You're making a scene," Geraldine said through her fingers.

With a growl, Daniel turned to Petra and sprayed a puff on her.

Petra only had a moment to recoil from the fine, earthy-scented mist before Geraldine said, "*Stop that*," in a knife-edged tone.

Both Daniel and Petra were frozen. Petra had never heard anything like that voice come out of her before.

Daniel unfroze before Petra. He stepped close to Geraldine and snarled, shaking, "*Get it over with*."

Geraldine didn't flinch. Instead, she reached up and took the bottle out of his hand, as quietly and surely as someone taking a box from a shelf. Then she said, "Get yourself together. Have you no respect for yourself?" To Petra she said, "Please excuse me for a moment, Petra."

As she turned, Daniel seized her arm, jerking her closer. "*No.*"

Petra didn't even think—she just swung her bag at his head. Daniel grunted. The strawberry lip gloss and bottle of mace probably had not had much of an impact, but the two volumes of nineteenth-century poetry probably had. When he didn't fall over or back down, Petra swung it at him again, and once more for good measure.

"Stop, you lunatic!" he hissed finally, clutching his temple. At some point in Petra's beating, he had released Geraldine. She was backed several feet away, holding her hand over her mouth. "God. You've probably given me brain damage. What do you have in there?"

He sank to the floor, careful not to crush his takeout boxes.

Petra realized that her heart was racing. Her arms felt liquefied. "Should I— Should I call the police?"

Geraldine still had her hand over her mouth; she spoke through her rings. "No. Isn't that right, Daniel?"

"Call them on this crazy girl, maybe," muttered Daniel. He linked his arms over the back of his head. Voice muffled, he added after a moment, "I'm not sorry for calling you a beast. You are a beast."

"And you're a sack of meat," Geraldine said, "but we are more than that too, aren't we?"

"Speak for yourself," growled Daniel. His fingers were white-knuckled in his hair. He looked more shaken than either Petra or Geraldine.

Geraldine said, "Petra, I must have a moment, I'm so sorry. I will make you some tea."

Petra got herself together. "No, please don't—"

"I need a moment," Geraldine insisted. "It would help me a lot if you would find something to read to me. Unless you are too bothered. I understand entirely."

Petra was sort of still too bothered to just forget about the previous minutes, but her options were doing as Geraldine asked or simply leaving. She shot a gasoline-tinged look at the top of Daniel's motionless head before retiring to the couch Geraldine preferred to sit on during readings. By the time Geraldine had returned from making tea—in an entirely different dress, Petra noted—Petra had selected a poem and calmed her pulse.

Geraldine sat. "What do you have selected?"

"'The Listeners' by Walter de la Mare," Petra said. "Unless you have something else you'd rather hear."

"No, that sounds perfect." Geraldine picked up her tea and put it back down again. "I remember liking that one."

Petra said, "I'm sorry, I don't have a background on this one. I just like the way it sounds."

"That is good enough for now."

"The Listeners" was ordinarily a satisfying poem to read aloud, a ghost story with only the promise of ghosts, and usually Petra would have thrown her back into it. Instead she wandered through the first few stanzas, only finding her stride near the end.

Glancing over to Daniel—the source of her discomfort—she saw that he had lifted his head to listen as well. All of his anger had vanished, and there was something else in its place, quite lost.

Petra read,

> And he felt in his heart their strangeness,
>   Their stillness answering his cry,
> While his horse moved, cropping the dark turf,
>   'Neath the starred and leafy sky;
> For he suddenly smote on the door, even
>   Louder, and lifted his head:—
> "Tell them I came, and no one answered,
>   That I kept my word," he said.
> Never the least stir made the listeners,
>   Though every word he spake
> Fell echoing through the shadowiness of the
>   still house
>   From the one man left awake—

Geraldine fell from the sofa.

It happened so gently and without remark that at first Petra didn't understand what had happened. It was only when Geraldine remained on the rug before the sofa, a soft chiffon heap, that Petra realized that she had passed out.

"Geraldine!" Petra tossed the book away from herself. Kneeling, she said her name again. There was no response. Petra felt for her pulse at her neck— tentatively, at first, because this sort of touching felt clumsy and invasive, and then more firmly.

Tears marred her vision until she found Geraldine's pattering pulse.

"Call 9-1-1!" Petra told Daniel.

"What? I'm not doing anything."

"You monster!" Fury cleared the tears and Petra scrambled to her feet. Snatching out her cell phone, she called 9-1-1 first, and then she called Marla. While she waited, she crouched beside Geraldine with her arms around her, crying. Everything seemed impossible. This thing was not Geraldine! It was a pile of clothing. Daniel remained where he was. She hated him.

Geraldine's eyes fluttered open.

"Oh, dear," she muttered. "Oh, dear, Petra, don't."

Petra felt a great sob of relief. "What's *wrong?* I called everyone."

"I just felt so faint."

Finally, the door opened to Mr. Goodminster and his pigtail and his duffel bag. Petra stared at him.

"Where are the paramedics?" she asked. "Where's Marla?" The great well of adrenaline inside her was beginning to wash out, making it all seem even more imaginary than before.

"They're unnecessary," Mr. Goodminster said. "But we all appreciate your vigilance. Marla called me and filled me in. I was still waiting for the, ah, ah, train. She fainted?"

"Petra, love, give me your arm," Geraldine said. "This is unseemly."

Bemused, Petra helped Geraldine up, and found Mr. Goodminster on the other side of her, holding her other arm.

"I'll take her from here. Geraldine, we spoke about this. I did warn you. I really did," Mr. Goodminster said. When he saw that Petra was still holding one of Geraldine's arms, he added, "I'm going to take her to her bed and have another little talk with her. You can go home. Edith will call you later, I'm sure."

Petra reluctantly allowed Geraldine to be led from her. Her desire to have the responsibility taken from her warred with her lack of faith in Mr. Goodminster. "Will she be all right?"

Mr. Goodminster said, "Will she what? Oh. She just needs to eat."

The two of them hobbled beyond the ferns, beyond the screens, to whatever faraway place Geraldine's bed was in. After Petra could no longer hear Geraldine's shoes scuffing on the rug or Mr. Goodminster's murmuring voice, she sank down onto the sofa where Geraldine had been sitting before she fainted. Then she cried, silently and snottily. She didn't want to go home. She wanted it to be a normal afternoon.

After a few minutes, Daniel stood over her, a paper towel in hand.

"Why are you crying?" he demanded.

"I thought she died!"

"Why are you crying?" he repeated.

Petra blinked up at him. "She saved my life."

This was melodramatic—the Petra version of melodrama, not the Barbara version—but still, it was true enough. Petra had not really been going to die from embarrassment. But she wasn't going to live with it either. Whatever she was now, and it certainly wasn't the Petra who first agonized up those stairs—it was because of Geraldine.

"Oh," Daniel said, sounding cross. He thrust the paper towel to her.

"What's this for?"

"Your face. It's disgusting."

Petra took it and used it. He had not lied. After she'd finished, she asked, "Aren't you going to call me an old beast now and spray me with whatever that was?"

Daniel cocked his head with comical curiosity. Then, in a low voice, he said, "You really don't get it, do you?"

Petra blew her nose. "What is there to get?"

He said, "I'm supposed to be eaten."

"To be what?"

"You heard me."

He waited for her reply. For her to understand.

"Don't look at me like that," he said finally. "Like *I'm* the crazy one."

Petra merely frowned more deeply; she could think of no elegant response.

Impatiently, Daniel said, "I'll show you."

"*Show* me?"

"Get up."

Petra allowed him to lead her to the far end of the painting area, near the windows. There was an empty easel here, which he moved, and a few glass jars with brushes in them, which he also moved. A great oriental rug covered the space, and he kicked up the edge of it.

The weight of it gained inertia and it rolled back, revealing: slaughter. There was no mistaking it, the twist of blood stained the floor. Something sizeable had bled here. A lot.

"Tell me this isn't blood," Daniel said. "It's right in front of you! Look, this curtain is even newer than the others. They had to replace it because it got blood on it. *Tell me* that's not blood!"

Both dramatic Petra and practical Petra believed that it was blood, but neither of them was prepared to accept that it was the blood of a hypothetical Geraldine-victim. She chose her words carefully. "There are a lot of reasons for bloodstains that are more logical than attacks by the elderly."

"I'm telling you, I'm here to get eaten. That thing is supposed to eat me. She was supposed to eat me ages ago. That was the deal."

"By that *thing*, do you mean Geraldine?"

Daniel impatiently spread his hands. "Yes."

"You did notice that she was an old lady?"

"Lady? Ha. Lady-*like*. She was collected in Malaysia or something years ago. She's been in the family for decades, they told me. Only eats once a year, and only feeds at night, and is so rare, ecological treasure, blah blah."

Petra gave him a withering look. She couldn't even be angry at him anymore: he was being so earnest and not sullen that she could only pity him.

"Don't give me *that* look, either! That one's worse," he snapped. "The cage? You saw the cage. You must have."

"Yes," she said. "So?"

"Come on! Put it together. All this old shit? It's because she's been around since the 1800s, getting fed trash like me every year or so by this crazy family who wants to preserve the species."

Petra was beginning to feel a little jittery; whether from aftereffects of the shock of Geraldine's faint or from proximity to mental instability, she couldn't be sure.

"I'm going," Petra said.

"Fine, go," Daniel replied. "Whatever."

She got her coat and made a big show of putting it on. As she went to open the door, she turned. He was sitting on the edge of the sofa where she had been crying, his eyes closed. He had made a tiny tripod of his thumb and first two fingers, and his forehead rested on it.

Petra asked, "If she *were* a man-eater, then why didn't she eat you? Or me, for that matter?"

"That's the point," he said. "That's why Mr. Goodminster's here. Old bat doesn't like hospital food, apparently." He laughed humorlessly.

"You're awful," Petra said. She didn't know if she believed him or not. Of course she didn't. "Really awful."

"I know," said Daniel. "That's why I offered to come here."

. . .

At home, while the babies watched television and gave each other very wispy cornrows, Petra paged through her poetry books and slowly felt herself considering Daniel's explanation. It was not the bloodstain that swayed her, nor the presence of Mr. Goodminster. It was the cage. She tried again and again to imagine what might fit in that cage besides a person-shaped something, and she just couldn't.

Petra tried to think if there were any poems dealing with cannibalism in her current collection.

Don't be stupid, Petra thought. *You can just ask her.*

. . .

Petra climbed the stairs to Geraldine's apartment and found that she was not out of breath, though she was still sticky with sweat. At some point, Petra realized, she might simply climb these stairs and not think about it. What an impossible thing.

Geraldine answered the door after three knocks. She looked tired, or hollow-eyed, but not like she was starving. Petra had to allow that she wasn't sure you could tell from the outside. She couldn't really tell what Geraldine looked like, anyway, because she'd looked at her too often to see anything but . . . Geraldine.

"I'm sorry that I'm not really feeling well enough to make tea," Geraldine said. "Do you mind terribly if we do without?"

Originally, in this scene, Petra brought in a poem to trick Geraldine into talking about whether or not she was a man-eater. During revision, I realized that I had already written the exact same scenario when Petra was trying to get Geraldine to confess if Marla, Edith, and Frances were really her daughters. In the first scene, Petra realizes that this kind of trickery is unnecessary, so having her resort to the same method here was an accidental step backward for her character. During edits, I changed this scene to reflect all the things Petra has learned about herself.

Petra did mind—she didn't miss the tea, but she missed the Geraldine who was well enough to make tea. As she stepped in, she saw that Daniel was already peering at her. Petra glared back, as she hadn't forgiven him for the misty assault of the day before.

"I could make you tea," Petra said.

"Oh, no, not on my behalf," Geraldine protested. "Your words alone are enough for me. Do you mind if I sit?"

The two of them settled in their usual sitting area. Petra was distressed to see that one of the ferns near the window was striated with browning leaves. It needed watering, and no one had been watering. Petra's heart jerked a little.

"Geraldine," she said, "I'm going to read you this poem by Tennyson."

She went quite pink, surprising herself. It was not quite the same sort of blush as before, because it was just her neck behind her ears and the apples of her cheeks. But the shock of feeling it reminded her of how long it had been since it had happened.

"You're red!" Geraldine exclaimed. "I'm sorry, but it's been so long."

"It's because I'm nervous. Here. Just listen."

> I loved her, one
> Not learned, save in gracious household ways,
> Nor perfect, nay, but full of tender wants,
> No Angel, but a dearer being, all dipt
> In Angel instincts, breathing Paradise,
> Interpreter between the Gods and men,

Who look'd all native to her place, and yet
On tiptoe seem'd to touch upon a sphere
Too gross to tread, and all male minds perforce
Sway'd to her from their orbits as they moved,
And girdled her with music. Happy he
With such a mother! faith in womenkind
Beats with his blood, and trust in all things high
Comes easy to him, and tho' he trip and fall,
He shall not blind his soul with clay.

"Oh," said Geraldine, content.

"I'm reading that because it's the mother poem I *should* have found you before," Petra said. "And because it's how I feel about you."

Geraldine's mouth said O but her voice didn't.

"I love you, Geraldine," Petra said, earnestly. She took a deep breath. "So I don't want you to be upset with me about what I'm about to ask you." She remembered just a little while before, when she had tried to trick Geraldine into confessing whether Marla, Edith, and Frances were her daughters. How things had changed!

"Ask, dear heart."

"Please tell me if you're supposed to eat Daniel."

The tenderness ran off Geraldine's face, replaced by a frown. Touching her elegant throat, she turned away. "It's so crude to talk about the unseemly parts of ourselves in public even if we are not ashamed of them."

Petra's breastbone thrilled in horror and confirmation.

"Does it—does—" Petra realized that she didn't know what to ask. Was Geraldine a cannibal like Hannibal, first question. Was Geraldine a vampire, second question. Did she stab them first, third question. Was this real, fourth question. None of these questions were possible using Geraldine words. Petra collected her thoughts and then said, "Just give it words that you like. Say it in a pretty way."

Geraldine, recognizing her own sentiment, turned back to Petra. "There are no pretty words for this, Petra. It should remain untitled."

Petra's mind was still going wild. Dramatic Petra couldn't quite believe that this time, the dramatic truth was the real truth. But surely Daniel's version had to be wrong. She waited yet another moment until her words had come together in her head, and then she said out loud, "Like an Emily Dickinson poem, without a title. Can you just tell me the poem and leave the title out of it? Give me only the context."

Geraldine tilted her head to one side, regarding her thoughtfully. "Clever Petra. All right. All right. Daniel, though, you must get off the floor. I can hear you listening, so I might as well be able to see you as well. Come here and hear a story."

To Petra's surprise—everything was to be a surprise today—Daniel joined them. He didn't sit. Instead he crossed his arms and stood by a screen with two peacocks painted on it. But he was there.

Geraldine did not stand, but she sat straight, as always, and held her hands out as if inviting them into her mind. She began.

. . .

"Once there was a *she*. She lived in the north of
Pahang, a place of spiky rattans with dragon's blood in
their veins and great tualang trees tied with strangling
figs and ferns hiding pitcher plants hungry for meat.
The forest in Taman Negara was a place of wild
secrets, and *she* was one of them.

"Back then, she was faster and sleeker.

"She lived among the ferns, skin like honey, eyes
colored like the water of Tasik Chini. Her language
was the birds', the monkeys', even the wild boars'. If she
heard a sound she loved, she learned to make it herself.
The finest sounds of all were the ones made by the
men who forayed into the jungle to dig roots.

"She learned to make their sounds, their *words*,
and when she called their words to them, they plunged
deep into the forest after her. She did not need to eat
many of them to survive. But she was a wild, savage
thing, like the rivers after rainy season, and so, like the
river, she rushed and killed without purpose.

"She—and those like her—were legends. Men did
not enter the jungle at night.

"After some generations, another one like her
appeared in the trees. *He* was there to pursue her, but
he did not make lovely sounds. So she moved farther
away from him, to the edge of the forest. She darted
and flickered through villages to eat, and she became a
wilder legend than before.

"That was when she was caught.

"Not by the men who hunted roots nor the men
who gathered fish. White men from a foreign shore,

with bright, strange clothing and beautiful, strange words. One of the officers called her Geraldine, and he made her clothing to cover her honey skin. During the day he taught her to dance and speak, and at night he displayed her in a cage while his company drank wine. He fed her prisoners when she grew hungry. Sometimes ladies or their men would draw too close to the cage during the dances and she would be able to reach them through the bars. But she never got to eat them, no matter how surely she caught them. 'Geraldine,' the officer whispered, 'you must learn manners.'

"In London she learned manners. In Dublin she learned poetry. In South Africa she learned that men died whether or not she killed them. In New York she learned that she, too, would one day die. She was no longer fast and sleek, and now she had manners. Now she had learned all of the beautiful words that she wanted to learn, and she tired of hunting men and ruining her clothing. She tired of ugly things entirely. She wished only to have and to touch and to hear things that were lovely; she wished only to *be* a lovely thing herself. She had put away childish things and become a lady."

Geraldine put her hands in her lap. "That is my story, Petra, without a title."

Petra closed her mouth, which had fallen open in an unseemly way. She had no words, but Geraldine didn't expect her to.

Instead, Geraldine looked to Daniel. "Now, Daniel," she said, "perhaps you'll tell us your story."

"Once upon a time, there was a monster," Daniel said. "The end."

He walked away.

. . .

Petra called Marla. And Edith. And Frances. The three sisters stood on the biting sidewalk outside of the building, turned toward each other, three different brands of fancy. Edith was the fanciest of them all. She looked like a young Victorian queen, with her hair done like Geraldine's.

"You didn't tell me Geraldine was a cannibal," Petra said.

"Technically," Frances's words fluttered from one branch to a higher one, "she's not a cannibal, as humans aren't the same species as her."

Petra continued, "And you hired me and sent me up there all alone all this time!"

Edith pursed her lips. "We did make sure you weren't there after dark. You remember we took great pains."

"But what if she got very hungry? Like now!"

Marla patted Petra's shoulder gingerly. "Oh, you were always perfectly safe. Geraldine has very particular tastes. You've seen her apartment. She only wants to eat a certain sort of person. And you, well, you're so plain, Petra. We knew right away you would be an excellent companion."

"The risk was nonexistent," Edith said. "After all, you saw how fancy Daniel was, and she won't touch him, stubborn thing."

"She just doesn't want him because *we* picked him out," Marla agreed. "She wants to be able to pick something out herself, which is impossible. And so even though she would have liked Daniel fine if she had seen him on her own, she just won't take him out of principle because I found him."

"Now we play this ridiculous waiting game!" Edith said.

Petra's mouth opened, but then she remembered to think her entire sentence through before saying it out loud. "You three are *afraid*. That's why you won't ever go up. You think she wants to eat *you*."

Frances's laugh nervously hopped to another branch. "Well, *look* at us."

"She ate her piano tutor," Marla said with annoyance. "I think because she had ringlets."

Petra pressed her fingers to her eyes and then lowered them. "Why did you keep her?"

Edith sounded impatient. "Surely you see that she'd never survive now if she was turned free. You ask us to kill her?"

"She kills people!" Petra said.

Frances's hands flew into the air. "Shh! Shhh!" There was no one on the street to hear, though.

"*Killed* people," Edith corrected. "And not very many, if you compare her to, say, malaria."

Petra allowed her face to say what her mouth couldn't.

"She's been in the family for ages," Marla said, clearly upset that Petra remained baffled. "What were we supposed to do? We knew she'd outlive

Mother and Father. And Edith always says it's about preserving the species, but it's not that. We don't want her to die."

But she eats people, Petra wanted to say, but didn't. She didn't need to say it out loud again. Also, it was Geraldine. Petra didn't want her to die either.

"We love her," Frances whispered. "We grew up with her."

"It's really a pity we grew into things she would eat," Edith noted.

"Please don't stop visiting her," Marla added. "She does so enjoy it."

What an impossible thing.

Petra pulled off her gloves in order to be able to open the door to the building. Crisply, she replied, "I'm headed up now, in fact. I don't suppose you'll be joining me?"

The three sisters peered at her and blinked. They were not.

"Please convince her to eat Daniel," Edith said. "It's getting expensive to send him takeout."

.   .   .

Petra climbed the stairs, knocked, was allowed in. Daniel was not sitting by the wall. She felt a burst of conflicting emotions: Geraldine had eaten him, she would get better. And Geraldine had eaten him: there was a horrific stain in here somewhere.

Petra didn't ask Geraldine—there were no Geraldine words to ask her if she had eaten him.

"I'm still alive."

Daniel's voice came from somewhere over one of the screens as Geraldine edged back to a chaise. As Geraldine eased herself down, Daniel appeared from behind a banana tree with a stack of books in his hands.

"I thought you'd been eaten," she said.

"I knew you would. I'm just bored senseless of sitting there and I don't even . . . don't come close," he warned, as she drew near to both Geraldine and him. "I smell. I used her big claw-foot tub, but I had to put on all the same clothing again afterward." He laughed, but it was a miserable sort of laugh. "I never thought I'd be here long enough for it to matter. I didn't pack."

Both of them looked at Geraldine, who lifted her chin in a vaguely rebellious fashion.

"We should talk about solutions," Petra said. "I just spoke to Edith and Marla and Frances. If you don't want to eat Daniel, can I help in some other way?"

Geraldine said coolly, "Don't help me. I know why I'm making my choices, and I am fine with them. Daniel is the one you should be counseling; being eaten is a poor answer to life's problems."

"I thought I was being civic minded," Daniel shot back. "I should have just used pills."

Petra lowered her backpack to the sofa beside Geraldine. She didn't feel like reading any more than Geraldine seemed to feel like being talked to about food. "How *did* you come to be here?"

"How did *you?*" Daniel snapped. "Did they come find you on a poetry reader's forum and fetch you back for her? Did they put out a classified ad 'looking for pretentious girls with pretty clothes to entertain centuries-old killing machine?'"

Petra didn't move. "That was singularly unkind."

He rested his forehead on the shelf. "I know. I'm an asshole. I can't stop. I want to stop. I want it all—"

"You can just say sorry," Geraldine broke in. "And answer her question in a civil way. That would be an excellent start."

Daniel's expression was petulant for a long moment before clearing. "I don't have a good story of how I came to be here. I didn't start in a Malaysian jungle or whatever. I just live in New Jersey and sell advertising space to companies that sell shit, and I dress like this so that I can forget that I go home to a shitty apartment with gray carpet and no furniture in it. There is no sad part where I tell you that something bad happened so I wanted to get eaten. I just looked down and saw that my life wasn't really what I had pictured when I was a teenager. Edith found me on a suicide forum and said I had good taste in shoes. The end."

"I'm not who I was a few months ago," Petra said. "When I first came here, I wouldn't have been able to talk to you without going red. I was miserable. I hated everything about me except for poetry. You can change. If there's one thing about yourself that you like, you can keep that and the rest can change in no time at all."

Recall how in the introduction I reasoned that Geraldine and Petra must have complementary character arcs. Daniel is the third wheel on this people-eating plot-wagon, and his story has to fit in, as well. Ideally, his story needs to make theirs more meaningful, and vice versa. So Geraldine has made herself into the elegant creature she wanted to be, Petra is learning that elegance is something that *can* be made, and Daniel has made himself into something he thought was elegant and really is just empty. Can they all learn from each other?

Daniel looked at her. His expression was ugly. "You think that because you're not even a person yet. You're what, seventeen? You don't have any idea how you can make one sort-of bad decision, and then another one, and then another one, and then it's just so many of them piled up on each other that there isn't any way out of it. You haven't had time to become something stupid and incurable."

There was silence. Petra was thinking that he really was a jerk, but didn't want to say it out loud because it felt both counterproductive and like she would be agreeing with him, which was the last thing she wanted to do.

Geraldine finally said, "Well, I'm afraid to say that I'm not going to be eating you, Daniel. Petra, I'd very much like to listen to some poetry now."

Petra said, "I'd like to solve *your* problem, though, Geraldine! This is terrible! Can't I get you . . . a different kind of food, or something?"

Geraldine reached over to pat Petra's hand. "Petra, please. There's only one thing I can imagine I'd like to eat, and it's quite impossible. Please, let's not talk about it anymore. Please respect my decisions. My mind is not feeble."

Daniel made an incredulous noise. "I might as well go!"

He didn't go, though. He just stood there with the books in his hands.

Petra opened her mouth and then closed it. She very much wanted to talk about it some more, but instead she turned to Daniel. "I might only be seventeen, but you know who's older than you and figured some things out about changing herself, Daniel?" Then she turned to Geraldine. "All right, let's read."

What she wanted to say to Daniel was *she'll change you, too, if you want to be changed.*

But surely he could just tell that by looking at her. If he really wanted to see it, everything that Petra had learned about herself was visible from the outside.

. . .

Petra had to miss several days of visits because of the holidays, and when she next came to Geraldine's, Daniel opened the door at her knock. Geraldine was bedridden, he explained, and Mr. Goodminster had suggested she stay in bed to preserve her strength.

Petra hovered by the front door, coat still on, disbelieving that Geraldine was somewhere within the apartment, lying down. "And you're still here!"

Daniel said, "Two beasts in one apartment, right?"

She frowned at him. "You look different."

"She cut my hair," he said.

"Geraldine!?"

Daniel looked at the floor. "I brought her tea—"

"You did what!"

"I was bored," he said, his manner too deliberately careless to be anything near careless. "And after that, she told me how to wash my clothing in the sink and then she came into the room and she said she would cut my hair like she used to cut the officer's hair."

Petra struggled to imagine this scene.

"Wait," she whispered, finally. "You were naked?"

Daniel's ears went as pink as Petra's used to. "It wasn't like *that!*"

No, Petra expected that it wasn't. But—still.

"I read her some poetry," Daniel said, even more carelessly than before, and Petra's shock turned into slow pleasure. "And she told me I could stay here in this jungle of hers until I was ready to go back out into the world again."

Petra thought of the stairs behind her, stretching down and out into New York, a world that neither Daniel nor Geraldine seemed at all prepared to inhabit. Only a few months before, she would have thought either of them far more qualified to live in that city. And now, instead, Petra was the only one who seemed likely to wander those streets anytime soon.

"But what will she eat?" Petra asked in a hushed voice. "I don't mean that I want her to eat *you.* But she has to eat."

Geraldine's voice rang out from the other side of the room; she had heard them, impossibly, this entire time. "Petra, please stop going on about that and come read to me!"

. . .

At home, Petra filled out college applications, all of them for New York schools. Her mother said, "Petra, this letter of recommendation from your English teacher is ridiculous. She says you're personally much improved! What was wrong with you? Oh, I suppose she means your mumbling."

"Possibly," Petra replied.

"I'm glad to see all these local schools," her mother added. "Staying close to home."

"Yes," Petra agreed, and picked up her bag.

"Where are you off to now?"

Home, thought Petra.

. . .

It was the end of January when she climbed the stairs for the last time. She removed her coat as soon as she stepped into the stairwell, hung it over her arm, and jogged up the six flights. At the top, she smoothed her hair and knocked on Geraldine's door.

Daniel opened it at once.

"Petra," he said, "I didn't know how to call you. It's bad."

He shut the door behind her.

Inside, the apartment had subtly shifted since that week Geraldine had first told her story. The plants were lusher and greener than ever before, as Daniel had taken over their care. He had moved aside some of the screens and view blocks to allow Geraldine's bed area to have a better view of the rest of the room. The result was a space that was lighter, smaller, more comforting and less mysterious. Less Geraldine, too. More Daniel.

He led Petra back to Geraldine's bedchamber. It was against an interior wall, so most of it was dark brick hung with wall planters. Ferns draped down behind her, some curling on the mattress itself. The light came through the windows in the opposite wall, checkered through banana leaves and palms. The bed itself was high and ornate, with old brass knobs.

Geraldine was curled small at the head of it, withered in a way that her plants were not. She was terrifyingly still.

As Daniel hovered by the screens, Petra skidded to the bedside and knelt beside it, clutching at Geraldine's hand. It wasn't *warm*, but it wasn't cold: she was still alive. But Daniel was right: her eyes were open only a crack, and her breaths were far apart.

"Geraldine," Petra said. "What can I do?"

Geraldine cracked her eyes open a little wider. "Keep being you."

"I should have found you something . . ."

"I always wanted to pick for myself," Geraldine said. Her gaze wandered around the room at all her fiddly, particular, beautiful things. Here, at least, was still very much like her and very little like Daniel. "I never would have eaten Daniel. I wanted someone . . ."

She trailed off, but Petra knew what she meant. Someone like Geraldine's other things.

"It's too late now, anyway," Geraldine said. "But it's all right."

Petra closed her eyes so that the tears would stop blurring her vision. Geraldine put a knobby hand on Petra's cheek, palm over the tears. "There, there," she said. "I would have eaten you, Petra, my love."

Petra sniffed, but the tears kept making her nose run anyway. "You would have?"

"I knew after the Dickinson," Geraldine said. "You would have been delicious, I could tell."

Petra's heart was at once swelling and collapsing. She was an explosion under water. "Why didn't you?"

Geraldine traced Petra's cheekbone. "Because if I ate you up, I wouldn't have you anymore."

Petra opened her mouth, but she didn't have any words to say. Geraldine already knew her thoughts, anyway.

"Don't let Daniel stay here forever," Geraldine whispered. "He has to leave the jungle eventually, when he's less young and savage. And take the Dickinson with you."

Petra wiped her face with the back of her hand.

Geraldine smiled then. "And read me just one more."

"Which?" Petra whispered.

"You choose," Geraldine replied. "Something with a satisfying context."

Petra thought for just a moment and then said, "Daniel, would you get me the Dickinson?"

Daniel scuffled to fetch it. He'd also brought Petra a handkerchief for her face, which Petra used. Shuffling through the pages of the little green book, she found the poem she was looking for.

Then she said, grand and oratory and tearful, "I'm going to read you a poem by Emily Dickinson. You're the context."

Three character arcs with three different endings—how to make them all end neatly within a few pages of each other? The answer is: not in the first draft. Don't get discouraged if you get to the end and it's terrible. Take it from me; I have thirteen published novels behind me, and all of them are terrible when they're first done. The beginnings are wrong, the ends are wrong, and probably the middles as well. That's what revision is for.

This story had all kinds of endings. Some of them involved eggs, if you can believe it, and some involved coffins, and some of them just involved really nice furniture. I like this one the best. That's why it's the end. Because I buried the others in a place where no one else will ever find them.

Petra read,

I died for beauty, but was scarce
Adjusted in the tomb,
When one who died for truth was lain
In an adjoining room.

He questioned softly why I failed?
"For beauty," I replied.
"And I for truth,—the two are one;
We brethren are," he said.

And so, as kinsmen met a night,
We talked between the rooms,
Until the moss had reached our lips,
And covered up our names.

/fin

CRITIQUE PARTNERS

Tessa

This is about audience. You need one. Writers write for or toward something, and that something is a reader. As the writer you can only imagine being in the place of the reader, but the space you occupy is the dangerous space of performance. You need a stage manager. You need a spotter. You need a reader stand-in.

Critique partners aren't readers, though—like the name says, they're partners. They're in this *with* you. Like the midwife to your literary labor, a critique partner should be familiar with the writing process and understand genre, intentions, and the relationship between book and reader. They should know the rules and be able to witness your writing pains from a slight distance in order to keep the level head you can't.

You are *in* it; your critique partner is sitting next to you, checking the gas gauge and watching for cops. (A critique partner will say, "Gratton, that is a lot of metaphors up there.")

Brenna

Critique partners are people you can count on to be your objectivity when you've worked on something for long enough that yours is broken. They want your story to be the best version of itself, which is not the same as telling you what you should do or how they would write it. Once you've known each other for a while, they begin to learn how you write and what you're capable of, and then when you get discouraged or burned out or just plain lazy, they say, "Hey, do better! Because I know you can."

Maggie

Okay, great. You're convinced. So, where do you get one of these critique partner people? Not all readers are created equal, and not all readers are on the same page (pun, pun, pun) as you. I went through many writing groups and critique partners when I first began putting my writing out there, and even though I was happy to get feedback, it never felt exactly right. I always felt as if the other person was asking me to write a slightly different book than the one I had in my head. It wasn't until I realized I needed to find a critique partner who enjoyed reading the same kinds of books that I enjoyed writing that I began to really have success. Tessa and Brenna are not my clones, but their reading and writing tastes are similar enough to mine that they enjoy my writing for what it is. Plus, they know that a good critique partner helps you to craft the best version of the book *you* want to write, not the best version of a book that *they* would write.

There are places to find critique partners online—that's how I found Tessa and Brenna—but you can also look for them in local book clubs, in writing groups, and in your classroom. But be leery of picking someone who will take it easy on you, like your mother or best friend. Critique partners can become great friends, but it's a little harder for friends to become great critique partners.

Part Two

World Building
and
"Desert Canticle"

by

Tessa Gratton

INTRODUCTION

This story began with bombs.

IEDs, to be exact. Improvised explosive devices found in every pothole, burned-out car, and pile of rubble in Iraq. Reading about them in news, nonfiction, poetry, and novels from and about the Iraq War has been an uncomfortable obsession of mine in the past few years, and I tend to work through my emotions about the world I live in by writing stories about it. I make up stories to process my political and cultural hopes and fears, and doing so calms the angry, desperate part of me that wants to understand the world, that needs the world to be a better place than I'm afraid it is.

Because I'm me, I was thinking about what IEDs made with magic might look like. IEDs are hidden bombs meant to ambush, meant to be secretive up until the shocking moment they are not. And they're desperate bombs, planted outside your house to keep the enemy away, even at risk to your own safety. Who would make magical IEDs and how? Would they still be surprise bombs—the kind that take you unawares even if your *job* is hunting for them? Could you hunt them if you weren't a wizard? How might they affect the body and air and land? I love the dissonance in pairing death and beauty, so I imagined magical IEDs to be beautiful, deadly bombs that explode in glorious colors, ripping through anything in their way.

I wondered what sort of world and context could lead to magical IEDs that were just as lovely and elegant as they were bloody and deadly.

I have six thousand words of notes to myself asking and answering that question over and over again. I thought about landscape and religion, family groups, refugees, rebels, and occupying armies. The thing about IEDs that scares and fascinates me is that for the most part they are made and laid by the people who are *home*. IEDs are a desperate resort used by people willing to destroy their own safety in order to drive an enemy away. That couldn't change just because I was making my IEDs magical.

Magical IEDs came with some suggested themes: secrets, occupation, imperialism, refugees, postwar devastation. My own feelings about the larger real-world context of IEDs in Iraq are angry, sorrowful ones, tinged by a sick understanding that your own country can betray you and its own ideals. So that was floating around in my imagination, too.

It wasn't difficult to invent a world for my magical bombs—only time-consuming. I knew I would have at least one occupying force, I knew the landscape I chose would be devastated. I knew magic needed to be part of the land, because the key to IEDs is the *improvised* part—they're made out of material on hand.

This is where I say, Research research *research* **research**. You have to know everything you can know about a few things before you can even begin to layer in all the complexities of a world. Of course making things up is the goal, but you need to build the meat of your world on a skeleton of true information so people will understand and believe it.

But all of this above only tells you about where the world came from and hints at how I slowly spiraled out from that central idea: the magical IED. How did I get to the story itself? That didn't start until I turned my attention to characters, because the only thing that brings a world to life are the characters who literally live in it. If the basic elements of story are a pyramid, then world is the thick base, character is the middle, and the tiny tip is plot, because characters are created within and grow out of a world, and plot is *only* the action rising from the conflict between what your characters want and what they cannot have.

(Of course, you can reverse engineer that pyramid if you begin with a plot/conflict idea. Work your way back to character and world, but in the end it should *feel* like your plot is a natural progression from your characters' desires, and those desires are dictated by how characters fit or don't fit into the world itself. I just happen to begin with world and work upwards from there.)

When inventing my characters, I made a list of things I wanted from the magical bomb story:

- kissing
- inherent political/cultural tension
- secrets and secret motivations

Kissing is there because it is always there. Sorry not sorry. I like romance of every kind and rarely conceive of a story without some element of it. But this gave me the initial information about my characters, other than that I would have at least two main ones and I would need sexual attraction between them. Beyond that, I didn't immediately assume gender or sexuality or very much else at all—though I knew because of the war-zone setting that there would be ample opportunity for trouble and forbidden love.

Political and cultural tension had to be an important aspect of the characters because it was the basis for why there would be magical bombs in the first place: war between two (at least) nations. My characters needed to personify that tension in some way. I knew they would be on opposite sides of something. Possibly the war itself, possibly just on opposite political sides within the same culture.

Secrets and secret motivations occurred to me very early on as a major theme because IEDs are usually (always) disguised in some way. I wanted at least one character to Have A Secret that could "go off" like a bomb at the right/wrong moment.

I brainstormed more about the war zone I was creating. The money, politics, religion, and what sort of people would be necessary: a soldier and a wizard seemed obvious, and sometimes I'm happy with the obvious characters if they fit the world right. I could use them to explore the military and magical systems that are the two most important aspects of magical bombs. Weaponized magic requires the militarization of magic. This was the point where all the possibilities opened up. Is my soldier from the occupying nation or an insurgent planting bombs? When does the story take place? During the war, after the war? Is my wizard an expert in making magical bombs, or did she just stumble onto the key to defusing them? Is she a rebel or an expat or an occupier? I could have chosen any of those possibilities and made a story out of them. Like we've all said in this book: you can make any idea into a good one. You just have to choose.

What I needed next in order to choose was the core emotional conflict.

Because of the world I'd begun to create, I knew it involved secrets and cultural misunderstandings, and there was a niggling sense that I needed to make the conflict about rebuilding connections. *Connections?* my brain said. *Kissing is connections.* OH HEY HOW ABOUT THAT FORBIDDEN KISSING.

Sometimes a kiss is like a magical bomb.

As soon as I thought that, I realized how I could weave in culture, politics, secrets, and kissing. (SPOILER ALERT: I'd tell you but it would spoil the explosion.)

I had an emotional plot.

All I needed now was a hero for point of view, and a way into my hero's narrative.

The choices I made at this point were mostly just about what I wanted personally, and that is maybe the most legitimate way to make a choice as a writer. *What do you want to talk about?* I wanted to write about magical bomb disposal in a postwar landscape with kissing and identity angst. So I made my hero a young man in the occupying force who returns to the place of his war to clean up the mess his country helped make, who thinks he knows who he is and what his country did and what he wants, who was formed in wartime and unapologetically a soldier and very good at his work. I made the wizard (and love interest) a native of the war-torn land, connected to its spirituality, magic, and traditions in a way that would be challenging and controversial to the hero and his imperialist notions.

I hope you enjoy "Desert Canticle."

—Tessa

DESERT CANTICLE

The desert is all the colors of fire.

That's the thing I said when they asked the first time I came home—*What was it like, over there?*—in hushed, or jovial, or unconcerned tones, like the desert was a different world, not merely a war zone.

It was better when I was with Aunt Lusha, because she'd answer for me: *The Sweet is a seeping wound, a bloody gash in the earth that we put there!* Her violence, her insistence, her politics—everyone immediately dismissed me and listened to her. Glad to have a woman to hear out instead of only a second son.

The truth is, the desert is beautiful. It *hums*. That's why I went back.

· · ·

Usually world building is just choosing what details to focus on and when. Here you already learn that not only is the narrator a boy, but he's also not important compared to his aunts, and that's reflected in the greater world: women matter more than sons. A lot can be extrapolated from that.

I thought I understood hypocrisy.

After all, I signed up to serve in a war we could not win and had no intention of winning. An Riel and the Eruse Confederacy have fought over mineral rights or minor insults every few generations for as long as we've both existed, and the Sweet has always been between us. Our battleground. Our game board. Our collateral damage.

I volunteered despite being a few months too young. My great-aunt signed papers forcing my commission because I'm not only a son, but a second one at that, and what better way for me to distinguish myself? Everyone expected there would be no more than a half year of combat left before our Queen Mother and the Eruse Chancellor signed a new treaty. I expected a few months of difficult work, of miserable heat and raw skin, bad sleep, crap food, scorpions, and heat exhaustion. I expected the thankless task of rooting out the star clan rebels who did not flee the desert when our war machines rolled in, who did not join their expat families or become refugees in Eruse.

I never expected to be so good at it.

. . .

Aniv haunts me. Those striped, jewel-toned robes she wore, green-blue-ivory, sliding along the orange adobe cobblestones of the fortress city. Her sheer veil, marking her a star clan mage, distorting her image so I could barely see her dark eyes, the long end of her nose pushing against the veil, her always-painful smile. I think about her too often. I think about *him* too often.

It was this line, "I thought I understood hypocrisy," that gave me my first real window into Rafel's emotional worldview. It made me realize the third-person point of view I was using focused too much on world, politics, and setting and not enough on Rafel's heart. The story is about magic bombs, but the core of the story is about setting off the hidden bomb in Rafel's heart, so to speak.

NOTE: When world building in first person, you can only reveal information your narrator knows, cares about, and believes is relevant.

Good at being a soldier, or good at hypocrisy? OR BOTH? #theme

It's important to remember that every word should be doing multiple jobs. This entire section is both characterization and world building. It's a lot of info, but it's tinged with how Rafel sees it, experiences it, and thinks about it.

Once she said, "I know you cannot understand, but you will not tell me I am wrong."

When one of the curtains here in my mother's seaside manor flutters, or an aunt turns a corner quickly enough to make her pant cuffs flap, my entire body tightens with hope that it's Aniv.

. . .

I'm writing it down, all of it, everything I can remember and some things I only think I remember. Because I'm losing her the longer I'm away. I feel her draining out of my memory so there are only these impressions on my heart. I have to retain as much as I can so I can be *honest* about it. All I want is some honesty, and I must begin with myself.

. . .

And the flower mines.

Invented near the end of the war by a mad star mage whose entire family, they say, was massacred by one side or the other. To the star clans it's sacrilege, using magic to kill, against the laws of their gods. That's why they say she was mad to do it.

When the mines explode they change the air, and the wind smells sweet, like burning sugar. There are the tiny pansy bombs that only maim, but can be fairly easily scattered;

This section used to be more informative, but Maggie and Brenna both thought Rafel lacked emotion in the first half of the story—he was telling it too coldly, as if he had PTSD or was trying to distance. That is not what I wanted. This was the first place I started to layer in his relationship to his emotional state.

Many military names and nicknames are incongruous to their meaning for humorous or ironic reasons, and I wanted to highlight that desert magic is meant to be beautiful and spiritual, and so here is this beautiful thing being used to do terrible things. Therefore, the bombs are named after flowers.

crater-making tulip bombs that ruin foundations and kill more people via cave-in and collapsing walls; impressive dandelion bombs that cannot be hidden, but when set off propel a hundred small grenades in every direction; rose bombs so violent they splatter blood in a huge radius; and the intricate, special orchid bombs nearly impossible to defuse.

We weren't expecting firepower like that. The desert gives off a magnetism that ruins mechanics and gunpowder projectiles, forcing even a sophisticated army such as ours to rely only on our sabers and bows. The war might've ended a year sooner without the flowers mined along every road, in forts and cities, oasis camps, even dry riverbeds where we dug for water. They gave a generation of furious young star clan girls and boys a powerful encouragement, taught them we empires could be defeated.

That was a lie, too. We beat them still, with special service fireteams like mine.

. . .

I want to—

If I could—

. . .

I want to write about being a pacer. Meeting her. The honesty of sweeping for mines and aiding the star clan mages in defusing mines. It was my second tour, and no matter what *else*, destroying bombs is a good thing to do.

But.

My first tour I wasn't concerned with *good thing to do*.

I was a natural at killing in the desert. I was vicious and artful, but patient and precise. Skills I'd not had an opportunity to realize in the luxury of my mother's home in An Riel. Though the soldiers in my team were older, I proved quickly that I had the drive as well as the talent to find any rebel hideaways. They say I'm especially observant or particularly subtle, but I know it was that peculiar desert *hum*. I always found what I was looking for by listening to it, letting it pull me one direction or warn me away. My fireteam confirmed more kills and cleared more walls and lost fewer lives to flower mines than any other. They named me the Gardener, *not* for how successful I was at pruning the weeds of insurgency, at identifying the mines, at stalking targets through ruinous adobe houses and cracked, dry riverbeds; I was the Gardener because when we found rebels, my men and I sliced them to pieces with our sabers and marked the locations with blood-spattered flags torn from the colorful robes of the dead. When mortuary services arrived, they found a rainbow garden of streamers and pennants.

I did it the first time on instinct: to leave a clear mark so my fireteam could move on.

It wasn't until Aniv asked me that I could say the real reason I continued the tradition: because it made me feel better, in a terrible, slick way, to create something new out of those dead bodies. Like art, I told her, quiet as a confession.

. . .

The Sweet was declared rebel-free three months after
the treaty with the Eruse Confederacy and six weeks
after my seventeenth birthday. The war was over, and
I came home to commendations enough they weighted
down my dress reds.

They'd told us not to think about what we were
doing. Death and killing, heat and backbreaking work;
it was just our job, and we should save our consciences
for when we got home. Easy for me and some of the
others. At first I thought it would all be easy.

Except I hummed.

I did it under my breath, tunelessly, and hardly
noticed myself. When my mother complained, I
struggled to explain and said only that An Riel was too
quiet, not like the constant noise of the Sweet. (What
an irony that is to me now.)

Mother said the crashing ocean was louder than
any desert could ever be, and Aunt Lusha peered at me
as if I'd offended her. She said the desert was stuck in
my brain.

But if I didn't fall asleep humming, I didn't fall
asleep at all.

. . .

I dreamed of the flower mines.

They weren't nightmares. I never woke sweating or
angry, choking on tension trapped in my subconscious.
In my dreams the mines were beautiful, like the desert.
They exploded slowly, in great waves of color, layers of
death like petals spiraling out from the zero point.

I would wake, stare at the stucco ceiling of my childhood bedroom, and imagine painting tulips or roses there. I'd realize I was humming.

. . .

The mines were in the news every week, even though the war was over. They killed the native star clans flooding back from Eruse, exploding sometimes immediately, sometimes not for days and days because the triggers could be so specific. I read about murdered children and grandmothers missing limbs, blindness and burned skin. The star clans stopped coming home; their numbers trickled to almost nothing. It made me vaguely sad, and it made Aunt Lusha apoplectic.

Then a massive wreath exploded at the Irisu Dam, loosing the power of its river onto the red adobe city of New Spring. The entire place flooded, water setting off more bombs until it took a triplet of star clan mages to put up a barrier spell locking the water inside. One of them died in the casting.

They'd never recover New Spring, the center of star clan sacred ritual for generations.

Because of us.

I felt a sting of anger for the first time. At the rebels who kept planting those bombs, who didn't destroy them when they'd lost finally and for good. At my own An Riel for creating

New Spring was always the set piece for the finale: a flooded city. I mentioned it here as the point at which the Queen sent her soldiers back to the desert because it needed to be immediately relevant to Rafel's character arc. During revisions I connected this early shift in Rafel's feelings to New Spring so it changed not only his political landscape, but him as well.

the desperate situation in the first place. At the Eruse Confederacy, who'd been our enemy for generations, but now I wasn't sure if we weren't our own worst enemy. At strangers minding their own business in Mother's market square. At my aunts.

What a mess of politics and death. I'd never been to New Spring, but I could imagine what it would be like to never go home again.

. . .

My mother's household became a center for debate between government parties; my aunts didn't even agree on what the Queen should do. Lusha argued violently on behalf of aiding the star clans because without the An Riel–Eruse War, the Sweet would not be scattered with mines in the first place. Mother argued just as viciously that it was the star clan rebels themselves, trying to force An Riel and Eruse out of the desert, who planted the flower mines, and so An Riel bore no responsibility for getting rid of them. Let the star clans erase star clan magic. Eruse certainly would not divert resources to it; why should the Queen?

The Queen ordered a vote in her parliament, which she had done rarely since coming to power. Lusha whispered that her mother wished to pass any blame onto parliament, should they vote one way and it go wrong, but Mother insisted the Queen genuinely did not know what was best: she had never been to the desert and only could rely upon the words and advice of others.

Nobody asked me for my opinion. Gardener or no, in my mother's house I was still only a second son.

If they had asked, none of them would've been as surprised as they were that, when the Queen and parliament ordered the special service to coordinate with the provisional star clan counsel and render aid in a venture called the Restoration Campaign, I immediately presented myself at the quarter house to volunteer again.

Anything to get back to the desert. To the *hum*.

. . .

When I set foot in the Sweet again, I terrified the translator who greeted me first in camp. A star clan expat who somehow got swept into service, he shied away from my teeth: it was a thing I'd forgotten, that baring teeth is an intimate gesture there, of either aggression or heartfelt smiles. I could not help it. The *hum* was in my teeth again and my mouth could not contain it.

. . .

I'd been recommissioned as a pacer, partnered with one of the star clan mages to find and disarm as many flower mines as possible. There were five disposal teams of fifteen men and women with our group, each led by a

This section could be cut entirely without affecting the story, because it's almost 100 percent world building. BUT I wanted this political background because that's part of my theme: the messy politics that create situations like this. I did my best to make it reflective of Rafel, too, and reaffirm his place in An Riel culture and his world.

I rewrote this section based on editorial feedback asking me to clarify and refine the explanation of what a pacer does. A lot of this was peppered throughout the next four pages instead of in one simple, informative place. Sometimes it's best to just hand the information over. It worked as a better transition between sections, too.

mage-and-pacer pairing. We worked three teams at a time, moving slowly through the winding, narrow streets of Shivers.

Mage and pacer went first, eyes peeled for potholes or rubble or shadows that most likely hid bombs.

Behind us came the snails—An Riel special services explosive-arms disposal teams—to clean up and make sure nothing remained that any rebels could use to rebuild bombs, and to collect pieces for evidence and study at home. They were called snails because ordinarily they moved oh-so-slowly and wore heavy blast armor like shells. If these had been regular bombs from a regular war, the snail teams would've hunted and destroyed them in controlled detonations. Unfortunately, when detonated, the flower mines disrupted all the magic in a place, so we were forced to disarm them instead of blowing them up.

This is here because in real life most IEDs are dealt with in controlled detonations, not disarming. I needed disarming for story purposes, hence this explanation gave me more chances for world building.

After the snails, star clan natives brought up the rear, carrying desert-made shields and some supplies the mage might need in her work. They were there to be our guards and also as proof that An Riel and the star clans were working together on this even beyond the mage-pacer pairing.

When anyone spotted a potential threat, everything stopped. Only a mage could verify the presence of an armed flower without setting it off, and it was her pacer's job to go with her, create a perimeter, and identify any signs of wreathing or additional triggers. Once he cleared the area, the shield rows and snails spread out, shields facing the blast site, protecting it and themselves. Only the mage and pacer were exposed and defenseless while she disarmed the bomb.

I suppose they assumed I'd excel at pacing because I'd been so skilled at finding hidden rebels.

I've heard other pacers say it was a job that required calculation, dissociation, patience, and a command over fear—or ignorance of it. Truly, all it requires is a reliable coping mechanism.

The pacers I knew—Belen, Sars, Leonor, and especially my friend Jarair Man AnGraya—all had their ways. Jarair would clap you on the shoulder and jerk his handsome chin and say, "Think of the aunts and daughters back home who'll fall to their knees for such stories!" Leonor began every mission by saying, "No luck today," an old An Riel blessing that hoped for things to go so well luck became unnecessary. Belen would return to camp buzzing with tension, dive straight for his bunk, and bury himself in blankets too hot for the desert until the sun set. He emerged quiet, but having shed the thrum of anxiety.

For me, it was total immersion. If I kept my distance from the air and mud, if I let my mind alone do the detecting, I would have been dead too quick.

It was more like I became a walking piece of the city, of the brick walls and lighter limestone cobbles. I breathed the city; I felt its empty roads like dried-out channels of blood from my own body. It *hummed.* I listened.

> Rafel doesn't realize he's talking about transformation here, about becoming something he is not. #theme

. . .

I saw my mage the first time from a distance and did not know I was to be hers. Her pacer. She stood alone in the blue shade of the canvas wall that marked the line between the An Riel service camp and the star clan refugee camp. On our side. It was dawn, and the watery red sun just peeked over the pinnacle of the city to our east, the walled, orange adobe fortress we'd been assigned to clear first.

Her black hair fell in two thick twists to her knees, waving slow as sun-warmed snakes in the morning breeze. Otherwise she was still. Her eyes were closed; one hand rested against the canvas as if she listened to something on the other side. She wore layers of striped robes: green, blue, cream, and the softest seashell pink, falling from her shoulders and waist like a waterfall, but leaving her muscular arms bare. I knew she was a mage because she wore none of the rings or bracelets the star clans were known for, nor had she painted her desert skin with the pale lines I'd seen on most of their women and children. Her feet were bare, toes reddened with desert dust. In her other hand a sheer white veil was bunched in a ball, the only sign she was ill at ease.

"*Dinah?*" I said quietly, giving her a star clan honorific for their most esteemed mages.

She turned to me in surprise. She had dark eyes, as do most of her people, and a long nose. She was not pretty, but striking and young—even younger than me, I thought—with thin lips and long lashes and bursts of color darkening her already desert-dark cheeks. Before she responded, she studied me as closely as I had her.

> I like this slip of his: it's thematic in that he corrects himself into more exact honesty, but also a hint of his emotional confusion regarding Aniv.

> Repetition of language Rafel uses when talking about being the Gardener. Repetition of language in various contexts is a good world-building technique to draw comparisons.

> This was originally her first appearance, before I added the earlier section of Rafel thinking of her haunting him. I needed to bring her introduction up more: she IS the second most important character to the story, and THE most important character to Rafel himself.

I took satisfaction in knowing I looked like a soldier: brooding, heavy eyebrows, scars from a childhood disease marring half my face, a thick nose. My first tour I'd still been as slender and boyish as a poplar but since had grown into a man's frame. I have square shoulders and a square face, and my uneven reddish skin makes me more like a fortress of rough adobe bricks now. My hair was only long enough to tie back from my face and neck. The mage could not have known me for who I was, rank or family, for I only wore the dark red jacket of special services, with no sign of my rank nor any of my achievement medals because of how they amplify the *hum* in discordant ways.

Her first words to me were, "You pronounced it well."

"*Thank you*," I said, in the star tongue too, inexplicably pleased. I pronounced it again in my head, *dee-NAH*, glad to have remembered.

She introduced herself in her language, and I knew many of the words. I picked out that her name was Aniv and admitted in Rielan, "I only know a small bit of your tongue, Dinah, that I learned during the war."

Her expression tightened. "I can imagine what other phrases you must know."

I glanced at the gravelly desert floor, not ashamed exactly, but hearing it all again.

Stop!

This description was the first thing I EVER wrote down about Rafel. Before he had a name, when it was still in third person, this paragraph was the "birth" of Rafel. I wrote down "willow" instead of "poplar" originally in my notes because I didn't have a setting or landscape yet.

Vaguely cheating world-building technique, like that time in *Goblet of Fire* when Hermione told everybody how to pronounce her name.

Where are the weapons?

How many of you are there?

Burn them down.

I am sorry your daughter/son/father/grandmother is dead.

Come with us.

Keep back!

The Dinah continued, "You seem too young to be a veteran, but I did hear An Riel was sending children to murder children in the end."

That snapped my eyes back to hers. Her brow rose in challenge, and I remembered suddenly the first time I slit the guts of a boy younger than myself. It *had* been terrible. But it was not his face or small limbs that stuck in my dreams, but the slick, calm, *easy* way I'd done it.

The memory made me defensive. I said, "And now the clans have sent children to dismantle bombs too."

She stepped nearer to me, and the morning sun set fire to the curve of her eyelashes. "It bothers you not at all," she said. She was nearly as tall as me, and I smelled desert sweet tea on her breath. It was like the burned-sugar scent of an expended flower mine. I swallowed nausea.

"I am a soldier," I managed to say, very low and quiet.

"I haven't seen you in camp before. You're the new pacer, aren't you?"

The *hum* of the desert swelled in my ears, like rushing blood in a conch. I did not have to nod or acknowledge: she knew.

"I hope you're better at it than my last: he missed

> Until now, Rafel has been rather cool and distant from his violence, emotionally speaking. His moments of emotion are because he's writing it all down from a later point. Linearly speaking, it takes Aniv to get Rafel to react emotionally *in the moment*.

a secondary device *and* the rebel waiting to trigger it."

I held her dark gaze, imagining gardens of the men I'd hunted.

The Dinah said, "You are going to be magnificent at it, killer."

Killer.

Even from the beginning, she threw me off-balance.

"Come," she said, touching my scarred jaw. "Tell me your name."

Though I wanted to pull away, I did not. I'd heard that the star clan mages used senses other than sight to work their magic—hence the veil twisted in her other hand. As I answered, my jaw moved against the delicate pads of her fingers. "Rafel Sal AnLenia."

"Rafel," she repeated.

"Dinah."

. . .

For centuries the citadel of Shivers has stood upon the desert bluff overlooking the southernmost bend of the Irisu River. Built and molded from stones and mud bricks, it blends into the orange and red layers of the desert from any angle. It climbs the slope on seven terraces, like the shelf farms of An Riel's seaside cliffs.

The city was more blood-soaked by fighting than most. Control had traded

I chose names for An Riel based on vaguely Spanish names, because there's a history of imperialism there as well as of old wars with desert nations, and when I rolled the names around in my mouth alongside the initial character ideas, the sounds fit. They're not meant to *be* Spanish, only to evoke a commonality because we English speakers will probably recognize the rhythm and sounds shared by the An Riel names. For the star clans I developed less, and merely chose a handful of syllables and made rules about how many syllables names would have for which gender and place in clan hierarchy. If this novella was a novel or series, there would have been a lot more rules and specifics. But the amount of work and world building should fit the project.

Comparison is another good world-building technique. Twice the information, and more chances to reference something the reader will recognize.

between An Riel, Eruse, and star clan rebels over
and over and over again. The rebels' first priority
was leaving it uninhabitable for the imperial armies,
and so they churned the mines out, planting them
everywhere they could as they fled. Maximum damage
to the enemy, even at great risk to themselves.

I'd spent nearly a month here, hunting rebels,
when it was temporarily in An Riel's possession. The
Gardener, gardening.

Now I was here to dig up flowers, not create them
in violence.

. . .

Our first day together, Dinah Aniv said nothing to
me before moving out, though her eyes lingered on
the alterations I'd made to my red uniform. We were
all instructed to remove metal insignia and the extra
weight of ribbons and medals, to leave behind sidearms
because the worked metal interfered with the magery.
We were allowed our sabers so long as they were twins,
one for each hand, for the star clans said they balanced
each other out that way. "Marries the humors, or some
such thing," Commander Saria AnYar said dismissively,
never hearing or feeling the *hum* herself.

For my uniform, I'd gone a step further and
snipped off buttons and pried away the grommets
from my boots. My jacket tied shut now, and my laces
threaded directly through leather. Dinah glanced
down my chest and even to my feet before meeting my
eyes in brief approval and striding away with a grand
gesture that we all should follow.

. . .

We were designated Sky Breaker team, after one of the star clan gods incarnate.

. . .

As we picked our way through the deserted city, I kept both hands on the pommels of my sabers. I felt the singing energy connect, like a circuit closing through my body. Wind blew sadly through empty homes, ruffling threadbare window dressings and rattling old door chains. Our collective boot-steps were a rhythmic beat, kept in time by a sergeant in the rear shield row tapping the hilt of his saber to his shield.

Not even rodents or wild dogs had taken up residence on this terrace, though there were signs of both near the bottom fortress gates. I suspected the desert cats kept them away more readily than flower mines. The triggers were nearly always too sophisticated to be blown by anything smaller than a child.

I heard the cry of an eagle but couldn't see it in the painfully blue sky.

Sweat prickled my scalp. The *hum* held gently in my teeth.

I studied everything: patterns of brick and shadows, rubble, alleys, sniper perches, unhinged shutters, scraps of old canvas. I caught myself hunting signs of rebels instead of mines. Men were my specialty, and so I touched my tongue to the *hum* in my teeth, paced Dinah, and waited for a bomb to be found.

It only took a block and a half.

. . .

That first mine hunkered in a long, thin crater in the street, crowded with rubble for disguise. It was at an intersection of our wide boulevard and another road cutting immediately up to the next terrace on narrow stairs. I remembered that narrow stairway from my Gardener days; it was a dark cut-through once the sun was low in the afternoon, nearly impossible to see into even from the fourth-terrace neighborhood above it. Excellent hiding for rebels.

Dinah Aniv moved forward. I kept to her elbow, "pacing" her, as she walked slowly and evenly with her bare hands before her, fingers splayed. Her veil covered her face and hair, falling just past her chin. Sheer and undyed, it's meant to mar her vision only enough that she always remembers not to rely upon sight. Sight is imperfect, the star clan mages believe, more so than smell, hearing, taste, or especially touch. Eyes can be fooled, even the eyes of magic.

We stepped carefully in case any trigger waited hidden under the stones of the street. That was rare, but not so rare we shouldn't consider it. Once we stood near enough to crouch and touch the mine—a mash of ceramic and clay, as large as a hound's head—Dinah stopped. She glanced at me, and I could just see her open eyes through the veil.

I did my job: paced out the perimeter, marking with chalk any irregularities I noticed, inspecting windows and rubble within the limits of the perimeter. Took half an hour of silence but for the scrape of my boots and the low breathing of hot men behind me.

When I finished, I had three places marked for Dinah to investigate, though none required her immediate attention. The stair alley leading to the next terrace was suspicious, but there were no signs of recent movement or habitation. It was only my gut wondering if rebels still used it, if there were still insurgents hiding here, waiting to ambush. I signaled to the shield sergeant, and the rest of the team spread out to protect the perimeter lines.

It was Dinah's turn.

I softly asked where she would have me, and she gave me my lead.

Jogging to the nearest wall, I hooked an arm into the low window, then used it and the ones above to climb up the wall to the roof. I sat, straddling the brick ledge, one boot dangling into the courtyard, the other flat and solid on the orange roof patio.

From there I could see everything. I heard the team's quiet shuffle on the bricks, felt the breeze, saw over the houses to the rest of the city: there was colorful movement six blocks over and one terrace down. Cloud Swallower team.

I breathed deeply the dry desert air, and watched. Not only what I could focus on, but all of it. My peripheral vision, the patterns my mind recognized and didn't. The *hum*. I settled into that space, learned it, understood it, so that any slight shift would not be missed and I could warn her in time.

Dinah knelt at the bomb.

She reached with both hands in a single, elegant motion and skimmed her fingers along the surface.

I shivered as if she had touched my spine.

As the sensation passed, I realized I was humming along with the desert, too soft to hear even myself, only the subtlest vibration in my sinuses.

Nothing happened.

The wind slipped lazily over rooftops; the eagle called out again. Tore through the tension like an alarm. Several men below me shifted, wiped away sweat, glanced up.

All around, the orange and red city *hummed*.

Dinah slipped her fingers along the ceramic bomb, touching every inch of it, caressing it, reading it.

Sweat dripped down my back, caught at my belt, along my belly, soaked the cloth above my eyes.

She bent lower, twisted to put one bare foot on either side of the pothole, and slipped her veil off her face. From my perch, I saw her eyes were closed. Her lips moved, and she put her mouth against the bomb.

My stomach tightened, and I wanted to touch the hilts of my sabers for that circuit of electrical balance.

Dinah stroked the underside of the bomb with her fingers and lifted it out. She stroked it again, with her lips. She murmured, and maybe her tongue slipped out to touch the bomb, too.

All the servicemen from An Riel stared. The star clan men averted their eyes.

Setting the bomb upon the road as gently as she would a baby, Dinah put her veil back on and then pulled small items from invisible pockets in her robe: petrified wood, an opal the size of her eye,

I wanted this to be uncomfortable, but also sexy and dangerous. Like the flower mines are both beautiful and deadly. It's the way of desert magic to be two opposing things at once, and Rafel and the Rielans (and the reader) can and should have visceral reactions to the difference, the otherness.

river-bored limestone, the long black feather of a crow. She removed a chalk pencil and string. She laid the black string around the bomb precisely, in a series of squares. She drew letters directly onto the bricks. I couldn't see well enough from my perch to decipher them.

Everything fell still. Not even a breeze shifted the hem of the mage's veil.

I absorbed the *hum*, the quiet beat of my pulse in that strange tranquility.

Suddenly, Dinah said, "Ah!" very loudly and with a full yawning breath. Not a few of the men startled.

She directed her voice along the spine of the bomb.

A pale pink cloud of air puffed out from the bomb, shaped in swirls like a full blooming rose. It would have gone for blood if it had exploded.

Instead it fell to pieces.

The Sky Breaker team visibly relaxed, smiling some, shaking hands. The star clan members kissed their fingers.

I leaned off the wall, climbed down to the second-story window, and from there leaped to the ground.

It was a good landing, firm and exactly how I intended.

Dinah glanced at me as I rose and seemed to catch herself staring. Through the sheer veil her expression was washed out, but her black eyes and her mouth were apparent as she cast an amused smile at me, as if knowing I was trying to impress her.

I realized I was, at least a little bit.

. . .

That first day went better than the second, though the routine of disarmament never quite got boring. We found too many sun-bleached bones for that.

I fell into a good rhythm, and so did my team, as we systematically cleared the third terrace. Though there was always some tension between Rielans and the star clan refugees while in camp, once we set off as Sky Breaker team the mission goal put a stop to it.

Twice the first week I went off alone, signaling to the team I would return shortly, and on the second foray I found what I was hunting: a rebel crouched among broken pottery and dusty rolled rugs, waiting for us to pass so he could trigger a secondary device.

I slaughtered him too easily. The trigger was maged into his palm, so I sliced off the hand before marking the house with a flag made from his striped yellow and blue tunic. It was only then it occurred to me Dinah Aniv and likely the entire rest of the team might be horrified at what I was bringing. So I dragged one of the rugs under his ruined arm to soak up any blood that leaked out of him—the star clans collected all the blood of their dead—and wrapped the severed hand in a cloth.

I'd been gone no more than half an hour from Sky Breaker team's perimeter. I didn't know how to do it gently, only that I should. I brought the sergeant in charge over to Dinah and carefully unfolded the stained blue cloth from around the hand. "Here is the trigger I found on a rebel," I said, "and the body is

During revisions I added a few words to give more insight into Rafel's emotional connection to the events so he didn't come off as terribly affected by PTSD or a sociopath. I hope it did the trick.

marked for mortuary; also I arranged for his blood to be as easy as possible to collect."

"Rebels still in the city, sir," the sergeant said, not a question so much as gravelly acceptance.

"Not many. We'll need to keep an extra eye out. I want to make a few sweeps before we continue the mine hunt." I glanced at Dinah's face. Her veil was rolled around her neck as always when she was not disarming. The mage's lashes fluttered as she stared at the seeping wrist, the smoothly cut skin, broken bone.

"You have to tell us if it is disarmed," I reminded her softly.

Her mouth trembled as she opened it to speak; then she thrust forward her own large hand, finger out. She touched the pale line of magic painted to the palm. Dinah jerked away, gasping. "Warm," she whispered. "Warm and soft."

The sergeant glared at me, as if I'd upset her on purpose. "We should retire to camp, sir, to take care of this locked and safe."

I reached for Aniv's wrist. "*Dinah?*" I asked.

She did not allow me to touch her, but took the hand and its cloth wrap from me. I could see the tendons tight in her neck, the quiver of her brow, as she folded the cloth around the hand again. "It is dead, unable to trigger anything," she said in a tight voice, and she left to give the hand to one of her star clan soldiers.

.   .   .

After that I was recognized as the Gardener. It changed how everyone looked at me: the Rielans with admiration or at least shared pride of country, the refugees with fear or suspicion or anger.

Jarair Man AnGraya lifted his chin, clapped my shoulder, and declared at breakfast mess, "Excellent to have a gardener to help us get rid of all the weeds!" The men laughed, and I smiled a bit, but uncomfortably. I was good at my job. I liked to be. But I finally realized I probably shouldn't be so glad to be so good at *that* particular work.

. . .

Dinah came to me the next morning as I emerged from my tent, still tying my red jacket closed. I nearly ran into her. Her eyes were narrowed and dark, her hands folded into the skirt pockets of her red-pink-violet-yellow-striped robes. She said, "You are like the cree bark tree, whose berries are poison but whose roots hold water."

Tension at the heart of their relationship, and the relationship between An Riel and the Sweet.

I was more afraid in that moment than I'd been since returning to the Sweet.

"You are a very good pacer," she whispered.

"You are a very good mage, Dinah."

"You have murdered so many of mine. You are famous for it."

What could I do but nod? I thought of arguing over the word *murder*.

She shifted her feet; it seemed her hands clenched inside her pockets, and yet she did not remove her flashing eyes from my face. "Rafel the Gardener," she murmured. "Did you know we plant flowers for the dead, too? Did you know we water gardens with the blood of our fallen?"

"Yes," I said.

Her surprise made clear she did not expect me to know.

I wanted to touch her—the way she touches everything, to understand it. I left my arms dangling at my sides. I said, "They are your enemy too."

"Who is?"

"The men and boys who plant the bombs. The ones who hide in the cities, in the riverbeds, waiting to blow us all up. The man I killed yesterday was not one of yours."

"He was star clan," she whispered.

"You would have died. And the seven men of your clans in Sky Breaker team. Not only us Rielans."

She tilted her face up, her long nose like an arrow pointed at me.

I said, "We are your allies—I am your ally."

"Can a man from An Riel ever be allied to the desert?" she asked, but she immediately turned and left me. She did not want an answer.

If she had, maybe I'd have told her about the *hum*.

. . .

The refugees in the camp were the first star clan people I had a chance to observe who were not prisoners or enemies. It surprised me, coming from An Riel, how little they seemed to revere their women, despite the magical gift from their gods coming only *to* women—so I thought then.

During the war, most of the rebels had been men—unless their cell had a mage with them—and we assumed it was for the same reason most An Riel soldiers were men: because we are far more expendable. Second and third sons, nephews, men not needed for keeping a family strong or keeping a country strong. We are the tools, the servants, the branches of the tree. Our mothers, sisters, aunts are the roots and heart.

The most important word in this paragraph is "assumed."

I wondered for the first time if this distinction was why the star clans fled to the Eruse Confederacy instead of to us, because the Eruse do not even allow their women to inherit property.

It was not that the star clan women were treated poorly, that I saw. They and their men dressed rather alike, and both seemed to hold positions of respect within the refugee hierarchy. It was that in watching them interact, I noticed a deference on the women's behalf toward the men, except where the mages were concerned. It baffled me, for it was the opposite of Rielan ways. I wanted to ask Aunt Lusha, who'd spent time in the Sweet. I wanted to ask Dinah.

But Dinah, of all the star clan in camp, was the one treated most differently. I could not tell if it was awe or fear that kept them from gathering too closely around her, men or women. To a certain extent it was true of all five star clan mages in camp, but Dinah Aniv was most definitely set apart.

I decided it could only be for reasons similar to my own outsider role: she was famous for how skilled she was at her work. There was no doubt in any of the pacers' minds she was the fastest cleaner. Perhaps that made her the most powerful mage and worthy of their awe.

Special services had hardly any women with us in camp, except for the mission commander—a third cousin to the Queen—and her second daughter. It made the star clan women something of a focus for the flirtatious attention of some of our soldiers—the newer ones who didn't know better and weren't already husbands. In the service we were expected to keep our urges in check, and if we absolutely must we should confine our releases to each other, so there was no danger of getting ourselves all over a woman who didn't wish it. The commanders and aunts tended to look the other way so long as we kept it within our own rank.

I instructed my fellow pacers to speak to their men about the impropriety of flirting with star clan women, unless they intended to invite one home to An Riel for marriage. Jarair guffawed when I said it, which made me feel defensive about the idea. Thinking already of Dinah Aniv, unconsciously.

Some star clan women flirted back with our men, but only if there were no star clan men present, and I heard from Leonor that he didn't think any of the refugee women but the mages were unmarried, except those too young for it. And too young to the star clans was different than it was for us—some of the married star clan women were only fifteen.

But.

It was not my mission to figure out the finer

aspects of star clan personal or political relationships, and I tried to put it from my mind.

I tried to.

I wonder now, if I'd asked Dinah, how the rest of my tour would have changed.

World building as foreshadowing!

.   .   .

Three weeks into my mission, Sky Breaker team had cleared all but one of the mines on the third terrace of the city of Shivers, and we were about to shift our focus to terrace six.

We'd only just cleaned and balanced a dandelion bomb, and I remained perched atop the peak of an adobe roof to watch Dinah and two star clan men help the snails grind the ceramic shell to dust so it could never be reassembled.

The *hum* was smooth and low, vibrating my toes as I studied Dinah and the wavering air around her. She was graceful, strong, careful. Her mass of hair knotted in a ladder down her back, her robes the same green-blue-pink of our first day. I remember I was thinking at the moment how she had almost no discernible breasts under the robe and if that was part of the reason for layers. Her robe cinched at her waist but did not spread over hips. She was slender as the poplar I used to compare myself to.

I caught myself wondering if because she could not paint her arms or hands, she painted the star art of her people onto her bare belly, or asked a friend to trace constellations at the small of her back, or arcing down her thighs.

It was not the *hum* my body was responding
to anymore; I realized it suddenly and with sharp,
burning shame. My skin was too hot, and I looked
desperately over the cityscape for clarity.

Just then something in the distance popped, and a
wave of force shook dust from every roof between me
and the Moon Shard team above us on terrace four.

Everything froze for a split second—then I saw the
telltale bowl of orange energy with a yellow-bright flare
at the top. A tulip. The colors dissipated fast in the
burned-sugar wind, lost against the orange adobe city.

I leaped to my feet and yelled down to Dinah and
the Sky Breakers, "Tulip, fourth terrace, a hundred
meters east of my position."

And with that I took off.

I ran hard as I could, climbing and jumping from
roof to roof, into a courtyard, through narrow alleys
I had to shift sideways to pass through, adobe dust
scraping onto my red uniform.

I arrived mere minutes after the blast. Swathes of
cobblestone road were simply gone, only rubble now,
and the sides of three houses were collapsed inward.
Moon Shard's sergeant had already organized half his
men to the perimeter, checking for secondary devices,
and the other half used shields to pry rubble away
from the zero point. Two lookouts were down with
broken bones, and all bled from lacerations.

They were digging for their star clan mage and
pacer, both caught in the blast and buried under the
broken bricks from the nearest house. I helped dig. I
hummed low in my throat, hoping some answer would

lead me to them, as the *hum* led me to mines and rebels
and sleep. But I could not hear it over the ringing in
my ears, even though the *hum* is not truly a sound.

By the time Sky Breaker arrived we'd found
Belen—the pacer who always curled in his bed
between mission and mealtime—crushed completely.
Ten minutes later we uncovered the star clan mage
Virva.

It was Dinah who dragged me away, who wiped
the hardening layer of adobe from my face, roughly
and frowning, tears making mud on her own cheeks.
"Go," she said. "Be in the perimeter force while we
star clans gather her up. Your man, the pacer, will be
laid out too."

I put a hand on her neck, thumb aligned along her
jaw. I opened my mouth but had no voice. I let her go,
though her large dark eyes did not ask me to.

This section is for tension: the sexual tension growing in Rafel's awareness and the reminder that this entire world/job/situation can kill you if you do anything wrong. Literal and emotional tension.

. . .

The star clans asked us four remaining pacers to stand
guard for Virva's funeral, at sunset the next night.
Because they held their memorial out in the desert,
because they worked with blood, there was always a
danger of desert cats or wild dogs disrupting. It was a
kindness and an honor for them to include us. A hand
of friendship I was not sure we deserved.

But we all said yes.

. . .

It was impossible to know if the tulip's detonation
had been the fault of mage or pacer. The lookouts

and shield rows of Moon Shard team had not seen a mistake by either, though obviously there had been one, and the after-investigation revealed only that it had not been set off by a secondary trigger or hidden rebel. All we knew was something had gone wrong in the cleaning and balancing, and the tulip's blast threw both mage and pacer into the wall of the house, which then collapsed upon them, along with the roofs. It made a crater of the road.

I was glad we did not have one or the other of them to blame.

. . .

As I stood alone as a funeral guard, under the vast, starry desert sky, the *hum* was overwhelming. I felt it in my eyeballs and in my hair follicles. I felt it buzzing along my spine and in the soles of my feet. I knew none of the other pacers felt it. I knew that if they had any sense of the *hum*, they were unsettled by it, not part of it. Not alive with it the way I was.

As I stared at the dark line of horizon, where stars gave sudden way to black bluffs as empty of light as the deepest part of the ocean, I wondered if there was something wrong with me.

. . .

Belen's service was quick, without much ceremony. His body—what we could assemble—never touched the ground once we wrapped it in ocean-blue cloth. He was boxed up to be carried home between two horses, hanging from ropes only a foot off the earth. With

his family in An Riel he would be set to sea,
his bones to feed the great whales so that they
might sing his memories.

In the desert, we carved his family name
upon a flat stone and settled it near the gate
so anyone who entered or exited would see it,
walk over it. To remind us we move forward
on the achievements of our fallen. He was the
first from this tour to die, though I am sure
I was not the only veteran remembering the
spreading patio of name-bricks marking the
gate of every base camp during the war.

. . .

Two days after the tulip exploded, Sky Breaker
team was back to work. We finished our
terrace, then skipped to where Moon Shard
had been—their team was dispersed now
among the rest, awaiting a new mage and
pacer. I finally realized that I'd been assigned
here so late because Sky Breaker—Dinah
Aniv—had lost their first pacer in a similar
explosion. I got the story out of Jarair: that one
had been the pacer's fault. Everybody, even
the sergeant and all the Rielan lookouts, had
agreed. He'd disregarded a word from Dinah
and arrogantly knocked over a just-defused
dandelion. Its dying energy had snacked on
his leg. He was out of service, back in An Riel,
but because he hadn't been killed there was no
name brick for him, and I hadn't suspected.

Funerary rites are my number-one
favorite kind of world building. Not only
are they fun and challenging, funerals are
one of those things that link and distance
all cultures from each other, and one of
those things that might separate us from
the animals of the world. Sometimes all
we have to study about an ancient culture
is the evidence of how they treated their
dead, and so I love playing thought games
about what funerals do and don't, can
and can't mean in reference to the living,
to the story I'm telling, to the narrator,
and how they reflect (or contradict) the
culture I'm building.

Dinah Aniv knelt delicately before a rose bomb,
skimming the very tips of her sensitive fingers along
each of the curving petals of this strange mine. We
were in a tight, triangle-shaped courtyard with brittle,
overgrown vines and a trellis that made it impossible
for me to perch upon a roof and still observe. So, after
walking the perimeter, I'd chosen the farthest corner
of the triangle and crouched so I was eye-level with
Dinah and the bomb. It had been hidden here where
a fountain should have been. Long ago, this was the
private garden of some city dweller rich enough to
have plentiful water carried up.

The rose was too big for the courtyard, too, and
even the team's shields would not save any of the men
from the blood-hunting power if it detonated. I'd
ordered them to the alleys and streets just beyond, into
the houses themselves that created the courtyard. The
adobe would protect them. Only Dinah and I were in
the kill zone.

I measured my breathing and listened to the *hum*
in my teeth. I watched every corner, every brick, for
shifting shadows or falling dust. For the slightest tilt of
curled, brown leaf against the wind.

Dinah's veil did not wave at all, not even to show
she breathed. The ends of her thick black braids
curled on the mosaicked stones behind her heels. Only
her strong arms and hands moved: slow and steady,
exploring every surface of the bomb.

Sometimes rose bombs took hours upon hours to
clean and balance. It only required the removal of one

thin petal and the entire thing fell to pieces. But pull the wrong one, and that was the end.

It was one of the least interesting defusings to watch, as there was little in the way of outward magic, but for just that reason it took the most skill. I barely breathed as Dinah caressed the rose, as she lifted away her veil and put her mouth against one petal, then another, as she tasted, smelled, as she breathed it in.

She leaned back, pinched a petal near the top between her fingers, and with a firm, quick motion slipped it free.

The *hum* of the desert clicked, paused . . . shuddered.

I was running toward her before I knew it, to throw myself between her and the armed rose.

Dinah quickly pulled out a second petal, and the *hum* fell into its place again.

I skidded to a halt nearly at her side, panting, sweat covering every inch of me. I was dizzy, light-headed; my heart roared. My fingers were numb, my ribs tight.

Breathe, breathe, I told myself. She is all right, the rose did not explode.

Dinah stood and turned to me in the oppressive silence of the shady old courtyard. Her eyes were wide, her cheeks blotched with unusual color. "Rafel," she whispered, shocked.

"I thought—I thought you'd pulled the wrong one." I struggled to calm my panting, the rush of blood in my skull.

"I did," she said, stepping nearer to me. "There was a trick in it."

"You—you defused it, though." My chest was loosening, my head losing the clutch of terror. "I thought it was going to explode. It should have."

"Yes," she said calmly, though her posture added, *of course.* "How did *you* know, Rafel Sal AnLenia?"

Just then our sergeant approached, scowling at me. "You had us all choked, sir," he chided. "What happened?"

I licked my dry, salty, sandy lips. "I thought she'd made a mistake and the rose was going to explode."

The sergeant narrowed his eyes, and behind him a line of star clan men were muttering in their own tongue. Our lookouts and shield men were gathering, too. "So you *ran closer to it?*" the sergeant said slowly, carefully, as if speaking to a particularly foolish dog.

He was right.

I stared at Dinah, and she stared back at me, shocked, amazed, appalled.

I'd tried to save her. Tried to outrun a mine.

. . .

Everybody knew I was crazy after that afternoon: crazy pacer, reacting like a madman. At least I'd been right that the bomb was about to go off. Dinah reported the trick trigger to everyone.

This was the first moment between Rafel and Aniv I wrote down: that he would not realize the strength of his feelings for her (because he isn't that in touch with his heart) until he instinctually leaps in front of a bullet to save her, so to speak.

I had to prove that he's very good at his job and very levelheaded at work, a good soldier, in order for this scene to work. He doesn't break rules, so when he does, it hits like a ton of bricks.

Also: it was the moment for Dinah to have an epiphany too.

148

They knew I wasn't just run-of-the-grinder crazy, either. It was *her*. Jarair and Leonor and Sars fed me bitter wine from An Riel, inside the privacy of my tent, and Jarair told me I was a fool in love.

I wasn't a drinker, but I did not stop that night until I forgot.

She found me in the morning, alone, wrung out, splayed undressed on the thin rug next to my cot. She sat me up and said, "I suppose this means Sky Breaker is taking the morning off," in a tight, annoyed little voice. But then she found water and washed my face, made me sip slowly, and left for long enough that I'd nearly dressed myself completely before she returned with a hot bowl of salty bean soup, greasy chunks of goat, crisp flatbread, and even a small pat of butter. I devoured it with my fingers, eyes pinched against the light, and when I finished, I felt like I remembered myself.

Dinah roughly combed my hair and used a thread from her robes to lash it all back into a twist like hers, though only as long as my neck. She did not speak while she worked, and I held myself rigid, enjoying the rose-oil smell of her skin, the soft touch of her strong hands on my neck and unshaven jaw, on my ears, and her nails skimming against my scalp. I held myself rigid and tried not to react beyond the tiny little shivers and slick sweat on my spine and chest.

She finished and shifted away. I caught one of her hands. Dinah froze, kneeling on my cot behind me. I put her palm to my palm. Her hand was as large as mine, with long fingers, strong-looking, but soft and supple from the repeated oiling, from the silk gloves she wore when not working. Star clan mages keep their fingers as sensitive as they can—not like mine. My hands are scarred and calloused, sun-roughed and salted from the sea so they are even a bit darker than my face. Dinah's were lighter than her desert face and black eyes. Her nails were perfectly shaped pale ovals; mine were trimmed too low, the cuticles ragged.

Slowly she drew her hand away.

But she did not stand up to leave.

I said, "The desert has a *hum*, Dinah."

For long moments she was silent. I felt her gaze upon me but kept my face forward, crushing my teeth together because the *hum* was making them tremble.

Finally, Dinah said, "You used it to hunt, didn't you. In the war. You use it now to sense what you are looking for. It's why you're the best pacer. Your cousins do not know the song." I nodded, still not looking at her. "You ran *toward* me."

"Yes." My voice is a rough whisper again, like we're back in that narrow triangle garden, under the trellis shade. It had been such a grossly stupid thing to do, for a soldier, for a pacer, for a man.

"Oh, Rafel."

"*Aniv*," I said, hollow and horrified with myself.

"This is terrible," she whispered, sadly.

Part of world building is what characters call each other and when. When do they use titles, what titles, are names appropriate?

This conversation was twice as long, but Maggie told me it was 90 percent redundant and she was right, so I cut it down to the real emotions. So much better now.

150

She stood. Her head nearly touched the canvas ceiling of my tent. So did mine when I struggled to my feet, too. There was something so compelling about her, so certain and lovely and different. She was set apart, and I decided in that moment it was because of her place in the desert *hum*. Dinah Aniv was a *harmony*, I thought to myself exactly then, when she stood there looking mournful and worried, but she drew her soft, large hands together and said, "Get your boots on, pacer, we have work to do."

· · ·

I did my job. I was not distracted by her presence, or ruined for pacing.

I was very distracted.

But I did my job.

I would have run again into the heart of a rose bomb if the situation had presented itself. The knowledge vibrated louder than the *hum*, and just like I'd been shocked to remember how easy it was to kill my first boy, I was shocked to realize I'd never felt that way before—never wanted to kiss or touch or be kissed or be touched—with any other person, soldier or lady, in my life. It only occurs to me now that maybe the oddity was that it had taken so long, not that it was Aniv who brought it out.

· · ·

Every evening when we left Shivers, Aniv and I spent the brief walk from fortress gate to camp talking softly. Of small things: her family, expatriate life on the border of Eruse, living with only women to learn the ways of magic. I told her about my mother and aunts, about my older brother Onor. About humming to get myself to fall asleep when I went home after the war. She asked me about becoming the Gardener, and I asked her if she was the most powerful star clan mage.

One night, after defusing a triplet of dandelions, I said softly to Dinah, "That last one felt different."

She glanced at me, surprised. "It was a decoy. Perhaps one in fifteen is so."

"Unarmed, you mean?"

"Yes."

I nodded, let my arm brush hers, and then forced myself to keep a few inches away.

We stepped on quietly, surrounded by the Sky Breakers. Thin clouds striped the dark purple twilight above us. I heard a creeping low of wind through empty homes behind us.

Usually our conversation ended after we crossed the city gate, but that night Aniv paused to let the rest get ahead. They parted around her and picked up the pace, hurrying back to food and rest in camp at the base of the bluff. When we were alone, she said, "It surprises me every time to realize again I've met a man from An Riel with desert sense in his blood."

I laughed, assuming she meant it jokingly; only women could be star clan mages. "Is it a miracle from your gods? Because I'm a man," I teased.

Her expression did not lighten with mine. She only stared, dark eyes wide to swallow me whole.

Faltering, worried I'd offended her with some sacrilege, I added, "I don't . . . I'm sorry."

"Rafel . . ." her voice trailed off, and she watched me strangely, and hopefully, I thought. But then I saw the exact moment she changed her mind. Her mouth squeezed in a quick frown, then she pressed her hand to mine. "I will see you tomorrow."

I remained at the city gate, watching her walk slowly, gracefully away from me.

#theme: secrets

. . .

At night, lying on my cot while the desert *hummed* in my teeth, I made wonderful plans.

When the campaign was over, I would tell her my thoughts, tell her how I wanted her to come home to An Riel with me, see the ocean cliffs, meet my family, marry me. She would like my mother and all of my aunts but for maybe Lusha and Agata. And they would love her; they would love me more for bringing a woman like her home.

In An Riel, a noble man is expected to make his family stronger by earning the admiration of a strong woman—a woman who respects him enough to believe him worth leaving her family for. He says to her, *Will you come to my home and be my family?*

I imagined sharing time between the ocean cliffs and the desert, teaching our daughters to hear the *hum*, singing the melody of it to our sons. I would not only be Rafel the Gardener; I would not only be

Rafel Sal AnLenia, lowly second son. I would be the husband of the first star clan mage in the royal family of Lenia, the father of Rielan magic. I fantasized about how Aniv's body would change with a baby, though I knew little of women's bodies. I only had seen one of my sisters swell as her most powerful muscle worked to make a daughter.

It all made me tremble to think of it: my great-aunt's pride, Aunt Lusha's wry acceptance, the salt-sea wind roughening the twists of Aniv's black hair, what the *hum* would do when we came together—I imagined it would be like the revelation of electricity I felt when I grasped both sabers at one time, the closing circuit, like my body and the blades were one.

That is what I anticipated. That is what made me hot. That is what I dreamed of, how I fell asleep every night.

. . .

It took nearly four months to clear the citadel of Shivers, though it would have taken more if not for Dinah.

We moved to the seventh terrace because Dinah Aniv was the fastest, best star clan mage, the most efficient. The first afternoon on that highest and smallest of all the terraces, the air smelled like smoke, and we paused to admire the clan flags that curled in the wind, hung from the tower there, piercing up into the sky. We were near enough to touch them, to hear them snap. To pick out the patterns of rainbow stripes, one for each of the star clans. Behind them the sky was unadulterated blue, the wind cooled the sunlight, and the valley stretched behind us, a gaping, lovely red desertscape. It was refreshing to look down into the lower six terraces of Shiver and know they were nearly safe, nearly ready for the laughter of mothers and running children, for games and gardens and love again.

Dinah guessed, based on the square feet, there would be thirty-some mines up here, and so we could clear it all in two weeks if we were lucky. We began our hunting and quickly located the first target: a small pansy, the size of my fists held together. Made for maiming and easily hidden, this one was buried in an unobtrusive gutter.

Normal perimeter established, all men in their places, and me on the roof of a squat public bathhouse, we watched Dinah work. After merely ten minutes or so she stopped. She backed away from the pansy, eyes on the broken bricks of that wide avenue.

Very softly, she said, "Rafel."

Not my title, not with urgency, but just my name, quietly, so as not to startle anyone.

Of course it had the opposite effect.

We all snapped to attention. I climbed carefully down to her. "Aniv?" I said under my breath.

She pulled off her veil. There was fear in her wide eyes. "Send the men all away, and go—only you—go and fetch every pacer and mage in the city below. I will remain and protect this mine."

"Why?"

Dinah's brows twitched in annoyance.

I said, "I will obey, Dinah, but why?"

Leaning in, she whispered against my ear, "This is the first of a wreath that I believe winds all throughout this top terrace, a wreath of thirty or more bombs, and I cannot disarm one without detonating the rest."

I shivered and glanced at my boots against the dark orange bricks. Wreaths were nearly impossible to set—the one at the Irisu Dam had killed the mage who linked them. As far as I knew, all the known wreaths had exploded or been carefully detonated by a group of mages. None had been destroyed without killing somebody. "Dinah, you should go with me."

She shook her head. "I have been working on a theory for dismantling wreaths, and today I will see if it works."

. . .

It was twenty hours before the mages and pacers of all other teams detonated their last bombs, cleared every other terrace, and joined us.

I spent those hours supporting Dinah, bringing her water and little pieces of food she could eat without breaking concentration. Once she was alone, she'd immediately engaged a net around the pansy with thread and river stones and tiny opal charms, sitting before it and adding her own hands and strands of her hair to the mix. Then she did not move for all those hours: sitting, sweating, staring through her veil at the wreath.

Darkness fell, and we remained. No light, no candles, for flame and oil would introduce chaotic

Magical details should fit the culture from which the magic comes, the culture and the landscape. Star clan magic is lovely and elegant and practical, hence local stone, on-hand items, and pieces of the opal lines that make the desert glow.

elements to her very fine balance. A net like this, she whispered to me, required flow. Elasticity and curvature, a boundary that would move with the mine, move with Dinah herself, and flex between them. There could be no rigidity, no flickering.

#theme

The stars expanded overhead as the sun set, and the moon gazed down upon us, bringing out tiny silver lines in the creamy white of her veil that I had never seen before.

The *hum* pulsed.

It was Dinah's heartbeat.

I tried to breathe in time with it, to make myself a part of the atmosphere, a part of the net—flowing, not rigid, though I am very good at being rigid.

#theme x2

She allowed me to lift her veil off her mouth and feed her morsels of cheese, dry meat, and olives until we realized she'd have to spit the pits back into my hand. Her shoulders dipped, I thought with humor, and she asked me to wet a cloth she could suck on, for she could not move her hands to drink, nor allow me to interfere with her line of sight so much as to put a cup to her lips.

Food choice is also 100 percent world building. What they eat and how.

Once I briefly left her to relieve myself, but she allowed herself no such luxury.

I settled beside her, alive and tense but trying to be smooth and easy. I listened to—felt—the *hum* and stared at the small, oddly shaped little pansy bomb. It shone in the moonlight as if made of metal—strange for a flower mine—and I stared at the triangles of net around it, wishing to understand how the tools engaged with the desert song.

Late in the night, when the air was cold, she leaned against me, just her shoulder to mine. I concentrated on being solid, on the sweet, cold air in my nose and the *hum* in my teeth.

Dinah whispered, "The woman who created this was truly mad, Rafel. Desperate in it."

. . .

With the dawn came Jarair and his mage, then Leonor and his. We waited three more hours for Sars. The star clan mages immediately replaced me at Aniv's sides, touching her shoulders and joining the rhythm of their breath to hers.

She whispered to them, and they dispersed. Each pacer went with his mage, and I touched Dinah's shoulder so she knew I remained.

. . .

It seemed like all the times before; the work was invisible to me, tense, with Dinah moving nothing but her hands; gracefully, certainly.

The sun lifted to its zenith, beating down upon us. My stomach growled, I was thirsty—I may have neglected myself in my effort to take care of Dinah Aniv.

The *hum* was a cord between us, between me and the city, me and the sun, the air, the Sweet itself. It was all around, and as I watched her, I held onto the awareness of my peripherals, doing my job, though what I wished to do was focus with her, see the magic, sense the wreath. She said I had magic in me; I wanted to touch it, not only listen to its song.

Dinah took a thin knife I'd never seen before from her robes and carved into the bricks. She scratched slowly, methodically, cutting through her net. She used chalk and drew pale lines that danced around the carvings. Around and through, weaving in and out. She moved, she stepped lightly. Her veil shimmered in the sunlight, the ends of her thick hair-ladder reddened with dust.

Then she knelt before the tiny pansy mine. She hummed a long, low song with only two notes. She lifted the thin blade in both hands. The sun caught the edge, flashing in my eyes.

When I blinked, I saw a vibrant, violent illusion: like lines of watery silk all around her, a near-invisible net. She was at the center, and it knotted around her knife. Strong ropes of it flared off, up and down the street. It was a wreath of water and air, of desert song.

Dinah Aniv cried a sharp, screeching note and drove the knife into the small metal flower.

The shock wave hit my chest. Knocked me off balance like an ocean wave. I braced, but there was no explosion. The bluff beneath us trembled, and the entire city shivered.

A thinner, gentler aftershock swept around my ankles, traveling back toward the center point, toward Dinah. Like the tempting undertow as the tide goes out.

Dinah stumbled back.

I scrambled down from my perch and raced to her. I put my arms around her from behind, and she leaned back into my chest. Her head lolled to my shoulder.

"Done," she gasped. "Safe."

And her knees gave out.

.   .   .

I carried her home.

Her knees tucked up to my chest, her head on my shoulder, arms around me. She was tall and lankier than I'd realized, but she settled well into me, loose and almost unconscious. I paused to awkwardly spool her laddered twists of hair around my forearm like a rope. I went carefully down through the city, slow as I needed to be, along the broad avenue of stairs that led from the seventh terrace straight down to the first, opened into a great red courtyard, and marched out the city gate to the rougher path down the bluff.

The sun beat down—it was after lunchtime—and many, if not all of the refugees and special service members not actively engaged in their duties lined the way. They all knew, somehow, from the released detonation teams I guessed, what we'd been doing—and what Dinah Aniv had done.

I nodded at the service members. They saluted me with knuckles to lips. The star clan refugees—men, women, children, all in rainbow-striped robes, their black hair twisted and woven in long plaits, dark eyes painted with respectful desert mud—reached out to skim their bare hands on Dinah's robes, or on her hair. They crowded in, murmuring blessings, murmuring *Dinah*.

I swelled with joy, with pride. Also with heat, and sweat smeared dust down my face and neck. It pooled in the small of my back, collected there by the belt of my red uniform pants. It rubbed in my boots. I tasted it on my lips.

The refugees created a path for me, leading me for the first time through the canvas partition to their side of camp. Here everything was bright and colorful against the desert. No raw canvas tents for them, but dark blue, purple, red, green, woven rugs and braided rugs, flags and fired pottery, striped robes hung out to dry—all of it faded from sun and time, ragged and dirty, but the colors shone through still. It was merry, despite the dingy press of time. It was a home.

They led me to her tent, one of five conical tents all in the same sky blue, at the edge of camp, facing east. One man pulled open the flap and tied it high enough I did not have to duck. Nobody followed me inside.

I laid her down in a nest of blankets and rough straw pillows. Carefully, I unwound the rope of her hair from my arm. The air smelled of roses—the hand oil, probably. In the dim light I saw two carved trunks, one set with many squat candles and a scatter of raw opals. I wondered if I should wake her gently and help her undress, get her drink or food or take her to a bathhouse. But her body relaxed away from me, sinking into the bed. All I did was remove the crumpled veil from around her neck and spread it carefully over the second carved trunk. As always, she wore no shoes.

Leaning back on my heels, I admired her. I wished to lie beside her, be near as I'd been all morning and night. I was exhausted too. I wanted to press against her back, her hips, hold her tightly and pretend it was all over. That tomorrow I could ask her to come home with me to the sea.

Instead, I brushed my lips to her cheek, barely enough to feel it myself, and left.

. . .

There was a celebration that night.

While I slept, soldiers and refugees pulled down the partitions and moved tents and the mess hall in order to create a wide public space—star clan and An Riel—for a great fire and party. Jarair woke me at sundown, dragged me to wash up, put a fresh uniform on me—buttons included—and dug around my tent to find my medals and rank pieces. I protested, but he only grinned and grabbed my collar. Nearly choking me in his insistence, he pinned everything in place and said, "Now brush your damn hair."

I did, and tied it back. He clapped my shoulder and said he approved. Together we went out where the other pacers waited, and as a unit we joined the celebration.

The food was fast-made, but delicious—both star clan and Rielan, with a lot of goat and cheese, olives from home, roasted desert beetles, even candied Sweet leaves. There was watery wine—better than nothing—and some special flasks of rice liquor. The fire danced taller than me, and we had our whistles, but the star clans brought out drums and gut harps and round, haunting pipes to add to the song.

The *hum* connected everything. Most of the drumming and all of the pipes seemed to affect it, to draw it thinner or faster, somehow. I felt it hard in my chest, making my sternum vibrate—and realized it was the medals, accentuating it, making my heart into a target.

I went around with Jarair, smiling, eating and drinking, but mostly quiet. I listened to the others tell stories about things I'd done—here and before, during the war that most of my current comrades had never seen. But mainly we spoke of pacing, of the mine and the desert, of the stars that spread as the evening wore on, filling the black sky with light.

The dancing began before I found Aniv. Just a few young refugees at first, and then a serviceman asked the wife of the star clan chief to dance with him. Our commander asked the chief in turn, and that popped the bubble. Soon the wide circle around the bonfire was alive with dancing and laughter. Jarair abandoned me quickly to join in, and I held to the edges with other wall-huggers, tapping the toe of my boot and drinking my watery wine. Commander Saria AnYar's daughter Yarlia, the camp second, took my wine and brought me out to dance with her—for show, she said, offering me a polite way to not enjoy myself.

Even though I've never come out and said "An Riel is run by the ladies," every time I've mentioned authority in An Riel there have been women there, especially compared to the initial dismissal of Rafel as "only a second son."

I assured her I was, though she barely heard me over the noise of the fire and the dancing.

And then I saw Dinah Aniv, a few feet away, in robes striped red, pink, purple, and black, with silver and golden threads that caught the firelight. Her hair was a great mass of darkness spreading around her head and shoulders. When she stepped toward me, little shafts of light shot through it, ribbons made of the same golden thread as her robes. I'd seen the robe—she only has three—but not the ribbons in her hair, not the dark paint around her eyes. Not the slippers on her feet.

I went straight to her, no hesitation, no pretense, and held out my hand. She took it. Hers were in thin silk gloves, nearly as soft as her skin. She smiled without teeth and I returned it. I put our palms together, and we danced.

It was star clan dancing—only our hands touched. I was not used to dancing at all, but when I had, it always had been in An Riel, where the woman chooses the path and rhythm. That night with Aniv, more was expected of me. I led, I pressed gently with my hand, one way or another, or I drew her to me by releasing pressure. She came and went with me, our eyes locked.

The *hum* was peaceful.

But I was not peaceful, I wanted more. I wanted to grab her hips and pull her tight against me. I wanted to embrace her, spin faster, bury my face in her thick hair.

Even in the flickering firelight, it must've been apparent in my eyes, in the way I couldn't stop moving my mouth; licking the bottom lip, chewing on the inside, pursing, stretching like I was going to smile, but stopping. Nerves, lust, anticipation; all of it unsettling me.

I gripped her hands, lacing our fingers together.

It ruined the dance: we were supposed to move palm to palm, gracefully.

Aniv faltered and then pulled me away from the fire and chaos of bodies, into the darkness of camp— the special services side, which was emptier, lonelier tonight than her people's side. When she found a completely secluded space along an alley of barracks tents, we stopped. I stepped close, almost panting, I was so eager. "Aniv," I said. Only the second time I'd said it aloud.

"There's something I've needed to tell you for days, Rafel." She shook her head once, abruptly. "No, weeks. Since you—since we . . ."

"Yes," I said.

She paused, mouth open, almost as if caught in a gasp.

I kissed her.

Her lips were parted, and mine, too, and so though it was a gentle kiss, we breathed together, and I felt her tongue touch mine and skim across my bottom lip the way she read the flower mines.

I wrote everything previous just to get to this kiss, of course. Remember? "Sometimes a kiss is like a magical bomb?" Well, it's about explode all over Rafel's character arc.

Then Dinah Aniv dug her fingers into my hair and dragged me closer, kissing me as surely as she did all things. I did not know what to do, how to kiss; I was a child, a new recruit to this particular service.

I fumbled, I pressed my palms to her ribs. I did what she did with my mouth and tongue, closed my eyes, and pulled at her.

Kissing should always, always, always build characterization and add to the story. It's sexy, but like everything, it reflects character and world, too.

But Aniv drew away, keeping our bodies apart. She sucked at my lip, exactly the gentle, patient way she'd sucked water from the cloth last night. And then she stepped fully away.

I stared at her, listening to the wind and the cry

of blood in my skull. She was so lovely, bright-black eyes and parted, mysterious mouth, colorful robes, hair like the night sky and all its sparkling stars. Tall, strong, lean and graceful. I remembered that when I first saw her, I'd thought she was only striking, but not beautiful. "Dinah," I said. "Aniv." Then I grinned: a face-splitting, delighted grin, with all my teeth because I felt everything we'd been told teeth meant to the star clans: intimacy and aggression both, a promise and a challenge.

Aniv put her gloved hands to her mouth, dragged them down her neck, and folded them over her heart. "I am so sorry, Rafel," she whispered.

The *hum* was there, buzzing my teeth, in the palms of my hands. It was the feeling of dread now. "What's wrong?" I asked.

"You will have difficulty understanding, my pacer," she said, in an odd, tired voice.

"Tell me—I'll find a way. That is what I am good at."

Aniv smiled sadly. "I am not what you think I am. I am not a woman in the way you will understand."

I shook my head, withdrawing a little from her. What a strange thing for her to say, I thought. Why would she? It was funny, at first. I almost laughed.

She pressed on. "I live as a woman, dress and behave as one. My heart is a woman's heart, Rafel— that proof is in my magic."

My laughter fell away; I was afraid then, afraid of rejection, that she was telling me mages are different from other women. That they do not love, do not feel the way others do. It was impossible for us to share anything because she was a star clan mage.

And then she said, "But I was not born with a woman's body. My parents had a son, until I went to live with the women."

I did *not* understand.

It was the wine, I was sure. The wine, the weariness, the dancing and crowd and energy and *hum*. All of it fogging my ears. I shook my head again, slowly, felt my face dragging into a frown. "A . . . son?" I said, staring at her through the fog and *hum*. "But you . . . are . . ."

I could not see what she was telling me. So blind I was, so confused, I did not understand how a person could be a son and then later a woman with a woman's heart. I imagined some magic, some strange desert secret we did not know. Transformation.

Aniv put her hands to her chest, her flat chest. She smoothed her thin robe against herself until it was clear the layers hid no breasts at all—I did remember thinking about that before.

She slid her hands lower, but when they reached her belly I swallowed a sharp pang of panic and fell away, turning. I stumbled a few feet back, caught my breath, and felt myself humming, deep in my throat.

The desert *hummed*, too.

Not magically different, that was not what she was telling me. He was telling me. Dinah Aniv was a man, only pretending to be a woman now.

My lips buzzed. I bit them back. They were soft, damp. Hot from her. Him. I didn't know. I glanced back to see Dinah Aniv standing exactly where I'd left her, watching me. Dinah Aniv as she always seemed. Herself.

Lying.

The word pounded through my thoughts, and I walked away.

. . .

I slept. I did not expect to.

. . .

I woke angry.

Still in my uniform with the medals and rank pieces. I tore them off, tossed them onto the foot of the cot.

In An Riel we are taught we are not as good as women, we are not so important. We are expendable most of the time, generally less good at thinking, too likely to be caught up in our emotions, especially aggressive ones like anger and the protective instinct.

We are supposed to love women; we are supposed to respect them. We are not supposed to *be* them. It does not happen in An Riel. Outrageous. I had never heard of such a thing. Surely if a man felt he should have been born a woman, he must ignore it; he must swallow it. *You are your body,* I told myself, flexing my hands. It is your vessel, your weapon, your canvas and home. *Your bones, your flesh, your beating heart—those things are what make you.*

We give our bodies to the ocean when we die because our bodies are the material essence of our spirits.

There are women who do not bleed, who cannot

#theme! World, politics, romance, war, bombs, all about the same damn thing.

This is world building as much as characterization: it was Rafel's world that taught him to believe these things. He was raised this way, and gender roles are insidious.

be the roots of a family. Not-quite women, but nearly, and we speak little of them if we can help it. And there are women true born who choose not to marry, to rule. They live like youngest sons. Little power, little influence. Of course you can always choose to be less than you are.

But it is offensive to reach above yourself. From man toward woman.

I could not even think what might happen to Aniv if she went to An Riel and this secret was revealed. Some old punishment we'd long given up for being too cruel, like being stoned to death or drowned in a sack, bound and weighted to the bottom of the sea so your bones would always be near the great whales, but never part of their song.

She and I were done.

I know now that was the thing angering me most; we were over, and we had never even begun.

The worst part, I told myself in my tent, shoulders heaving with emotions, was that it was hypocrisy that had led me there. An Riel's, and the star clans', and Aniv's, and mine.

We were all hypocrites in the desert.

. . .

She was waiting outside my tent with tea and a small box of breakfast. Calm, gloves on her hands. "You must have questions, Rafel."

What I hope is that when readers read this section they realize that I've been telling them (Rafel's been telling them) about Aniv's "secret" since the very first page. Whether readers guessed or not, saw it coming or not, I want them to look back over the first part of the story and be amazed that it was all there, woven in through the world building, so that if it's a surprise it's a good one, and if it's not a surprise, it feels like it was meant to be.

#theme! This line came with that very first line of Rafel's, "I thought I understood hypocrisy." And I wrote it down, waiting for the right moment.

"Dinah," I murmured, accepting her offerings and allowing her inside. Withdrawing into politeness. It is what I do when I am angry at my mother too.

The space of my tent was limited but ordered and simple: cot, open crate with folded clothes and my few belongings. It was difficult in the small space not to meet her gaze, though she helped by taking a blanket from the cot, spreading it on the rug, and setting out a picnic. She knelt there, her striped robe subdued in the dim sunlight that managed to filter through the canvas.

When she finished, she looked up at me. "Ask."

I towered over her, jacket undone, barefoot, hands hanging uselessly. And I stared down. She looked the same. Was the same. No particular hint of maleness—though her hands had always been long, as large as mine. She lacked all the outward signs I had, for example: the rough shape of my face, wide, square shoulders, muscles everywhere. A man was strong on the outside. Women were strong inside, their greatest muscles being their hearts and wombs.

That is what we believe in An Riel.

I opened my mouth and then only asked, "Why?"

She nodded. "Because women do magic in the star clans. Our gods gave that gift to me, and so to use it, I must be a woman."

"But doesn't everyone in your clan know?"

"I believe so."

"So it is a collective lie. An illusion you all . . . perpetrate among yourselves."

"It is not a lie. I have magic in me, and only a woman has magic. So, I am a woman, despite my body." She said the last firmly.

"Your *body* makes you a man."

"My *magic* makes me a woman."

"*I* have magic," I said, too loud.

Aniv stripped off her silk gloves. She rubbed her hands on the robes over her thighs as if nervous, sweating. "You sense magic, Rafel; you do not use it. You could not without being a woman."

"Your gods made a mistake then, didn't they?"

Her glance was cutting.

I said, "Either they make mistakes or they are fools. To do it accidentally." I would argue until the horizon, I so badly wished for this not to be true.

She touched her fingers lightly together. "Maybe the god of shapes and the god of the desert song did not speak to each other when forming me. One thought to shape a man, the other gave me a woman's gift. Should we be so rude as to point this out to them? I am a woman because I respect myself, and the desert song, and the gods and my clan."

"It's not natural," I said. "You say it's respectful toward your gods, but it is not respectful toward actual women. You are pretending to be what you are not."

"I am a woman," she said again, as if sheer stubbornness was enough. "Because of what is inside me."

So many of our problems come from using the same word to talk about different things, or using different words to talk about the same things. Language is all signs and symbols; it's messy and flawed just like us. I wanted to bring that in here because gender and sexuality, and war, are things I think we have a nearly impossible time discussing. We think we understand it, until we suddenly don't. Add in religion and, well.

My world building and stories try to ask questions. I don't always (ever) have all the answers.

"Inside you?" I held myself taut, else I would pace jaggedly, I would walk circles around her, or tear my tent to the desert ground. "How can you know what it is to have a woman's insides when you do not have a woman's muscles? You cannot know a woman's strength any better than I can, cannot know the pain of carrying death inside you, you cannot know those things than make women *women*. If you bled as they do, you would weaken and die."

She unfolded herself from the rug, standing nearly as tall as me. "I know because I grew up among them. I lived as a girl with other girls and women. I learned, I lived, I understand. I am a woman, Rafel Sal AnLenia. My spirit and my life tell me so. You may ask questions, but stop arguing with me—I know you cannot understand, but you will not tell me I am wrong."

I could not have written this argument or story if I hadn't studied gender studies and feminism in college and grad school. That's where research comes in, or life experience. Familiarity with the political and cultural discourses of the themes you're engaging with.

The strength in her voice immediately cowed me—as would my mother's or aunt's or the Queen herself.

Rafel is still subject to his world building and characterization. He MUST act in-character until I show through story that his character is changing.

I went silent. Staring at her, brow pinched so hard a headache began behind my eyes. I clenched my jaw against the desert *hum*. I tried to see the man. Him. Tried to see him standing before me.

I could not. I only saw her, even imagining the shadow of a beard on her jaw, or slicing off all her hair—none of it changed how my eyes would look at her. "Don't you feel a man's . . . urges?" I finally said, quietly.

She nearly smirked. "I feel many urges, pacer. Sometimes I want to touch a woman, yes, which must be what you mean. But mostly I desire what my sisters and girlfriends and cousins taught me during my life with them. What my spirit desires. What many women desire: a finely shaped man." Aniv's gaze then traveled down and back up my body, making her point clear.

My stomach twisted in its heat—it made me tight and hot all over. For a moment I didn't care at all, I just wanted her to trace my body's pathways with her reading lips.

And it *hurt*. That hurt exploded like rage. I could not have what I wanted, and so I said, "You can't make a family with those desires. What good is a woman who cannot be the root of a family?"

She drew up her chin and proudly said, "You mean I cannot make a family *with you*."

I whispered, harsh and final, "My family would never welcome a star clan refugee like you."

Aniv tilted her head away, the slash of her mouth bitter and, I think, disappointed in me. With no further looks or talking, she left.

I sank to a crouch on the rug, thrusting the food and tea away in a mess. I put my face in my hands, and I tried not to cry.

The *hum* the *hum* the *hum*, I thought.

. . .

I hope my world building has been good enough that readers know Rafel is wrong about this. And I hope my characterization has been good enough that readers know Rafel doesn't truly believe it.

That's why world building matters so much: the emotional epiphanies and breakdowns, the crises of character that drive the emotional engagement for readers will be believable only if the world is believable. (And characterization too, of course.) You do your building work up front and the payoff hopefully happens, comes together in the end.

It shames me now, that I was so afraid. Aniv was what I wanted, but not all of what I wanted: I had dreamed all those dreams, and they were shattered.

An Riel, the clans, me: we were all culpable. But Aniv only followed her magic where her family, her people, told her she must go.

An Riel used the Sweet for battleground, used it and left it full of deadly flowers. Worse: we returned under the guise of helping, as if we cared, but it was political; it was because we did not want dying, angry star clans fleeing into our country. We did not want the consequences of our war. But we pretended it was charity, kindness.

The star clans believe only women can do magic, and so when a boy was born magical, they twisted him into something he was not.

And I let myself fall, knowing it was unprofessional and distracting to even think of the Dinah, knowing I should clamp down on my wants. I disregarded the rules and reality, and I never looked away from her.

It was my fault.

Not Aniv's. The woman—the man—I loved had done nothing wrong.

That is what I decided, cowering on the rug in my tent.

But I had to get dressed and make a choice. A second son does not wallow and break; he holds onto the pieces, even if they are sharp and cut his hands. He acts. He steps forward.

I had to choose a direction.

I dressed again in the metal-free pacer's uniform

All of this was here, but in a totally different order. I rearranged it about sixteen times trying to find the right order of information, the right progression of thought. The right way to remind readers what the world is and what the Major Themes Are. Especially as far as Rafel is concerned.

with its little ties and lack of grommets. I pulled my hair into a tail; I washed up. I didn't eat, though. Only drank the dregs of spilled tea.

Hollow and stiff, I went to the star clan camp, directly to her tent, which I could easily find since yesterday. Smiling refugees practically pointed the way.

I paused at the folded-open flap of her bright sky-blue tent and said, "Dinah."

Her title. Not her name. Not the intimacy of her name. (GOD, NAMES ARE SO IMPORTANT.)

She emerged from the shadows with the end of her braid in her hand, wiping tears off her cheek with the soft hair.

It nearly broke my resolve.

She stared at me in raw surprise, and I suddenly saw it: the boy she'd been.

Lanky and tall, with large, soft hands and simple, thick braids, a long nose and thin lips, big black eyes, desert skin, solid shoulders and a tapering waist, with no hips under the simple dark robe like a man might wear to drink morning coffee by the sea.

He might have been a friend or comrade, my younger, paler brother if I had one.

Then the young man licked his lips, tentatively, and she was Aniv again, and I was thinking of her tongue on the smooth ceramic surface of a flower bomb.

Once again: bringing it back to magical bombs—connecting Rafel's sexuality, and his experience and needs here in the desert, to the flower mines. Beautiful/terrible. Secretive/explosive.

"Aniv," I said softly. "May I say something to you I should have said a long time ago?"

Now her name. He's removing a shield of politeness and distance. Taking a deliberate step nearer.

"Yes," she replied, letting her braid drop to her knees.

I bowed smartly and put my knuckles to my lips in salute. "I cannot be your pacer. I go from here to my commander, to request a transfer."

Tears shone on her eyelashes, and she shook her head, angrily. "You would not have said that a long time ago. You only say that since last night."

"No." It was a struggle to be calm, polite, distant. As I always *should* have been with her.

"We are the *best* team, and they need us together," she said.

"I am not my best when I am with you."

"How can you say that, you imbecile?"

My eyes lowered to her bare toes, showing under layers of dark robe. "I am distracted by you, Dinah. I always have been, and you know why. We are lucky I did not make some grave mistake, and that those mistakes I did make were countered by your great skills."

"No," she whispered.

"It was a great honor," I said to her feet and the desert floor.

· · ·

The commander was not happy with me when I walked into her office to resign as a pacer. "You think because of who your family is you can do whatever you want?"

I had no energy to answer any other way but truthfully. "Yes," I said.

Deleted a whole section here that was slowing things down, about how he spent his afternoon. It added nothing but words.

· · ·

Rafel.

My whispered name woke me, and my hands found my sabers.

"Wait," she whispered through the dark tent.

Aniv.

I rolled to my feet. "What's wrong?"

"Be quieter, please," she murmured, and the tips of her fingers began to glow. Or, rather, the fingers of the gloves she wore. Dinah Aniv was fully dressed, swathed in the traveling robes, veil, and thin boots the star clans traveled through the desert in.

"Where are you going?" I asked.

"To New Spring. Come with me."

I peered through the dull light. It cast her face silver.

New Spring was the drowned sacred city. Where the Irisu Dam had burst under the onslaught of a wreath of flower mines, triggering this Restoration Campaign. Said to be impossible to clear of the mines because of all that water.

Because I didn't answer, she kept talking. "Do you know why we were a good pair, mage and pacer? It was *because* we were connected, *because* you were distracted. You hear the desert, Rafel. We can free New Spring of all flower mines at once, like on the seventh terrace of Shiver."

My mouth was dry. My eyes groggy from sleep. I was glad of the zing of desert *hum* between my sabers, rushing through my arms and down my spine to spin urgently in the small of my back.

"Rafel, go with me."

She lowered her glowing hands. The light slashed shadows up her chin, mouth, nose, and creeping, long eyelashes.

This was "I," but I needed her to be challenging him about *them* specifically, not just randomly wanting suddenly to free the city. Make it about their relationship and her sort of Hail Mary pass to get him to understand. I played with it for a while, then ended up only changing that one word, but I think it makes a huge difference here.

I felt such sudden, piercing grief that this mage would never be my wife, the heart of my family. I thought I might die of it.

But I said yes. I would go, pace her, keep her alive if I could, and witness everything if I could not.

．　．　．

The days of traveling were like a dream. Even now, it is hard for me to space them out, order them into this, then. The two of us walking, sharing the burdens of the sun, following the *hum* and its patterns to water, to shelter. When the sun flashed, the spirit stone that striped the bluffs and chimney rocks would shimmer like living magic. There were well-known paths, of course, that the star clans used, that even the special service knew, but Aniv was worried we would be followed, caught, dragged away from Irisu Valley without the chance to save it, and so we strayed from those known paths.

"I forgot you knew so well how to slip unseen through the Sweet," she said to me the first day—it must have been. She had turned to instruct me on folding the veil she'd provided, but I'd already laid it correctly over my face to protect from the late sunlight and dusty wind.

I wondered if she'd tried to forget I was Rafel the Gardener.

We went in a jagged line farther and farther north, to meet up with the Irisu River just below the broken dam. It was long hours of walking over rough desert, climbing chimney rocks to look ahead and behind, cracked gulches, wishing for horses—at least on my part—and outwaiting the sun at its peak. Mornings were for boiling water for coffee and for softening the hard meats to eat with stiff, heavy crackers. Evenings we roasted a snake or little wingless dragon if we'd been lucky enough to catch one, rock beetles if we had not.

> New location (sort of), new world-building details! Keep the world and setting fresh in readers' minds, but with new details so it's not redundant or boring.

Aniv and I did not need to speak very much—even in our division there was an understanding. I knew what she needed, and she predicted for me, too. I knew when she should drink more; she knew when I'd reached the end of my energy. In such a way we took care of each other. I realized I was paying more attention to her needs than my own, but it balanced because she paid more attention to mine. Laughable, really, and dangerous.

I asked why she was so determined to save the Irisu Valley, and why now. She reminded me it was sacred to her, to her clan. She'd lived most of her life farther north, near the Eruse border, and then later in Eruse itself during the war, but her grandmother and great-grandmother had both been mages, both born in New Spring.

She wasn't telling me all of it. I believed her about her family, but this was about us. About proving something to me, to herself, maybe to the Sweet itself.

> Added this paragraph late in the game to make this conflict about them overtly, not just symbolically.

. . .

The first full night, we stretched in the lee of a layered rock whose wind scars shaped it into the profile of a goat. We'd been quiet since making camp near the roots of a short inyan tree, whose roots held water for years. Water that tasted like sugar when squeezed from the meat of the root, and when pulped, that meat was chewy and refreshing. A gift of the Sweet.

The stars pulled out from behind thin clouds, and Aniv lay near enough I could've taken her hand if I stretched out my own. Our heads were slightly nearer than our feet, our bodies wrapped up in travel robes that tied tight enough to keep spiders, scorpions, and any other such night-crawlers from us as we slept, but that fell away with one tug of the intricately woven ties. One of my sabers waited flat against my thigh inside the robes, the other outside it, near the palm of my free hand. The great canyon of stars overhead made me feel small, but Aniv and her desert *hum* made me feel larger.

"Aniv," I whispered.

"I'm awake, Rafel."

I liked how she always said my name back to me when I said hers. "Do you remember when I said my family would never welcome a star clan refugee like you?"

After a pause she said, "Yes."

"I lied." My confession was only a breath of noise, but I knew she could hear. "For weeks I had been imagining exactly that: taking you home to my family. I knew they would not only welcome you, but love you, be proud of you, and of me."

"Rafel—"

I talked over her. "I should not have lied—it was not worthy of myself or my family, and certainly not when I knew they would admire and love a strong,

This scene was one of the other core moments I wrote down in my notes before ever beginning to write the story itself. Just Rafel confessing this to her, aching and proud and ashamed. It meant a lot to me personally.

It can be hard to push through a draft because of a muddled middle or a loss of purpose or uncertainty about the ending or fear of your own lack of skills. I try to have core moments like this that I cannot wait to write, and the pressure to get to write them is what draws me through the middle and end of my draft.

beautiful woman such as you were."

She rolled toward me, touched my shoulder. I turned my face away, to the dark, to the stars.

"I'm the same person, Rafel Sal AnLenia," she murmured.

"I know."

It was true. I did.

Her soft, bare fingers touched the hollow of my cheek. When I did not flinch or pull away, she turned the touch into a caress.

"It hurts," I said.

Aniv stopped.

. . .

Sometimes, when we climbed hard and silently, saving our breath for the task, I saw the man Aniv again. The way Aniv's gait changed over rough terrain, becoming less elegant and sure, more irregular but still strong. It was my imagination, I knew: I was ascribing a maleness to it just because it was not the grace I was used to. But it was a relief to see.

Why a relief? Because it kept me from falling backwards into those dreams again, where Aniv could be what I wanted her to be.

. . .

What I would not give to be there again. To have those days back, even if nothing changed, if I changed nothing at all.

. . .

One morning I jogged around the striped rock marking our camp, having scouted ahead and used the time to stretch, let loose my hair, relieve myself. I skidded to a halt because Aniv was bare to the waist. Her back was to me, her golden, curving back. Her shoulders and the long, smooth muscles of her arms. All that black hair piled haphazardly atop her head in a messy stack. She sopped at her neck with a cloth, rubbing dirt and sweat away under the pink light of the morning sun. Her robe gathered around her waist, falling like a smooth gown to her ankles.

Paralyzed, I watched, half wanting to run away again, half wanting to go up to her and kiss her shoulders, her spine.

. . .

Mere hours later, we stopped to collect thick juice from a hava plant, which when added to boiling water thickens it to a soup that is almost tasty to eat. I crouched beside her, lifting the heavy fronds up so she could harvest juice without irreparably harming the plant. My face was inches from hers, and I could smell her sweat and the rose oil she still rubbed every day into her hands.

A shadow was on her cheek, at her jaw.

It took me a long moment to realize she was finally showing the promise of a beard.

See what I mean about food being a great way to establish world stuff? Many of these scattered traveling scenes are grounded in what they eat, because all they're doing is eating, sleeping, and walking.

There's an old joke about stew in high fantasy novels because it's really common as lazy world building that your heroes eat stew around the campfire at the end of a questing day. DON'T BE LAZY WITH YOUR FOOD.

I wondered if it would be fine and soft, or coarse and spotty like mine when I let it come in.

I said, "You should shave, Dinah."

She replied, "Why? I thought you did not want me to hide?"

I glanced back to our task and said no more.

A personal favorite moment of mine. It is really okay to have them, love them, keep them. You do not have to kill all your darlings. If you did, why would you bother sharing your story?

. . .

The night before we would reach New Spring, we camped on a high promontory of orange stone. The wind was sparing, the air cool, and we could see down into the great Irisu River Valley where the city waited—dark, invisible in the moonlight because no people resided there to light lanterns or fires.

Moonlight glinted off great swathes of water, though, for the valley itself was flooded.

I stood with one boot up on a rock, leaning over the edge of the cliff, staring down into the valley at the black shadows of the city walls, the towers and homes, the courtyards and avenues and palace.

An image of a flooded desert city—all terra-cotta and pale tiles, flooded about three or four feet deep with brilliant teal-green water—is what located this story in the desert for me. I know it seems like it must have been the Iraq/IED connection, but I played with setting it in a more tropical location for a long time. When I saw that image I knew FLOODED DESERT CITY. The desert I used for research and imagery was part of the Australian Outback.

Aniv joined me, the light breeze toying with her hair and the ends of her robe as it could not play with my heavier, fitted uniform.

I was thinking about such a glut of floodwater, surrounded by the desert.

#theme! Surrounded by so much of what you need that it's killing you.

She took my hand. Her touch startled me, for we'd been careful with each other all these six days of travel. She pulled me down to her.

She kissed me.

Surprise pulled the air from my lungs. I leaned away. Looked at the dark red desert under my feet.

"Rafel," she whispered. "This is the last night. Tomorrow we go to work, and it will be work and work and work—hard work—until we are finished."

"The last night for what?"

Aniv tilted her head and leaned in to kiss me again.

"Aniv, I can't." I pulled far away, heartsick.

Anger bent her mouth. "You want me, though, don't you? Tell me the truth, Rafel—you want my touch, you want my friendship and love."

I nodded.

"Then what is the problem? Your people do not care if men share any of those things with other men—that is what the Eruse say. They mean it as a curse, as a condemnation, but it isn't. Why do *you* think it is? Rielan men dally with other men."

"I have not!" I cried. I bit my lip. I added, "I have not . . . dallied . . . with anyone."

She looked at me suddenly as if I was sweet. Adorable. As if she loved that about me. "Let me show you," she said.

I really did not want this emotional conflict to be about Rafel being homophobic (inasmuch as that was possible, because to a certain extent he *is*), and I worked hard to make the world building support that it is NOT what is primarily holding Rafel back. This is really about gender, not sexuality—his or hers. It's about the very rigid gender roles in An Riel specifically—I built them to be different from ours (American), and hopefully they subvert ours well enough to make this point.

I put my hands to her jaw. She had shaved the tiny dark hairs that same night I'd mentioned them, and her skin was as smooth as ever, as soft. "I can't," I said.

There was a great, heavy pause. My hands slid off her as she studied me. She was nearly my same height, especially now that she wore star clan boots. Her black eyes were open wide, her long nose lifted toward me. And she asked the one single question I'd asked of her.

"Why?"

"Because," I said from a dry throat, "I can't bring

you home. I expected everything from you—unfairly, I know, without your input or consent, *I know*. But I wanted everything from you, everything there is in life, and I can't have it now, knowing the truth."

She made an expression like a spitting cat: teeth bright.

Aniv was as ferocious and beautiful as the ocean. She said, "Damn you, Rafel Sal AnLenia! I want you too. I want anything, everything you'll give me, Rafel, right now before I go into that drowned city and break everything, risk everything. If we both want the same, why are you being so stubborn?"

"It would hurt too much," I whispered, hoarse and ashamed. "To let myself think—to pretend—and then go home without you. Take myself away. Lose you. It will be hard enough without adding these memories."

Her face crumpled, and she truly looked like a man then, on the verge of crying, full of passion and sorrow. "I have fallen in love with a coward," she moaned.

> Choosing to Other yourself when you don't have to is very, very hard. That's what Rafel would have to do to be with Aniv openly because of how I've made An Riel culture and Rafel's family. SEE? SEEEEE? World (building) creates character conflict which creates story.
>
> *drops mic*

. . .

I can still hear her saying it, if I close my eyes and let the sea spit at me. It's what I deserve. Rafel the Gardener, a frightened boy. Tucked again in his bedroom in his mother's house on the cliff.

. . .

The city of New Spring glowed under the morning sky: polished cream sandstone and long strips of marble cut through with bloodred blocks and columns. It was a true desert city, built of rock and mud, beautifully gleaming tiles, and narrow towers connected by swaying bridges woven of mage-silk.

But abandoned.

Drowned in still, emerald water.

. . .

We approached by the main road, raised above the desert floor just enough so the floodwaters left it like a narrow bridge for us, from the edge of the valley directly to the main gates.

The *hum* vibrated through my entire body the moment I stepped into the valley, and I glanced, startled, at Aniv. She said quietly, without anger but with no encouragement, "The water reflects the song again and again. Amplifies it, you would say in An Riel. Hold on to your sabers if you must."

I did.

We walked carefully, but fast.

A large white banner hung from the carved wooden gates, blocking the crack between them. I'd seen such things before: a mage's flag, to mark that a place burns with magic. I supposed it worked to remind anyone who came here that the city was full of flower bombs.

Aniv strode to the flag. She stripped off her silk glove and put her hand upon the cloth. It was just high enough that she could reach the top corner and run her fingers down from top to bottom, then again farther to the right. She moved her hand up and down in columns, the way I might move my eyes to read.

I stepped to her shoulder and examined the flag;

it was dusty, stained, but there was no writing, nothing I could see. I reached around her to touch the edge. I felt tiny, barely discernable texture—not a weave pattern, but marks made into the stiff cloth. Aniv *was* reading. But with her hands.

She lifted the flag, handing it to me unceremoniously. She ducked under to kiss the hollow of a spiral carved into the gate, and flattened her hands in specific ways. Her forefingers found nooks I would not have seen, and she breathed heavily into the spiral.

The gates slid away with cranky groans. Water spilled out over our feet, washing pottery and broken wood past us into the desert.

Aniv took me into the great welcoming yard of New Spring, which she said was as far as we could go until we dismantled the system of mines. "Find a perch, pacer, and wait."

I stared at the knee-high water all around. "The mines could be anywhere."

"Yes. Be careful, and disturb the water itself as little as possible." She pressed my hand. I pressed back, then walked slowly toward a broken cart that leaned against the blue-green-white tiled wall of some public house. It was awkward but not difficult to climb and then swing up on an old pole from which a sign should have hung. I scrambled to the first balcony, then used windows and the tiny tile decorations along the rooflines to climb to the third balcony. This one was hardly large enough for me to crouch upon, being meant for flowers or pottery, not a man, but it had no rail to be in my way. I could slip down quickly, too, if

One of the first details I created about star clan magic was their refusal to rely upon sight when casting or performing magic. I expanded that philosophically in a few directions, including that they should or would have non-sight-based ways of communicating.

Much world building is only expanding outwards in all directions from a few key details.

need be, and see not only the entire yard but well into the surrounding neighborhoods.

Aniv stood in the center of the flooded yard, water lapping her knees, dragging at her soaked robes. She wore blue, green, and black stripes, with occasional thin shocks of orange. That orange was all that kept it from seeming she rose out of the dark water, a thing of water herself.

She spread her bare hands over the water, palms down, and remained still.

For hours.

The sun rose to its pinnacle. Sweat prickled my scalp and slid down my back. I was glad of the veil I still had tied over my hair, soaking some of the sweat away. The edges of it flared out on my brow to shade my eyes somewhat. I stared down at her, let my awareness grow, let the *hum* fill my skull and slither along my bones. I breathed, I watched, I studied.

Water rippled green everywhere, *humming* through abandoned buildings. The silk bridges were tattered in places, hanging and drifting like cobwebs. No sign of people, but plenty of bird droppings and evidence of rats, maybe smaller cats. The kind who can live roof to roof. Very few insects other than some beetles. No obvious mines, though I counted sixteen potential hiding places in the surrounding thirty or so meters.

I parted my lips to let the *hum* into my teeth.

Clouds pulled across the sky.

Aniv was a sundial, tall and straight. Her shadow pointed two hours past noon when I realized there was an *angle* to the *hum*.

"Aniv," I whispered hollowly.

All she did was turn her face to me and nod through the sheer veil.

I went, climbing carefully, and then slipped into the water with as little disturbance as I could. The water sank over the top of my boots, soaking my socks again; the only sound was the quiet lapping of it against me. Ripples rushed gently from me to her, then back again, making an intricate, interlocking pattern.

"What did you see?" she asked me.

"The water . . . it's . . . there's something about the water itself."

Aniv stared down at it. "The entire city is wreathed," she whispered.

"How is that . . . the water?"

Slowly, she nodded. She touched the tip of one finger into the water. "Rafel, it was not a star mage or insurgent. The mines were set, and the flood itself connected them. The desert did this. I can use the water to do the opposite."

"Alone?"

"I have you," she said, with a slant of irony in her gaze that I could read even through the veil.

The world itself connected these flower mines.

Swallowing, I glanced up at the sky. "Tomorrow might be better. We only have maybe five hours of solid light."

"No, now. I know the layout, I know the water level, and I don't want to risk it all changing because of wind or nighttime elements. I can do this, and you get as high as you can and watch. Listen. Feel."

This city was always wreathed, but it was Brenna's idea that the water itself somehow connected the mines—nature did what mages could not. Very thematic. I liked it, so I did it.

I took her hand. "Are you truly powerful enough for this, Dinah?"

Her mouth twisted. "Late to doubt me now."

"This task is immense," I whispered.

Wind rippled the floodwaters, teased at her veil. She suddenly dragged it off her face, pressed it to her chest where it would not get wet. "Rafel."

I gripped her elbows. The *hum* connected through my hands, as if I'd grasped the hilts of my sabers. I felt it in my teeth. "I believe you, Aniv. I will watch, and warn you if anything goes wrong."

As I let her go, she said my name again. "*Rafel*. Stay high, as high as you can. If anything goes wrong, it will go very, very wrong."

"You brought the wrong pacer for that," I said, attempting a smile. "I run toward explosions, remember?"

"Toward me." Her voice was thin, tense.

"Toward you." I kissed my knuckles to salute her and made my way slowly through the water again to find my highest perch.

. . .

Oh those hours.

Aniv did not put her veil back on, but spread it before her so it floated nearly invisible on the water. It drifted with the gentle, subtle flow of the floodwaters as they

I knew the climax of this story took place in a drowned city, and it involved Aniv and Rafel doing something only they could do—together—that also involved the flower mines. When I began, that's *all* I knew about the ending. But I didn't worry about it, because I hoped writing the story would reveal to me what it needed to be in the same way that working out world building often reveals to me new potential roads and solid answers. I was right: this climactic bomb brings together elements from basically every other example of a flower mine that I explicitly described.

Sometimes it's okay to trust yourself and just write and hope.

Smoothing out the bumps when you aren't totally sure as you draft is exactly what revision is *for*.

curled throughout the city. Like a sniper's wind-guide, I thought.

She knelt down so the water lapped at her chest and shoulders. Her bound hair turned even blacker as it soaked, the twists like snakes around her shoulder blades, coiling just beneath the surface.

I hummed. I pitched my breath to the *hum* itself, letting it inside me, vibrating my bones, making my teeth ache. I focused on Aniv, but also on the entire world of lush green water, white-red city, audacious blue sky, small balcony, heartbeat, breath, and most of all, the *hum*.

I sipped from my narrow, long waterskin, wished to remind Aniv to do the same. She would not, though, not without my putting it to her mouth. Interrupting.

I never needed to relieve myself even as the sun lowered enough to cast long shadows, and knew I was dehydrated. How much worse Aniv must have been.

My vision gradually washed with light that felt somehow the same frequency as the desert song. Perhaps it was a function of fasting, perhaps we needed to be deprived, sun-bloated, balanced on a precipice of nothing but *hum* and magic, between water and fire.

· · ·

She moved so suddenly, so unexpectedly, my humming faltered, my boot slipped.

There'd been no warning, no placing of a net, no altar of opals and carved charms, though how could there have been when water surrounded everything?

Aniv slapped her palms to the water's surface, then drove her hands under.

All of her followed.

She vanished underwater, swallowed up.

A pause just long enough for me to thrust to my feet—then the center of the yard exploded.

Water rose in a massive bubble, bursting up, tossing her veil away. It flowered out in hundreds of curved petal layers, a spray of orchid, the bulk of a rose, pink and vibrant purple, then scatters of yellow and white seed-explosions like a dandelion.

I did not see Aniv.

The water rushed away from the zero point, ripples of shock wave that I saw moving as if the water was a living explosion.

But not in concentric circles, not in every direction. From my vantage I saw it plunge *east*.

The ripple of magic traveled fast, only going a dozen yards before another watery explosion, then another, and another. They popped like beads around a pearl necklace, one at a time, unevenly spaced, running in one singular direction away from us, around the city.

I stood there, watching, listening to the angry, buzzing *hum*, and realized—*knew*—what was happening.

She'd set the wreath off one at a time, like dominos. But the wreath was a massive, connected, circular net, and the beginning point would also be the ending point.

Panicked, I nearly threw myself off the balcony, barely managing to take measured footholds, grip tightly, wait to find the right place to dig my fingers.

The entire city trembled. My chest shuddered and shook from the constant, impossibly loud echo of the wreath.

I fell the final few feet, landing hard in the water, then ran for her.

The *hum* grew louder and louder—the explosions that had distanced were returning. I heard thunder and slapping rain, I felt the pulse of it.

She was still underwater. I dove into the shallow flood, dragging my fingers along drowned cobblestones, mouth open to call her name, choking on water—all with that screaming wreath running back at me, running, running, bringing the city and floodwater with it.

. . .

I found her, the edge of her robe, and I struggled to bring her to the surface, dragging at too much weight. But I managed, yelling her name, pulling her, limp, against me. She was cold and soaked, but her mouth opened and breath was there. Her eyelids fluttered. I shook her, jumping up and down. "Aniv!"

The thunder was upon us.

She suddenly threw out her hands, toward the coming power, and knocked her head back like she would embrace it with her entire self.

I wrapped around her, dropping us both down.

I made myself into a shell for Aniv, my back to the approach of death.

It drove hard and sharp through me, into her.

Aniv's body flared with vibrating heat.

My skull shook, I ground my teeth together and roared, screamed just like the screaming city, as my entire body pulled and shattered.

In my arms, Aniv caught it all.

· · ·

I don't know if she'd have been fine, had I stayed up on my balcony, or if she'd have died. If I interfered and that's why it was so hard, or if I saved her.

#theme

· · ·

I drifted on water, floating faceup because she had turned me over. It was the only reason I breathed: my mouth was to the stars; flowing, comforting, healing water buoyed my aching body. No pressure of gravity to ruin my lungs even though every breath made the fire in my ribs burn and burn. I heard nothing but the water, the ocean of blood in my ears, dull, but filling everything. Maybe she said something, but her voice was blurred like a voice through water. Water blinded me, filled my nose, ruined my ears and all my skin so I felt nothing but the air on my lips and the fire in my rib cage.

· · ·

They found us floating, both of us unconscious. A team of special service and one of the other star clan mages, led by Jarair. They'd followed after us, and even Jarair heard the desert shriek when the city exploded. Later, I was told Dinah Aniv woke as they were taking me away, pulling us apart. She said my name, said, *Rafel Sal AnLenia, the Desert's Pacer.*

. . .

I still don't hear anything but the ocean of blood in my head. At least I can sleep.

. . .

It's been months. I can run again, after so long being unable to catch my breath, after waking every few hours with sharp pain in my chest or back, my body refusing to listen to my screaming mind, begging to breathe, to breathe.

Three of my molars fell out of my head, crumbled from grinding, shaking magic.

My ears are ruined. The roar of blood overwhelms words, the wind, music, anything I should be able to hear. My mother gave me a chalkboard so she could write down specific things she wanted to say.

Rest, stretching, slow walks with a cane, all of it embarrassing for a young man, especially the now-famous second son of the Queen's youngest niece. Though Rafel the Desert Pacer would not *be* famous if he wasn't so broken. If he hadn't done what he did in that drowned city.

With her.

Without her.

Running is hardest on the beaches below Mother's cliff house. Where the footing is loose and uneven, where I wish the pale, bone-colored sand were vibrant red or the orange of life and twilight. Where I can see the rhythm of the waves, but not hear it at all.

Sometimes if I stand still, if I kneel where the foamy surf swirls around my legs, sometimes then I can feel the rhythm of the ocean, the song of An Riel. It is not the *hum*, but it pounds in my bones and vibrates up my teeth.

. . .

I tear off my dull blue coat and toss it into the ocean surf. The salt water floods it, darkening it, until it is only a shadow of darker blue against the blue of the water. When I return to the house, shivering, I tell my mother I want something brighter.

. . .

When my mother talks to me, writing at the same time, I hear the tone of her voice, a blur of sound, and I see her lips move. Sometimes I can read it, and I think of Dinah Aniv caressing the smooth ceramic lines of an orchid mine. I think of her heavy black hair, her large, soft hands, and I think of her secrets.

Our secrets.

Aunt Lusha talks to me about my future, says I need work to focus my melancholy. Her handwriting is scratchy and bold, impatient. I tell her I'm not melancholy, and she lowers her chin, eyes me suspiciously and asks if I'm dumb then, in addition to being deaf, or lost in memories of the Sweet, or in love.

Oh, she's not surprised when I startle at that. She makes a disgusted sound I can't hear but can easily read in the shape of her mouth.

<u>I want to tell her all of it. I don't want this to be a secret. My heart.</u>

In the beginning, Rafel did not want to tell his secrets to anybody, but he's changed. I shouldn't have to put a line in the text reminding readers of his initial reluctance to share secrets, not if I've done my job right.

. . .

There are letters from all over An Riel, there are summons from ladies and the royal city, but not from the Queen herself, so I can ignore them for now, pretend I'm still recovering, pretend it's nothing personal. Besides letters, all my aunts come, and my sisters. Even my brother, the first son of AnLenia, Onor. His sons are with him, little fat boys with eager hands and smiles, reddish cheeks darker than mine because Onor's respected wife is as brown as amber trees. Onor's sons—three of them, unbelievably; the second one I've only seen once when he was a babe, the third never at all—draw sun and flowers made of sticks and triangles onto my chalkboard like words, and even though I can speak just fine, I draw the shape of the desert for them, and flowers shaped like roses and tulips and danger.

Onor cuts my hair, shaves my face, and only nicks my skin once, apologizing but not well. He calls me *Pacer* like it means *Worm* because I'm his little brother, but when his sons are with us, he tells them to be as strong as their uncle if they can.

Before he leaves, he tells me he is glad I was injured enough that I can never go back to soldiering. "If you went back again," he whispers, "I fear we would never even find your bones. And those crazy desert gods do not know how to remember men like you."

. . .

I write it all down because it sticks in my gut.

. . .

Jarair came to see me. He wrote his greeting on the chalk slab, but then just clapped my shoulder and grinned. His hair is shaggy, and out of uniform he dresses surprisingly well, like a middle son angling for the attention of fine, royal women. Good thing all my sisters already chose their men.

Before he could say anything, I handed him this entire sheaf of paper, everything up to this point, and he read it. His brow lifted in humor or wrinkled in surprise. He frowned, he frowned harder, his mouth went expressionless, and when he was done, he let the last page flutter down against the pile and stared at me. He only said one harsh word in response.

It was an easy curse to read in his mouth.

I said it back, with more emphasis.

. . .

I do not know what to do with myself but write. Feel the ocean's rhythm and pretend it is like the *hum*. I don't know if I can send her a cuff of mother's pearl and a note that it reminds me of her red-pink-purple robe. I only know she lives.

. . .

There's nothing left to say; there is everything left to say.

. . .

Today I—

. . .

Today I was told the great star mage Dinah Aniv, Gift of the Desert, is here in An Riel.

. . .

Invited to meet the Queen, in part because I never answered any summons when I was recovering, and the desire of An Riel to honor somebody for what we did is fading. They brought her because they thought, Aunt Lusha said, it would serve dual purpose: make a huge deal of the Restoration Campaign, and introduce a powerful woman from the star clans to the court.

Oh, oh. It made me laugh even as all that old ache in my chest flexed itself to make sure it was still strong.

. . .

I'm going.

I don't know what I'll do when I arrive, but I'm going.

I might—

I might kiss her in front of the Queen, in front of my aunts and mother. Everyone.

I might ask her to dance.

I might only stare.

I wonder if I will be able to hear her voice. Will she *hum*?

Maybe I will walk up to her and only say her name. Feel it on my tongue again.

Dinah. Aniv.

I leave at dawn.

THE END

Here is a story that began with magical bombs and ended up being about love and identity—national identity, gender identity—and ambiguity. Of course the ending is ambiguous, too, and very much about point of view.

All my world building is there to spiral around a few questions and point toward a few key emotional moments I hope will leave an impression on readers' heads and hearts.

REVISION

Brenna

Revision means getting rid of every needlessly convoluted twist that seemed like a good idea in the first draft. It means refining concepts and combining scenes and finding as many connections as possible between characters and images and ideas. Once these connections start clicking into place, I have a better sense of what's important, and that's the point at which I finally have enough information to sit down and figure out the exact shape of a story. Until then, I'm always just looking for where the edges line up.

Tessa

Drafting to me is inherently messy and chaotic—it is gathering the raw material that will eventually be a story. It's like mining. I dig into world and character, forming and shaping what I think I want and discarding what I don't. Sometimes I shape something, only to realize it's greatly flawed and throw that out, too. (Also known as burning down entire drafts— it's painful, but in a cathartic way because it only happens when I'm doing something very wrong, and therefore it's a relief to start fresh.) Every time I throw something out, it brings revision into drafting. But until I have a complete first draft (beginning, middle, climax, denouement, with all the character arcs within) I still think of it as drafting.

The real revision happens when I look at this mess I've made and start to make sure I'm communicating what I want to communicate. Because writing is all communication between writer and reader. Revision is when I look at the story I've put down and instead of focusing on what I want or need to say, I focus on making it understandable, relatable, relevant, clear, and desperately engaging to a reader.

Revision is the part I liken to being Doctor Frankenstein. You've gathered the raw parts from a variety of dark cemeteries; now you have to sew arms onto torsos, remove intestines and replace them with better ones, find the right heart and the best connective tissue to bring it all together.

Maggie

Writing a novel is a lot like being pregnant. For several months, you consider what this creature you're making will look like, contemplate names for it, dreamily imagine what it will grow up to be. You pester your friends about it until they begin to dread your number on their caller ID. They block your posts about it on Facebook. "Show me when it's done," they say. And you do. Only when you finally give birth to this thing, it's a tiny, hideous monster with a wrinkled tomato face and the voice of a bronchially challenged pterodactyl.

Well, that was anticlimactic.

It is precisely like writing a novel. The good news is, after you birthed this short-limbed Winston Churchill–doppelganger wombfruit, you now have its entire life to dress it in cute clothing, put hats on its weird-shaped head, send it to schools to learn Spanish, and teach it how to play a small assortment of pleasant sonatas on the pianoforte or recorder.

That is what revision gives you: the rest of the novel's life to make it (and you) look brilliant. It doesn't matter how ugly it begins—you're only graded on how it ends.

It's my favorite part of writing because it's when I feel like I have total control to fine-tune. I like my drafts like I like babies: they're the best when they start to get funny.

Part Three

Ideas and "Drowning Variations"

by

Brenna Yovanoff

INTRODUCTION

When I first sit down to write, I don't always know
what I'm trying to say. For some people, it seems
like the major events of a story leap into their heads
fully formed. Other people do so much planning
and outlining ahead of time that they know even the
tiniest details of a plot point or a character before they
ever type a single word.

My process is a messy, meandering one. When
I write, I'm really just taking stock of all the things
inside my brain and then fiddling around to find the
circuits and wires between them. I think a lot about
ideas—where they come from, what they mean, how
their insides work. I like the way that you can start
with a single event or image and then steer the part
that comes next in an infinite number of directions.
And if you don't like where you end up, it's totally fine
to backtrack and try again from the same jumping-off
point. Or a different one that you discovered along

the way. You might not be happy with Version One of something, but you won't ruin an idea just by using it to find out where it goes.

My contribution to this book is a little bit different from Maggie's and Tessa's. Even though the pretext of this project—of our entire critique relationship, in fact—revolves around writing fiction, the story that comes next is a strange kind of hybrid. At first I kept trying to tell just one part of it, but it turned out that I couldn't talk about how I relate to ideas without getting into all the ways that my own story is part of a bigger one. Or else, my story is the actual one, and the fictional parts are just different versions of the messy, sprawling world that lives inside my head.

A lot of what you're about to read is actually true, and when I tell you about poetry or drowning or Anthony Perkins, I'm talking about things that really happened. Those stories and that voice, that's me, but it's a constructed me—a character of myself. It's a version of me who is telling you a story about how complicated it gets to figure out the steps you took to reach someplace, and then go back and describe how you got there.

People sometimes ask where I get my ideas, and the answer is simple. Ideas are everywhere. They can start from a single line you read on the back of a jar of peanut butter, or something that your grandmother said when you were little, or remembering how once you saw a guy in a pig suit in the train station and it was weird. I collect ideas like I'm picking up shells along an endless stretch of beach, and it's easy to

Or trash along a municipal highway. One of those.

remember a specific moment that made me start thinking about something, but the evolution of an idea is hard to show without explaining the tangled structure of its roots.

The piece you're about to read is the story of how long it took me to find the true, beating heart of an idea and then use it to tell the story that I meant. The one I actually wanted to tell.

—Brenna

DROWNING VARIATIONS

I. THE SWIMMING POOL

There's a story I've been telling my whole life. Does that sound weird? The shape of it is lumpy and undefined. It changes in the telling and the retelling but never actually resolves itself.

Sometimes a specific moment can take on the weight of a stone—dense, asymmetric. Heavier than the sum of its parts. Afterward, you carry it around with you, tucked inside a coin purse or a pocket, and mine is this: when I was very small, I almost drowned.

It was in a public pool, on a remote afternoon when the lifeguard had turned away, in broad daylight. Probably in a yellow bathing suit, because for a long time that was my favorite color. Probably even in the shallow end. (I was still small enough that shallow ends weren't always shallow.)

I don't remember it the way it must have been: the concrete, pale blue around me, the water in my mouth and the way the light moved on the surface when I looked up. I don't remember the day or the weather, or what I was thinking right before, but I remember dreaming it again and again.

In my dreams, the water fails to hold me. I reach for something solid, but it comes apart in my hands. Overhead there's a web of reflected sunlight, and through it I can see the sky. For the longest time, there's only blue—blue and shadow below, blue and light above—and the fact that I can't breathe seems nearly inconsequential.

I'm never scared until I wake up.

II. THE RESERVOIR

Sometimes the things you live through take on a
second life inside you.

I didn't come out of the swimming pool *afraid*
exactly, but I was changed by it.

For most of childhood I didn't think I was
obsessed. When you've been obsessing about
something since you can remember, obsession just
starts to seem normal.

From my house, I could stand out on the deck
and look down at the reservoir—a murky body that
swelled in spring, then shrank to a muddy puddle by
November. I thought about the landscape underneath,
drawing crooked maps, imagining the rotting church
that everyone said was down there—left behind when
they scraped the houses to make the lake. I saved up
money and bought a snorkel and a mask, but I never
saw any sign of the drowned town. And still, I stayed
under as long as possible, searching for the wreckage,

holding my breath. The act of sinking filled some impulse in me but didn't quite cancel it out.

I swam in flooded quarries and jumped from piers and floating docks and out of boats. I wore canvas shoes, because all the duck ponds and creeks were dark and full of glass.

By the time I was ten I'd begun writing things down, recording my findings. I filled whole notebooks with charts and observations, trying to come to terms with the implacable weight of water.

The place I lived was nearly desert, and drought awareness was everywhere—on billboards and splashed across bus-stop benches, advising us to deprive our yards and limit our showers. One summer there was a citywide campaign warning against the dangers of overindulgent bathing. It cautioned us in giant font not to drown the duck, while a crowd of plastic bath toys looked on in concern. I grew up constantly reminded that the thing that had almost killed me was the one thing we didn't have enough of.

In my mind, drowning had become the worst, most magical thing that could happen to a person. I was stricken with it, consumed by it—deeply preoccupied with the animals that washed into the inlet by my house each spring, floating down through the concrete spillway, matted and puffy in the winter runoff.

I memorized poems and wrote them on the soles of my shoes, covering the rubber with murder ballads and smudgy water lilies. With lines from T. S. Eliot's "The Love Song of J. Alfred Prufrock." It wasn't the longing of the poem that struck me, or the creeping yellow fog, or the part about the patient etherized on a table, or even that perplexing question, *do I dare disturb the universe*. The answer to Prufrock's dilemma seemed obvious—largely irrelevant. The universe was already disturbed.

What I loved were the mermaids.

I was enchanted by the image of them calling to each other, and that one heartbreaking sentence, *I do not think that they will sing to me*. I wrote the line inside an empty seashell, in tiny letters, in black marker, and dropped it in a glass of water. It was strangely satisfying to watch the words bleed away. They dissolved in front of me, blurry and magnified, like I had hit upon some fundamental secret of the world and was holding it captive for study.

The part that struck me most of all, though, was the part at the end—an eerie, melancholy couplet. A promise.

> We have lingered in the chambers of the sea
> By sea-girls wreathed with seaweed red and
>   brown
> Till human voices wake us, and we drown.

That last line seemed like the most essential truth. All there was to know. I clung to Eliot because he understood—he knew that you could go into the water willingly. You could linger there, under the heaving surface, but only until the world intruded. (Till the lifeguard turned and noticed you were down there, hair curling around your head in a baby-fine cloud like

Yellow had already stopped being my favorite color, but the cheery insistence of it still blindsided me sometimes. In the poem, a cloud of yellow smoke moves through the city like a huge, imaginary cat, lazy and vaguely ominous. It seemed like something out of a horror movie, and I liked that.

a jellyfish, a pale and tangled octopus, and when he came splashing in and grabbed you by the arm and the water in your throat finally burned, when all this time it had just been stifling, that was when you knew. That was when the feeling of floating stopped being curious and started being dangerous.)

I was on familiar terms with a hundred versions of magic, tragic women—the Slavic Rusalki and the Latin American Llorona, and with the Lady of Shalott, who did *not* drown. But still. She died near water.

This kind of pattern spotting involves more than a little confirmation bias.

The lists I made were comprehensive—practical guidebooks to haunted wells, Japanese fairy tales, folk songs about jealous sisters and bonny swans. When we read about Ophelia in school, I drew pictures. She drifted peacefully down the margins on her back, blue-lipped and covered in flowers. I might be fuzzy on multiplying fractions and diagramming sentences, but I can tell you about more drowners than you ever wanted to know. The sad ones, the pretty ones, the famous and the infamous. The real ones, sometimes—Natalie Wood and Virginia Woolf. Anyone who might know anything about tiptoeing down to the water, slipping, falling, sinking under.

In a rational sense, I understood that drowning was ugly. It was purple and panicked. It meant scrabbling, flailing, choking. But my own encounter hadn't been like that. In my dreams, as in the stories, it was a kind of death that seemed strangely uneventful. Passive. Feminine.

When I looked back through the pages of my research, one thing stood out clearer than anything else: drowning is what girls do.

III. THE BOY(S) WHO DIED

I turned fourteen.

I turned fourteen, and eighth grade was not a world of ballads and fairy tales. I thought I'd outgrown my fascination with drowning, or else come to some tacit understanding of it. A reluctant truce. Then something happened.

Afterward, I wrote about it. To myself. In scribbles and fragments. I referred to it in the most nonspecific of terms or found ways to bury it in the middle of other things, referencing it obliquely, but avoiding actually saying what it *was*.

It wasn't until my freshman year in college that I finally wrote it down—all of it, in order, without generalities or evasion. It had been raining for a month. The ground was mostly clay, the clay had reached saturation, and the whole campus was underwater. I sat on my windowsill, looking down at the flooded parking lot. I held a blue, spiral-bound notebook against my knees and wrote and wrote and wrote.

I was fourteen the year that Kurt Cobain died, gone inside of a second, inside a shotgun blast. I'd always liked Nirvana but was still too young to understand them. I was too idealistic, or maybe just too nice. I had a dictionary definition of apathy, but I didn't know what it felt like. For a while, it seemed like the whole world was crying except me.

I was fourteen the year that a fourteen-year-old boy drowned facedown in the small stream behind my aunt's house. It was winter, and the water was less than a foot and a half deep in most places. The banks were rimmed with ice, and scraps of paper and cigarette butts floated in the eddies where the rocks jutted out.

On the news, they said he'd been so ***ked up that when he passed out in the creek, he just stayed there, breathing the water until it killed him. Only that wasn't how they phrased it.

Only, you know, the real word.

I was babysitting my cousins, and as near as I can tell, he died while *Psycho III* was on the television. My aunt had cable. Afterwards, I kept thinking, *Maybe if I'd gone outside, if only I'd gone outside . . .*

I'd opened the back door, just to check for Norman Bates. But in the dark you couldn't see that far. You wouldn't be able to see a fourteen-year-old boy lying facedown in the stream. At least, I ~~couldn't~~ didn't see him.

My aunt found him the next day, with ice in his hair, facedown like he'd fallen. His friend was lying farther up the bank, dry but frozen.

By midafternoon, the television crews were everywhere and it was on three channels. You could see his school picture on the front of all the newspapers. Everyone was talking.

I think it was because he had done something that no one thought was possible. When you are in the middle of a hundred-year drought and it's the driest season of the year, there's something magical about drowning in less than two feet of water.

I kept telling myself there was nothing I could have done. If he had managed to drown in a place where the air is so dry that your skin cracks and bleeds, then it was inevitable. Preordained, even. I said to myself, *There was nothing I could have done.*

Eventually, I sometimes believed it.

There's guilt in the telling, and I didn't mean it to be there. Or maybe I did. The fact that I felt it seemed important, but it was a guilt I couldn't quite explain. My sense of responsibility was impersonal, but very large. Not for my failure to circumvent someone else's catastrophe—I didn't believe I should have reasonably been expected to save anyone. When I felt a responsibility, it wasn't for any practical oversight on my part, but simply for the fact that I'd survived the pool.

Sometimes there's this small, stubborn, illogical part of you—a part that whispers how the thing that you escaped from can't really be that dangerous. There are different stages to growing up, and I think one of them involves the realization that on a personal level, the universe is unpredictable, a tangle of atoms and nonbaryonic matter and chance. It's hard to make peace with chaos, and so you just keep going over the basic series of events, just the facts, and telling yourself the world isn't fatal. After all, it was touch and go for a minute, but everything ended well. After all, you didn't die.

For weeks after my aunt found the bodies, I'd sit in my room and think about the particulars of the night—the order in which I had put my cousins to bed, the channels I'd flipped through before finding a horror movie. How fast my heart had beat and how empty the house had been, just me and Anthony Perkins. Me and two boys I had not been able to see or hear from where I sat, watching monsters in the dark.

There were two of them, but I was most concerned with the one who had died in the stream. I knew, in the tidiest, most logical part of my brain, that it wasn't really the water that had killed him. After all, the air was freezing, the toxicology report was definitive, and his friend had been just as unlucky. Even if he hadn't drowned, it probably would have happened anyway.

But he was the one I thought of when I thought about water, when I thought about winter. Because it wasn't just the randomness of it, or even the fact that he was exactly my age and we would have gone to the same high school the next year. It wasn't mortality that shook me. It was the creek. The fact that something could be sixteen inches deep and still have so much power. There was a wrongness to it, and I came back to it again and again.

For a long time, I thought that having the inclination to think about hard things and the words to write them down was the same as understanding them. But in this first attempt I still landed far off the mark. I came away thinking that it was somehow natural to feel guilty over a stranger—one who died near you, or someone famous who died so far away in personality and culture and geography that the only thing left was to feel bad that you didn't notice him enough when he was alive. There is a strange, protective magic in the act of not being sad enough.

There are all kinds of books instructing you to *write what you know*. I think now that *write what you know* is another way of saying *understand what you write*.

I spent a lot of time trying to understand the story of the boys, opening different doors to see if they would get me to the place the answer lived. The second time I tried to tell it, everything was wrong.

It starts off bad and just gets worse. Sometimes that's what happens when you're trying to figure out the answer to a problem, trying hard to understand it. The version that comes next is all the things I didn't want to think about and still, it was the only thing I knew how to say.

IV. BY DROWNING

There was a foot of standing water in Cora Fletcher's basement. When she touched the surface with her hand, it slopped against the walls, leaving a line of mineral deposit that crept up the cement.

The slow seepage had begun three days earlier, on the same morning she found Adam Clay's body lying facedown in the municipal stream that ran behind her parents' house.

The stream behind the house was shallow, too negligible to submerge anything so large as a person, but Adam had been wearing a gray jacket, and his hair was clotted with ice. In the January landscape, he was almost invisible. She saw his hand first, pale and resting half-closed against the bank. She stood over him in the bleached reeds, and the back of his neck was strangely bloodless. She knelt, touching his shoulder, then his curled fingers. The jacket was the one he wore every day, and ice had formed a fragile rim at the cuffs of his sleeves.

She was not a skittish girl. In the kitchen, she answered the police officer's questions. The discovery, which had horrified her tender mother, only made Cora feel unsettled. The fact that she had been the one to find him was as impossible as his drowning in the first place.

Now there was a foot of water in the basement.

· · ·

Since the morning of Adam's body, Cora had been waking up.

The previous night she'd gotten out of bed just after two and found a flashlight. Standing halfway down the basement steps, she held the light so it sent shadows splashing over the walls. For an awful, glorious moment, she thought she saw movement— there, by the shipwrecked washing machine—just from the corner of her eye. Adam, facedown in his gray jacket, hands floating limp in the foul water.

The flashlight dimmed suddenly, and when she shook it back to brightness, he was gone. She went back upstairs, remembering a day on the football field.

Alone under the bleachers, she'd plotted the meticulous lines of curves and vectors. He came across the field, unaccompanied. They had never spoken to one another.

Adam glanced over his shoulder, then swung his fist, hard, against the aluminum bleachers. The sound reverberated wildly, and Cora resisted the urge to cover her ears.

When his gaze shifted and he saw her there, he did not smile, but the shape of his mouth was tender, as though they shared a secret. He shook his head in response to a question she had not asked. "You don't want to know." His hand was bleeding in a thin smear.

Behind him, the sky was a hard, indifferent gray. Two and a half months later he lay in the weeds at her feet, all answers gone.

· · ·

Again, Cora woke in the dark to find the numbers on her digital clock fixed mysteriously at 2:18. In the bathroom across the hall, the faucet was running. She counted, first to sixty and then further, to eighty. A hundred. A hundred and twelve. The numbers glowed unchanging in the black clockface.

She considered Adam's declaration, his assurance that she did not want to know. It wasn't true.

She wanted his life. Not to live it, but simply to examine the hidden facets, his embarrassments and his sorrows. Had he been lonely? Had he fought with his parents, smoked clandestine cigarettes out his bedroom window? She wanted all the small, private moments that were so integral to a person. She wanted the hundred tiny miseries that drove him to the creek at night, the moment when consciousness faded and darkness swept in.

Across the hall, the water only ran, splashing into the basin, gurgling down the drain. Then it stopped.

She closed her eyes, imagining the current, how it would feel to breathe water instead of air. How vivid and real the world must seem in that moment. How inescapably true.

When she opened her eyes again, her room seemed small and strange. The clock said 2:19. She got out of bed.

In the basement, the smell was oppressive, cold as autumn. She flipped the switch and the bulb came on, illuminating the scummy waves as they lapped against the steps.

"I want to know," she said, cupping her elbows.

There was no answer, only the water. It ran down the walls, dripped from the exposed beams.

There in the shadows, she saw him again, but now he lay faceup, his mouth blue with cold and drowning.

She stepped down into the water. Her pajamas felt heavy, and the fabric clung to her knees. It was deeper now. It had been rising. She waded out to him, kneeling so the water washed over her thighs. His eyes were open, cloudy in the dim light.

"I want to know."

The hand came up then, catching her by the back of the neck. His grip was chilly and inexorable, pulling her down. His mouth on hers was cold, and she closed her eyes and let him do it.

He knew the dancing, gibbering secret of the world—what it was to die.

She pressed her lips to his dripping mouth and waited for him to share it.

V. WATERLOGGED

That story? Is one of the most unpleasant stories I've
ever written.

> And that's saying
> something.

Even now, I tend to think the best thing about it
is that it's short. I think I must have wanted it to be
a horror story. Or, at least, I wrote it because I think
drowning is horrific, and also, there's a certain clinical
comfort to sitting down and stating basic facts.

The problem is right there in the first line:

> There was a foot of standing water in the
> basement.

This is the essence of backing away.

I ignored everything about character or emotional
stakes and dove straight for the simplest component.
The part that scared me.

As I wrote, I cut out a lot of pieces that were
important and left ones that were mundane, or just so
obvious I didn't really have to think about them. I did

this because some of the pieces felt too complicated, and some felt too scary, or like they were pointing to something else, something bigger or more honest.

There was the ghost of another story underneath, but it was one that demanded so much more, and I didn't know what to DO with it, so I just gave up. I threw those parts away, rather than taking the time to figure out what they were good for.

Sometimes picking the wrong direction is part of the process, even though it looks for all the world like just wasting time.

The way I write is kind of strange. It's unusual. It's more than unusual.

I do not think in that neat, linear way that makes someone an ideal candidate for bullet points or notecards or corkboards covered in webs of string like they have in a TV show about the FBI. I will never be the proud possessor of beautiful color-coded charts or dry-erase markers or sticky notes. And this is disappointing, because secretly, I really want my office to look like a TV show about the FBI.

The problem (problem?) is that everything has a sound in my head—a rhythm that determines the words I use and the choices I make. This includes big rhythms, like scenes or chapters or the whole entire story arc, and little rhythms, like paragraphs or sentences or the individual letters inside one specific word.

I feel my way through a story, finding bits and pieces. When I reach a word or a syllable and don't know what goes there, I leave a little trail of commas

There are two things I wish someone would have told me when I was first learning to write, and they are these:
1) People have all kinds of weird, highly personal methods for how to get things done.
2) Most people's methods are still not as weird as mine.
2.b) And that's okay.

This will involve visual aids.

like tiny typographical bread crumbs—like so: [,,,,,,,,]. I do that in all the places where the parts are still missing, and then I move on.

For a long time I was very self-conscious about this and tried hard to change the way I did things. I wanted to be putting words on paper, in order, the same way other people did.

"If you keep writing everything in this disjointed way, you're just going to confuse yourself, and you're never going to finish anything," said one of my teachers. And I thought, *Oh, no! If I keep writing everything in this disjointed way, I'm just going to confuse myself, and I'm never going to finish anything!* Which was a huge and ridiculous fallacy, because I'm confused most of the time, even without worrying about all these blank spots and commas, and I still never once failed to finish an assignment. But for a while (too long), I believed it, because the teacher knew so much about writing, and I didn't, and I wanted to.

The reason it's important to learn how you write is that there are all kinds of exercises and techniques that are not going to work for you, and as you practice and experiment and try things, you'll start to know what does work. What will help you get an idea on the page, and what might not help you at all.

It's still totally reasonable to try everything once, though. Even if you don't really understand it or it sounds weird or you hate it. Trying things is a really good way to learn how you write. Techniques that don't feel comfortable or natural can still be good exercises, because even though the easiest way for you to write is sometimes the same as the best way for you to write? Sometimes it isn't.

When I revise, I comb through concepts and characters and ideas and take them apart like I'm repairing a clock or rebuilding an engine, or else putting a totally different engine in the original car.

When I finally came back to my drowning story, I was determined to find the engine. I wanted to say what I meant, or at least what I felt.

The first thing I did was change the point of view. In the course of trying to write this story, I've looked at it through a lot of lenses, shifting gradually from the real-world facts—my aunt's chilly December-morning discovery—to my own disjointed thoughts on a tragedy that happened near me, to the pretend story of a pretend girl who's strange and lonely and finds a body.

Again.

As I moved into fiction, the point of view drifted further and further from me. She was named *Viola* for a while, who then became *Cora*, who eventually becomes *Jane* in the next version.

Even at its starkest and most remote, I think this has always been a story about wanting things, wanting to act, wanting to have done the thing that needed doing. The third-person point of view wasn't working, so what about first? Someone tenacious, someone brave. I went down through the series of events, thinking of ways that every scene could show relationships. Which is kind of the exact opposite of Cora and her lack of human connection and her haunted basement. In fact, one of the main reasons I had such a hard time executing early versions was that I couldn't figure out how to get a real, actual *person* in the mix. Change the viewpoint and you change everything else.

(What about the person I wasn't, but wished I had been? The power of fiction is in its ability to explore the untrue—to consider what might be, what couldn't be, what needed to be but wasn't.)

The next thing I had to tackle was the problem of drowning itself. It had been the starting point and also the exact wrong point of entry. Instead of writing about people who wanted things, I kept trying to write about a creek, about a flooded basement. I was depersonalizing everything, alienating myself from my own story.

I'd spent so long collecting water nymphs and river spirits and the ghosts of drowned, weeping maidens. What was the point of all those years studying fairy tales if I didn't use what I had learned? Which was another way of saying, what if drowning is not a concept—what if it's a person?

The day I had that tiny, random thought was the day the story started to become more like itself. A tragedy is remote. It's wordless. You can ask a *person* questions. They can still be mysterious and strange, they can still be monstrous—mythic—but when you ask, they answer, and when they look you in the face, it is very, very personal.

I went back through all the scraps that I'd cut away, and the closer I looked, the more I started to see something else there, something that might be evidence of a real story.

In "By Drowning," Adam is practically a stranger—someone the main character knows from school and at the same time doesn't *really* know in any meaningful way. I wanted there to be some human aspect to that, but the relationship is just so remote and ugly and completely filled with ambivalence. In the following scrap, you've got Viola thinking back on

because remember, before she was Cora, she was Viola

a humiliating interaction that Adam had been witness to, and even though it's painful to her, she's still considering kissing him, and it's all just so impersonal, and so very upsetting.

> Now she tried to compile a list of shared
> encounters—anything worth treasuring—but
> all that came to mind were insults and miseries.
> Times other rough boys had teased her and
> Adam had stood by, wordless.
>
> The morning at the bus stop when Billy
> Creedy, emboldened by Viola's smallness and
> her silence, had torn the geography book
> from her hands and stood on it, his arms
> wide, mouth gaping. Adam had only smiled
> grimly, shaking his head. He'd drawn close, as
> though to whisper or to kiss her. Even now,
> the memory of his mouth thrilled her in a
> melancholy way. Then he had turned away.

This is sort of the worst thing ever, but also, there's want in there, and bitterness. There's story.

It turned out there were a *lot* of snippets like that, that I cut and then looked at later, thinking, "Wait, *here's* what I meant to say—if only it weren't so horrible and ugly." But the part that struck me more acutely than anything was this:

> At 1:45 she'd woken to a stifling heat, and
> she'd opened her window.

In the field behind her house, their voices had been clear. She'd leaned on the sill, pressing her cheek against the screen. They were laughing, the raucous cries of boys and girls together. They shrieked, then hushed each other, voices spiking with delight.

How she had envied them their blurry freedom. Their carelessness.

In the morning she'd gone down to the stream, and after several minutes of sweeping through the weeds for evidence of their wanderings, she'd found Adam's body.

and then the part that actually made it in

She wanted his life. Not to live it, but simply to know the hidden facets, to enter them in her notebook, his embarrassments and his sorrows. Had he been lonely? Had he fought with his parents, smoked clandestine cigarettes out his bedroom window? She wanted all the small, private moments that were so integral to a person. She wanted his unadulterated character, the secrets that loomed behind his flatness and his silence. She wanted the hundred tiny miseries that drove him to the creek that night, the moment when consciousness faded and darkness swept in.

If Viola/Cora wants these things, then there's more than a passing chance that as the writer, maybe I do too. Maybe the reader does. Maybe the point-of-view character wants and then *gets* these things, or tries and gets rebuffed, or has to be satisfied with a glimpse of them and a promise for the future.

My ideas about how stories work almost always rest on a bed of maybes.

The thing is, we use stories to make sense of the world, and now I think maybe the greatest failing of that first chilly, factual attempt is that . . . I wasn't.

When I started, I was writing about damp, existential horrors, so weighty and overwhelming—so brain-sucking—that I couldn't even finish my thoughts. The original file is littered with cryptic margin notes and unfinished sentences, those ridiculous rows of commas like tiny waves.

"I want to know," she said, crossing her arms over her chest.

There was no answer, only the water. It was running down the walls, dripping in constant streams from the unfinished ceiling and the exposed beams. It soaked the insulation, turning the cotton-candy pink a deeper, bloodier hue.

In the water, she saw him again, but now he lay faceup. He smiled, and his insolence was terrible. His mouth blue with cold and drowning.

Viola stepped down from the ,,,,,,,,,, and the water was cold, but only in the way that ,,,,,,,,,,, Her pajama bottoms felt heavy, and the fabric clung to her knees. The water was deeper now. It had been rising.

She moved closer to him, kneeling in the ,,,so that it,,,and washed over her thighs. She knelt over him, leaning to hear the whispered ,,,,,, His eyes were open, cloudy in the ,,,,,,,,,,

The hand came up then, frighteningly,, His grip was chilly and inexorable at the back of her neck, pulling her ,,,,,,,,,,

His mouth on hers was,,,,, The surge of water made her cough, but,,,and he pulled her down with him. In the,,,,she,,, and let him do it.

After all, what,,,when words could not convey the,,,? He knew the dancing, gibbering secret of the world—what it was to die—and Viola ,,,,,,, pressed against his ,,,,,,,, mouth, waiting for him to share it.

This is not what I wanted to write, but it was necessary—the clutter and the noise. I needed to tell the story in "By Drowning" in order to find what I was really trying to say. And so that next time I tried it, I could throw these parts away. Cora's story is the wrong one. It isn't what I meant at all, so let me tell you another.

VI. THE DROWNING PLACE

She wasn't one of those girls.

You know the ones. They show up to the party in sequined halter tops, flash through the crowd like shimmering fish. They toss their heads, bite their lips, suck suggestively on a never-ending supply of Tootsie Pops, and even though every movie and TV drama you have ever, ever seen has already told you to hate them . . . you can't. Because secretly, you understand that certain magic that they have. You know that everyone is going to look, because everything about them is golden, and really, you just want to look too.

She wasn't like that.

What I mean is, even when she came up over the top of the irrigation ditch and sat down next to our oily little bonfire, I didn't really think about her.

This opening is because of that thought I had—about how drowning is a person. I tried to figure out what it actually was that I was orbiting around when I thought about water. Water has a quiet insidiousness. It's always more powerful than it seems. Over a long enough timeline, a stream can eat through a mountain. Sometimes it looks shallow and murky and still. We underestimate it. We feminize it. Who is drowning? Drowning is the girl people don't even see.

It was late on a Sunday, and the way the scrap wood was sending up smoke in fat, blooming clouds made it hard to see the stars.

The field behind my housing development was where we went when we wanted to have fun without being bothered. It was on the other side of the jogging path, through a tangle of weeds, too far for Neighborhood Watch or Ari Loewe's dad to see us from the street. We were all cozied up in the empty spillway above the ditch, huddled around a metal washtub, watching the trash burn. I was sitting on the edge of the concrete wall that the skaters used for rail slides, with Evan DeSoto behind me, his legs resting on either side of mine and his coat closed around me. Against my back, his body was warm through his shirt. The cement was cold through my tights. He smelled prickly and comfortable, like thrift-store army wool and American Spirits and all the things I liked best about nights out in the field. About just being near him.

Evan wasn't my boyfriend.

I mean, he flicked me behind the ear in biology or wrote little poems about submarines on my arms sometimes, and he was always grabbing me around the waist and pretending like he was going to throw me off the sidewalk. Sometimes, when he scooted forward in his desk to whisper something funny about protons, I stared straight ahead and thought about how good his mouth felt against my ear.

But he wasn't my boyfriend—not *any*one's boyfriend—so the way he looked at her didn't bother me. And anyway, he didn't stare longer than anyone else. Because all the boys glanced up when she came across the ditch. They watched her climb the bank to us, as if there was nothing so strange about some sad-faced girl appearing out of the dark. Then they went back to poking sticks at our scrubby little fire.

Caleb Walsh was the only one who seemed to really *see* her. He looked across the spillway through the smoke, watching the way the flames reflected off her rings and bracelets like they were shining up from underwater.

She had long, wavy hair that looked nearly silver, and it wasn't until she got close and stepped into the light that I could tell it was actually green. She had on a leather motorcycle jacket covered in buckles and chains, and her smile was the small, expectant smile of someone who is used to being ignored. Her eyes were a washed-out blue, her lashes so blond they looked white. Even in the flickering light, you could tell she was almost colorless.

When she sat down next to me and Evan, her hip pressed against the outside of his thigh, which made the inside press against mine.

"Nice stars," she said, nodding at the rainbow galaxy printed on my tights, and I laughed, and Evan and I scooted over to make room. Her voice was husky and low, with a musical edge that floated underneath, and I liked it. I liked the way her hair fell in front of her face, and how the chains on her jacket clanked and jingled when she sat down next to us, so easy like that. But even before everything else, I still sort of knew she wasn't there for me.

That sounds so obvious, or like maybe I was jealous, and that's not what I mean. Just that it could have been someone else—Justin, because his dad was dead, or Michelle Fowler, who sometimes cut her legs and the insides of her arms with a paper clip and didn't always hide the scabs. Later, I understood that it could have been a lot of people, but there in the orange flicker of the bonfire, everything still just seemed harmless.

There was a foot of standing water in the ditch at the bottom of the spillway. It smelled like brackish swamps and old newspaper. She smelled sharp and clean, like ocean air or salt marshes. Like tears.

I didn't know that everything after that was going to be bad.

. . .

Evan walked me home at midnight, and we stood facing each other on my porch. My coat felt thin now, and sort of pointless without him pressed against me. My tights clung icy to my legs, and my ears were cold.

I'd twisted my hair into two sloppy knots on top of my head, like bear ears, and he reached over and tweaked one. "Don't you get bored, spending so much time messing with your hair?"

The way he said it was mostly just making noise, like he was looking for any excuse not to leave. I didn't mind. As long as he was here on my porch, playing with my hair, he was still standing close to me.

I shook my head, letting my bangs go in my eyes. "I only get bored if it looks the same for too long."

He leaned in suddenly, like he was going to kiss me there under the burned-out porch light and there was nothing I could do about it. I stood still and waited. It would be so easy to tip my head back and let him. To close my eyes, open my mouth, let his arms slide around my waist. It *sounded* nice, but there was a gnawing feeling that made me freeze. The thing was, he was careless with girls—flirting with them, making out—and I didn't want to get too close to that. I didn't want it to stop being Evan and Jane and start being Jane and every other girl with a pulse.

"I like it," he said, right by my ear. "Mood-hair. Anyway—" I could feel his breath against my cheek, making little flutters of heat there. "You know I'm all about the details. It gives me something to write in my diary."

I laughed into my mitten, but he wasn't joking. At least, not completely.

Evan was never exactly what he seemed. Or he was, but he was also more. There were all these parts of him that I was always thinking I had a handle on, and then he'd say or do something, and I'd have to start over. I was always having to relearn the shape of him.

On the outside, he didn't seem like a journal guy. He seemed like a knock-down, drag-out, punch-each-other-in-the-pit guy. He made a big thing out of his army jacket and his shaved head, but that wasn't all of him. The bare scalp was just a haircut, and a pierced lip isn't a whole person.

There were all these other, stranger parts, and one was the way he wrote down everything. He

collected the most minor things and put them in a
little spiral notebook with bent corners and a piece of
duct tape holding the cover together. The rest of the
time he was a clown and a show-off, joking around
like nothing mattered. I figured maybe he needed
the book because he had to put his extra thoughts
somewhere.

After a second he stepped back, and then I was just
standing in the dark, still half waiting for him to kiss
me and knowing that if he did, it would mean I was
nothing special.

The wind blew down through the cul-de-sac,
making the placuna shell chimes clatter and jangle.
The neighborhood was dark and shabby and mostly
foreclosed. I had an eerie feeling, suddenly, that we
were the only two people in the world. Then he put up
his hood and walked away, crunching out to the road
between my mom's half-dead chrysanthemums.

I went inside with my chin down and my heart
beating hard, telling myself how stupid it was to sit
around wondering about kissing him, when the smart
thing would be to just ask him if he wanted to. But
even if he did, so what? He wanted to kiss all the girls.

· · ·

Evan was the kind of guy who fell straight into the
category of ordinary and made your face feel too hot
anyway.

He wasn't beautiful, but he had a nice profile
and a good jaw. A long time ago, before we knew
each other—before he ever pulled me into his lap or

played with my hair—I used to draw pictures of him in my English binder and hope he would look up. It wasn't one of those pining crushes, but I was a more-than-casual fan of his chin and a downright authority on the shadow under his bottom lip. All I mean is that I noticed him.

How I met him was so random it almost felt like it wasn't random at all.

It was this gray, awful day in November, near the end of fourth period. I was out behind the school by the football field, sitting alone under the bleachers where the security guard couldn't see you cutting class from the parking lot. I was waiting for Ari and Justin to show up, hopefully with coffees from the gas station, and drawing pictures of the Canada geese honking and flapping around on the fifty-yard line.

Evan came out across the grass, and the geese all shuffled out of his way. He crossed to the metal upright at one end of the field and glanced back toward the school, like he was checking to make sure that no one was around. Then he took a deep breath and slammed his fist into the goalpost. He did it ferociously, like he was punching down the pop-ups on Whac-a-Mole.

The actual *moment* happened when he finally turned in the direction of the sideline and there I was, sitting cross-legged under the

Even though I liked how close to each other the characters were in the original scene, that blocking didn't seem to work as well with my new thematic overhaul.

I moved Evan to the end zone because I wanted to put a substantial distance between them. He's not invading Jane's territory the way Adam was with Cora, and in order to reach him, Jane has to see the distance and then still make a very conscious effort to bridge it. (Also, this conscious effort is sort of/kind of . . . FORESHADOWING!)

bleachers with my sketchbook in my lap. My coat was pink-and-black checkered, and I was very hard to miss.

For a second he just stared at me. There was blood on his knuckles, so red it made everything else look gray. I didn't say anything, but I could tell I was raising my eyebrows, like, *Whoa, guy, what is your deal?*

He shook his head like I'd asked the question out loud. "You don't want to know." His expression was cool—half a smile, and under that, a look so tired it seemed almost bottomless.

It was impossible to get out from under the bleachers in any kind of dignified way, so I didn't even try. I just flipped my sketchbook closed and crawled out on my hands and knees.

The whole time it took me to cross the field, he stayed right there next to the goalpost. When I got to him, he gave me a quick little nod, then leaned back against the post like he'd been waiting for me.

I took off my mittens and reached for his hand. It wasn't like a proclamation or anything. I wasn't claiming him. I just took his hand and wiped the blood off with my thumb.

"I'm Jane," I said. He wasn't wearing gloves, but his skin was warm.

He looked down at me, and his expression didn't change. "I know." His eyes were a clear, deep hazel-gray, like frozen ground or muddy water.

After that, he was always around.

It was hard to be sure what changed exactly, but when I'd reached for him, the lines of our territories shifted. Not like something earth-shattering, but he'd circled closer to me, the way a person can be around without it really meaning anything.

We teased each other over stupid things—my complicated hair, his secret notebook, the bruises he got at the shows he went to.

And maybe he never kissed me, but in a room, I always looked at him first, and the smell of his deodorant was enough to make my face hot. I could feel him come up behind me without even looking, and then my heart would start going a million miles a second, and sometimes the way you feel standing next to someone is all that really matters.

· · ·

Caleb Walsh was not my biggest fan, but most of the time he kept it to himself.

That wasn't some impressive feat or anything. He kept pretty much everything to himself. Generally he ignored me, but sometimes when I tried to tell a story or a joke, or got excited about something he thought was stupid or girly or overly pink—or *especially* when I had opinions—he'd give me these bored, disgusted looks, like I was a new toy that Evan had found lying around on the playground and would forget about as soon as something better came along.

The night of the bonfire, before the green-hair girl came up over the spillway and he fell headfirst into her strange, pale sadness, he'd looked at my star tights and said, "That's the thing about Jane. If you ever need an emergency rodeo clown, she's got your back."

Then Ari tore the pop tab off her beer can and

flicked it at him and we all laughed, and he just sat there, giving me the worst look, while I tried hard not to care.

I forgave him for that look, and for his sarcasm and his sulky bullshit, and for anything else he'd ever done when I found his body the next morning, lying facedown in the irrigation ditch at the bottom of the spillway.

Later, the newspaper made it sound like I was some kind of psychic. Like it was a miracle, me walking out through the weeds, straight to the place where he lay. The evening news said that joggers and dog walkers might have passed his body all morning and never noticed, if I hadn't gone out behind my house and across the footpath, picking my way down to the stream.

I wasn't psychic, though. I was looking for Evan's notebook. He'd texted me ten minutes earlier because it wasn't in his coat, and he asked if I could go back to the ditch and look for it. The sun was barely up. It was freezing out and I hadn't finished drying my hair, but the notebook was Evan's most important thing, so I pulled on my boots over bare feet and went to find it.

The ditch was shallow, running with a foot of dirty slush, not nearly deep enough to submerge a person, but Caleb was wearing a gray mechanic's jacket, and his hair was full of ice. In the reeds, he was almost invisible.

I saw his hand first. It was still and pale, lying half-closed against the bank. Even when I got close, it took me a minute to understand what I was seeing, to follow the pathway from his blue fingertips back to the rest of him.

He looked like he was waiting for someone. That's what I didn't say to the police.

He looked sad and patient, like he was only resting, waiting for some well-meaning stranger to wander by and offer him a hand. He just needed someone to help him to his feet.

I stood over him in my unlaced boots. The collar of his jacket was turned down, and the back of his neck looked bloodless in the morning light.

I had this crazy idea that maybe he was sleeping. I'd touch him and he would jerk awake and sit up, ask if I knew where Evan was and if I had a cigarette he could bum and why did my hair look like a wet wildebeest. But even before I reached for him, I knew he was never getting up.

When I finally crouched down, I did it slowly, touching his shoulder first and then his curled fingers, feeling the rough canvas of his jacket, the icy smoothness of his skin. The jacket was the same one he wore every day, and his face was turned away, sunk ear-deep in the stream. Ice had formed a fragile rim at his cuffs, like broken glass, and I went back to the house with the cold aching in my fingertips.

When I opened the sliding door to the kitchen, the overhead light was so bright and yellow that for a second, it made me dizzy.

A lot of this is the same description—right down to some of the exact same words—that I used in the Cora/Viola version. Here, though, I've kind of pushed all the physical details into the background. The images of the body aren't the main focus anymore, they're just a backdrop for Jane's thoughts and reactions. Because remember: this is a story about people wanting things, and not just an account of something that happened.

My mom was at the stove, frying bologna. "I called someone to look at that Dutch elm out front, but they can't come until Friday," she said. "Do you want toast?"

I didn't answer.

She glanced over her shoulder. "If they say we have to dig the whole thing out, I don't know if we can afford—Jane, what's wrong?"

"Caleb Walsh is dead in the creek," I said, and I said it so flat and so matter-of-fact that for a second, she just stood there, holding the spatula with her head tipped to one side. She smiled, like I might be joking, and I could see the lipstick on her teeth. It was poppy-orange, and I wanted to close my eyes. I wanted her to wipe it away.

. . .

Later, the police came. They sat in the living room and asked a lot of questions, but even when I took deep breaths and nodded and told them all the little stupid details of the night before—how Michelle had been drinking apple wine out of the bottle and when she tried to put her ultra-black Maxx eyeliner on Bethany Bledsoe, it came out all crooked; how Ari had tried to juggle burning branches like the boys were doing and accidentally lit the end of her ponytail on fire—none of it seemed connected to the way it really was.

They wanted to know all kinds of things about Caleb, like did he drink (*yes*), and did he use drugs (*I don't know*), and most importantly, had he seemed upset or sad or unusually quiet? (*Um, what does unusual mean? That's how he always is.*)

I tried to answer them like it was all just routine procedure, the way people did on TV, but no matter how straight I sat, how tight I held onto the points of my elbows through my sweater, my voice sounded strange and far away.

"You're doing a great job, Jane," the tall one said. "I know this is hard, talking about your friend."

But the more I thought about it, the clearer it was how much I didn't even know Caleb. He was Evan's friend, not mine. He didn't even *like* me. We hung out together, but being used to someone wasn't the same as knowing them.

Yes, he was the kind of boy who carried a pocket flask and liked thrasher music and probably had a thing for cheap weed or even something completely grim, like huffing paint or keyboard cleaner. Maybe he didn't talk much, but he and Evan were close. At least, I thought they *must* be. They'd known each other since kindergarten. Yes, he was rude in class and broke rules and sometimes he seemed depressed. No, even with all these things taken together, I didn't think that he would kill himself on purpose.

"It's like it's not real," my mother said again and again while the police sat in our living room, drinking coffee. "Something like this can't even be real."

She was perched on the edge of the couch, clutching a soggy tissue, wringing it into oblivion, and I had to stop looking at her. It felt too gross.

"It's so terrible," she said. "What am I going to do about Jane? What if she's traumatized—or emotionally scarred?"

"Mom, I'm okay."

One of the officers leaned forward, setting his cup on the table. His eyes were kind when he looked at my mom, who was sitting with her head bowed, picking at her Kleenex.

"Oh, God." She held the tissue tighter suddenly, pressing it to her mouth. "My God, it's like this isn't real."

When I'd touched Caleb's hand, his skin had been icy, too cold to stand. In a lot of ways, the frozen body at my feet was the only real thing that had ever happened in my whole life.

. . .

At school the next day, everyone was talking about it. They stood around the halls in little clusters, but their voices sounded fake. Even the ones who hugged everyone they saw and cried into their friends' hair were just going through the motions. Yeah, they were crying, but it wasn't the same way they'd cried after Kylie Morgan's car accident last March. Kylie had been on student council. Secretary, treasurer— one of those reliable, unfancy positions. She'd been popular, while Caleb had mostly just been like the rest of us.

"Oh my God," Melody Vickers said to me in gym class, opening her eyes wide. "Did you really find his body?"

I nodded. We were in line for volleyball drills, and the knobby little freshman in front of us was taking her sweet time serving over the net.

Melody leaned into me with her hand on my arm, like she was steadying herself. "Jesus, what was it *like*?"

I gave her the bare-bones version, how I went out for Evan's notebook and found Caleb at the bottom of the spillway. I told her how he'd looked, lying there in the water, but left out the ice in his hair, the way I'd touched his hand.

Melody moved closer. Her breath smelled pink, like bubble gum. "Was it totally awful? Did you just want to scream?"

I looked straight into her wholesome face and tried to figure out if the question was rhetorical.

. . .

"We shouldn't have left him there," Evan said at lunch.

We were sitting under the big cottonwood tree behind the school with Ari and Michelle. Up until then we'd kind of been avoiding it, talking about nothing much, and even though my hands were cold, like they'd turned to ice from touching Caleb's skin, I was feeling better, feeling like maybe it was enough to just be sitting here with each other—that we were all still okay. But as soon as Evan said that, the other girls got up and disappeared so fast, like I was the only one in the whole stupid world who'd know how to fix it. Like because Evan and I pinched each other and made paper airplanes or whispered about how creepy Mr. Hobart was, I would somehow have the magic words to make him not care that his friend was dead.

"Someone should have stayed," he said again, hugging his knees and staring out at the football field.

And it was true. Someone should have stayed, made sure that no one was the last to leave, but that seemed too obvious, and there were so many ways to measure the responsibility, assign the blame. If Evan hadn't walked me home. If Michelle was sober or Bethany was assertive or Ari and Justin weren't so relentlessly attached at the face. There were too many *ifs*, and I just didn't see the point in entertaining them.

I pictured Caleb, facedown in the water, and tried different sentences in my head. There were all these tidy, reasonable things I could have said, but I picked the worst one—something awful and stupid about drunken-bonfire safety, and Evan looked away. He sat with his back against the tree, smoking a cigarette and ignoring his greasy triangle of pizza.

I wondered, if he were someone's boyfriend, whether he would talk to them—tell that special imaginary person what he was thinking. I knew he probably wouldn't. Evan never said anything serious without it being half a joke, but still, I couldn't help thinking that if we were anything real, I'd somehow know the right words.

"I'm sorry," I said, tugging on my necklace, which was a clunky secondhand atrocity full of pop tabs and spare hardware. "That was . . . it was *bad*. It wasn't what I meant."

Usually the sound of all the screws and bolts and lock washers jangling together made him smile, but now his eyes were fixed on some far-off point and I had a horrible idea that he would never smile again.

He just shrugged, chewing on his cigarette. "It's true, though."

He didn't say anything else, but he didn't have to say it out loud for me to know what he was thinking—that Caleb was dead because of us, because we'd left him there.

When the two-minute bell rang, Evan ground out the cigarette and stood up. I picked up our trash and walked him to history. He was quiet the whole way there.

All day, I kept thinking I smelled the ditch, even at the most random times—in the halls, dissecting earthworms in lab. At home in the shower spray. The smell was everywhere, dank and swampy. It was all over my hands.

. . .

They buried Caleb on Thursday, out at Oakridge where they'd buried Kylie after her car accident.

Evan wasn't in school. If he'd been there, I would have driven out with him and stood at the gravesite, held his hand if he wanted, the way I did on the day we first met.

But he wasn't there, and without him, skipping class for Caleb's funeral seemed indecent. Like I had no right. All during algebra, I sat alone at my table, staring down at the chapter on factors and imagining the others, sobbing graveside in a little cluster.

Michelle and Bethany were back in time for English, whispering during free-reading and holding hands between their desks. Their eye makeup was heavy, smeared with tears, but when they talked about Caleb they sounded almost like they were talking about a stranger. Some dead celebrity who everyone had magazines and posters of, but no one had ever actually met.

"It's like it happened just to show us how messed up he really was," said Michelle, scraping at the skin under her eyes. Her fingernails were painted a chipped plummy purple. "Like there was no way he was ever going to be okay."

Bethany leaned across the aisle to touch Michelle's shoulder. "Don't. Don't say that." Bethany was always the tender one.

"Why not?" Michelle whispered down at her desk.

By now, the coroner's report was public knowledge. It was the kind of thing health teachers had been warning us about since seventh grade. Beer and vodka mixed with over-the-counter pills—no one knew what or how many. They were talking about an overdose, but if he'd gotten that messed up, he must have started after Evan and I left.

I listened to Michelle and Bethany whisper dully back and forth, but I was thinking about the girl—the green-haired one. I wondered if she'd stayed. Given him some kind of tab or drink we didn't know about. If anyone else had seen the way he'd looked at her.

Michelle was hunched over her desk, worrying at her lip until the skin was picked ragged. I was sure that in a minute she was going to draw blood.

On other nights when we'd all gone out to the spillway and sat around the fire, Caleb hadn't seemed too hormonal about any of us. It was hard to picture him all wild and handsy like Ari and Justin, stuck to each other every chance they got. But then, everyone assumed that Evan and I were doing it. Maybe it was just as misguided to assume that Caleb wasn't. For the first time, I wondered if maybe that girl was the kind of thing he wanted, when before he had never seemed to want anyone. So had she stayed? Did she talk to him? Was she as strange and hungry-faced as I remembered her?

"Who was the last one there with him?" I said, and I said it too loud for homework time. Everyone looked around.

Michelle twisted in her seat, still picking at her lip. "Ari was there after us, I think."

"No," said Bethany. "No, that's not right. She went home when Justin did."

"What about the girl?" My voice sounded weird and cool and not like mine. "The green-haired girl?"

The question seemed vital suddenly, more urgent as soon as I'd said it out loud.

"Maybe," said Bethany. "I don't know."

Michelle didn't say anything. The way she'd liked Caleb was that wispy, lonely way. The kind that gives you a radar for any time the boy you like looks at someone else. She didn't say anything, but her eyes were red and shiny, and I had an idea that she did know.

. . .

I saw the girl the next afternoon, on my way home from school. She was standing in the weeds near the place where I'd found Caleb's body, with her collar turned up and her hands in her pockets. Her hair looked much greener in the daylight.

When she glanced around and saw me there on the edge of the footpath, she smiled. It was a tight, toothy smile, but it kind of made me want to go to her anyway.

I stepped into the dead grass and went crunching out toward her. Behind her, the spillway sat gray and deserted. Our makeshift fire pit above the ditch seemed almost shabby in the daytime. It seemed so much smaller.

"What are you doing here?" I said.

"Nothing. Just hanging out." The way she said it sounded strange—foreign almost, like she was speaking a second language and really meant something else. For a second I thought she might turn and start for the ditch, but she just stood there in the knee-high weeds, waiting for me.

"Were you with Caleb the other night?" I asked when I reached her. "Do you know what happened?"

"He drowned," she said, looking sweet and sorry. "Didn't he?"

Up close, her eyes were a pale, slippery color that wasn't quite blue, but wasn't some other color either. She was taller than me, with a pointed chin and a high, smooth forehead like a fancy doll.

I stood looking up at her with my hands stuffed in my pockets, trying not to shiver. There was an icy flatness in my chest every time I thought about his body. "Yeah, he drowned."

"Oh," she said. "That's sad."

"There's one word for it." My voice sounded hard, colder than I was used to, and she turned away.

Her hair hung down like a veil, and the green looked nearly see-through in the setting sun. "It's an easy word for things no one wants to think about. It's what people fall back on—more poetic to call something a tragedy than say what it really is. Ugly. Pitiful. Wretched."

I felt myself get hot inside, like I was growing bigger. "Look, he might not have been my favorite person, but I'm not about to start calling Caleb ugly or pathetic, because he *wasn't* those things. He was mean and angry, maybe. He was obnoxious. He was a real dick. But he was *sad*."

"What do you know about sad?" she said. Her tone was vicious, like it was so utterly impossible that I could even comprehend it. "You don't know the first thing. You have no *idea* what your boyfriend writes in that notebook, do you?"

I shook my head, keeping my chin high. "He's not my boyfriend." As soon as I said it, the look she gave me made me feel like I was lying when no one else's knowing smiles or teasing ever had. "And what he writes or thinks or says in private, when it's not to me, is none of my business."

"If his thoughts are so private, he should be more careful about where he leaves them." She leaned closer, holding up a little spiral notebook. The battered cover was familiar, held together by duct tape and good intentions. "I found it in the grass behind the wall the other night."

"Great, then." I held out my hand. "I'll take it."

She was working her teeth into her lip, studying me. Everything about her made a cold tide rise in my chest. She closed her hand around the book and shook her head. "I'd rather give it to him myself." Then her voice lilted up, and she didn't smile exactly, but her eyes got wide and bright. "Unless you want to read it first?"

I wanted to grab her by the hair and make her expression change. "That's his personal property. It's *private*."

Her mouth twisted, making her look predatory. "Private?" The way she bit down on the word made me step back. "Nothing's private, *Jane*." She said my name like a swear. "No matter how fiercely they deny it, no matter how tricky they try to be, people wear their hopes and fears right out in the open."

"And so you just know so much about it then? You're like some kind of expert on whether total strangers have emotional problems? That's not even how things work!"

She shrugged, and it made an army of tiny shivers under my skin, like something was trickling down my spine. "Your boy Caleb was in a bad place. You knew. Your *friend* Evan knew. I knew it the minute I saw him, but mostly, I knew it by how he saw me right back."

Her mouth curved gently, almost a smile. Her bottom lip was full and glossy, so pale it looked bloodless. Her face was peaceful, like a carved saint, and I could see a hard, ugly hunger in her eyes that made my skin crawl. I could see her craving things. Bad things—desperation, frustration, desire. Whatever it was that made boys like Caleb drink and swallow pills and drown facedown in a foot of icy water, where candy wrappers and cigarette butts made circles in the eddies.

I could see a need so big it was nearly wicked, and I had a creeping conviction that she might devour me next, just for the crime of missing my dad sometimes, or because in Current Events, Ms. Halverson made us read the news every day after homeroom, and it was always full of diseases and complicated wars, and polar bears that drowned from global warming, or because the elm tree in the yard was dying, or because I was there.

"What did you do to him?" I said, stepping closer, weeds crunching under my feet.

The girl looked down so that her eyelashes made fringy shadows on her cheeks, like the secret flutter of feathers. The air coming off the ditch was cold, and the sun was getting lower.

"I kissed him," she said. "That's all. It was what he wanted. Since when is it a crime to kiss someone?"

She smiled then, showing small, straight teeth, like she was remembering something good to eat. Suddenly, I could see her looking around the circle of firelight, studying the faces and then settling on Caleb. Wanting him, but not the way Michelle wanted him and not the way Ari and Justin were always wanting each other.

She'd wanted all the things I sometimes wanted from Evan even though I didn't deserve them—his secrets and his hopes and fears, anything that made him Evan-for-real and not the boy who dove into the pit or swore at our teachers or kissed anyone who would stand still for it. She wanted all the sad, uncertain parts inside, and I closed my eyes for a second. My heart was beating so hard I thought I'd choke on it.

"Do you want to know what it was like?" she whispered, and I opened my eyes again. She was inches from me now, getting closer all the time. "I can show you if you want."

"No," I said, staring at her full, pale mouth. "I don't."

I thought she might do it anyway. She leaned in, and for a second, her breath smelled so much like the wild plums that bloomed along the ditch in May, sweet and alcoholic and temporary. Then I stuck out my chin and squared my shoulders, and she flinched and there was nothing but the swampy reek of the water.

"You can't tell me you've never wondered about the dark corners," she said, and she said it between her teeth. She was still holding Evan's journal, offering it now, and in my chest, the wanting beat and beat.

"You could have it," she whispered. "You could have his mysteries and his secrets. I know what it's like to be hungry."

The tenderness in her voice was awful. Her mouth was soft, and I believed her. People wanted so many things that didn't belong to them, and I was no exception. I was just as hungry as anyone else.

I left the spillway without it, without answering and without looking back.

. . .

Monday was hard and dull and ordinary. Things were starting to go back to normal. People were already starting to forget.

Evan had his notebook again. The cover was warped and the pages looked wrinkled and fat, but he was writing in it anyway. His arm was curled around the book, and his eyes were tired, purple with shadows.

At lunch, I sat in the cafeteria with my elbows on the table, knowing that even if I said something kind and understanding or asked him to talk about it, he would say what he always said. *You don't want to know.* That maybe girlfriends got to ask the hard questions, but I wasn't his girlfriend or his best friend or even someone to make out with behind the gym.

All I could think was how this was not a conversation I was equipped for. That I would never know what to say.

I sat with my chin cupped in my hands, watching as his pen scratched its way across the page. "You found your book."

He nodded without looking up. "Yeah, it was under some stuff in my room."

But even if I hadn't been out to the spillway, hadn't seen the notebook, bent and soggy, cradled in the green-haired girl's hands, I would have known from his voice and the way he avoided my eyes that he was lying.

"Do you want the rest of these?" I said, holding out my cardboard sleeve of chicken nuggets.

He shook his head, still hunched over the notebook. I hadn't seen him eat anything in days. His cheeks looked hollow and his jaw stood out. He'd been smoking a lot, which was weird because he didn't usually. Caleb was the one who smoked. Who had smoked.

I wanted to put my arms around him, but the time and the place were all wrong and we hadn't touched each other since the night Caleb died. The almost-kiss. I wanted to wrap myself around his body and hold on, but it didn't feel right. I didn't know how to touch him when he wasn't arrogant or sarcastic or brave.

"Are you going to bio?" I said, trying to sound casual and not like I was checking up on him.

He bent low over the notebook, keeping it turned so I couldn't see what he was writing. He still wouldn't look at me. "Maybe."

Suddenly, it seemed so awful—so pathetic—that I could wipe blood off his hand when he was almost a stranger, but I wasn't strong enough to hold onto him when he was sitting there across from me, looking smaller than I'd ever seen him.

He had always seemed so indestructible.

I slid my hand along the table, reaching for him, but as I did the bell rang and he stood up in a jerky lurch, fidgeting like he needed to do ninety things at once. He was scraping his books together, sticking a cigarette behind his ear, tugging the metal ring in his lip. Running a palm over his shaved scalp. He yanked my jacket off the back of my chair and tossed it to me, even though I was right there and it would have been easier to get it myself. Before, he would have made the whole thing into an excuse to touch me, maybe tucked the jacket around my shoulders or pretended like he'd zip me up, but now he wasn't even looking in my direction. He just yanked my jacket off the chair and tossed it to me.

I put it on and watched him go. He looked tall and shaky and exhausted, like a person who had stopped caring.

. . .

It was the end of sixth hour and Ari was swearing like a trucker and ignoring our microscope, trying to unknot a long piece of green string that Justin had tied to her belt loop. Evan hadn't come to class.

I reached into my coat to get my keys so Ari could cut the string, and when I did, my fingers skated over something rectangular and lumpy, like waterlogged cardboard and duct tape. I froze. Minutes ago the book had felt like nothing at all, and now it weighed down my pocket like a stone.

I sat through the rest of the class with my hand in my coat, fingers pressed against the cardboard, touching and touching it.

After the bell, I walked straight past Bethany and Michelle and my locker and the hall to my computer class. I slipped into the bathrooms and shut myself in the last stall and stood with my back against the door, waiting for seventh period to start. Waiting for quiet and stillness and the faucets to stop running.

When the late bell finally sounded, the last girls filed out and everything got so still there was only the ghost-white sound of the fluorescents buzzing. Even then, I just leaned against the door, holding Evan's notebook and trying not to breathe so fast. The pages were a mess, stuck together in places, and I had to pry them apart with my fingernail.

The first entry was nothing earth-shattering, just this list of homework problems for algebra and then a paragraph about how much he hated his stepdad and how he wanted to buy his cousin's Honda but that it would probably be March before he saved up enough.

The book was a disorganized record of every tiny, random thing that he'd collected—snappy quotes and lines from songs and snippets of conversation, the same way I collected pretty rocks and pop tabs and dropped pennies—putting them away in the notebook, no rhyme or reason, like a junk drawer for his thoughts.

I had an idea that I was seeing a part of him that wasn't quite familiar, but still wasn't that much different from the part that pinched my arm or played with my hair. It was gross to read about him kissing Taylor Mackinaw, who drove an ancient orange Datsun and had the kind of slow, heavy eyes that made everyone fall a little in love with her, even just for an hour. I skimmed through it anyway, though, because it was part of the story. He didn't belong to me. I wondered if maybe the book was a way to tell me that, or tell me that no matter what I was hoping for, it was never going to be about me and him.

Then, after something that was either poetry or song lyrics, and a sprawling, messy description of a party I hadn't been at, about a third of the way in, I found a single line, sitting all by itself in the middle of the page.

Jane Dunn is the most badass girl I know of.

The sentence was gouged into the paper in dark blue ink, printed in blocky capitals, traced and retraced and underlined, with fireworks and little lumpy stars scribbled all around it.

There was no date, but then underneath that, there was a line about how Aaron Lloyd had pulled the fire alarm and everyone had to evacuate the building and it was raining. I remembered, because it was the kind of stupid fiasco you don't forget—going outside in our PE clothes and freezing our tits off for almost half an hour. In front of everyone, I'd walked up to one of the angry-trench-coat seniors smoking out by the bus lot and told him, "Okay, I need your jacket because I'm about to die of exposure," and even though it was practically freezing, he'd sort of laughed. He let me have it.

That was at the end of October, three, maybe even four weeks before I walked out across the football field to Evan and wiped the blood off his hand and didn't ask him what was wrong.

Jane Dunn is the most badass girl I know of.

I flipped frantically through the book until I found the story of how he'd punched the football upright and

I'd crawled out from under the bleachers. Nothing about what or why. Just, *Jane talked to me today. It was like a scene out of a Wes Anderson movie or something just as good. It was kind of epic.*

Suddenly, for no reason, I felt like I might start crying. Not because it was so terrible or anything, but because it was true, and I was happy and sad and too many things that didn't have names. The book was in my coat because he'd put it there. He wanted me to read it. I smiled, feeling like maybe things weren't so terrible. Evan was sad, and he would keep being sad, but there was still enough of his old self left to want me there in the hard parts with him.

It didn't take long for things to get terrible.

Not the things about me, how I was bright and interesting and hard to understand.

Jane is colossally cooler than me. Like she knows how to be her actual self and everyone else is just pretending.

Jane is so up-front about everything. She always does exactly what she wants. If I had any kind of chance with her, she wouldn't keep me guessing. Anyone else might turn it into some kind of game, but Jane isn't like that. She doesn't screw around. She'd just tell me.

I think sometimes I'll find some other girl and forget. Then I try it. Next morning, I wake up thinking I'd trade anything else just to stand close to her.

She's always drawing pictures of Ari and them, like
she sees all their best parts. I wish I had some of those
same best parts. She never draws pictures of me.

I held the book so tight, thinking of all the
pictures I'd drawn and how I'd always been so careful
to never let him see because it was embarrassing for
him to know I looked at him. Like I had no right.

The book was a whole tiny gallery of Evan's
life, and not everything was about us. It was almost
overwhelming, seeing every random scrap of noise
that crossed his mind, and sometimes the only way I
could take it all in was if I leaned my head back and
closed my eyes.

I *had* to close my eyes at the part about his
stepdad—how he told Evan all the things he'd always
been most scared of, that he was a loser and a slacker.
That he was never going to be anything but trash, just
like his brothers and his dad. I bit my lip at *It's my fault*
Caleb's dead. At *I never told him he was my best friend* and
It's so bad without him and I feel cold all the time and it
kills me that I knew he was so messed up but I didn't ever do
anything about it.

That part that was the worst—all the pages and
pages—words shaky, handwriting drunk, maybe.
Evan, trying to figure out how to live with it, to have
known the truth or suspected it, and not have done
anything about it. I held the book tighter, thinking
how impossible it was to help someone.

I kept waiting for him to talk about the actual
night Caleb died—the details and the facts—but all

he said was, *There was this girl who came by the spillway, like we were waiting for her or she already knew us. When I saw her again, she was weird and sad. Or maybe I was. It was hard to tell where it was coming from. She was a good listener. At least I got my book back.*

School was almost over by the time I got to the end, the last scribbled lines, written in the cafeteria while I sat across the table from him and didn't reach for him or touch his hand, didn't ask about it or about anything.

Jane, this is really hard. I wanted to do it right or better or something. I'm not sorry how I feel about you, but I'm sorry I could never say it.

. . .

I called him. I called him a million times, and every time it went right to voicemail.

As soon as I was out the double doors, clattering down the steps to the parking lot, I was already hitting his name in my favorites, looking around at everyone filing out of school and knowing he wouldn't be there. I walked home in a panic, my hands going cold and numb from every time I took off my mittens to tap his name again, while every other part of me felt like I was hooked up to a car battery.

Finally I gave up and called his house. His mom answered, agitated and out of breath. In the background, I could hear his brothers shouting. For a second she just sounded confused, like she couldn't figure out why I would call the landline when we had a portable technology for that.

She told me Evan wasn't home, but I could leave a message if I wanted. I could hear her sighing into the receiver, scratching around in the junk drawer for a pen. Then she said, "Oh, for heaven's sake, he left his phone on the counter."

"No message," I said. "Just tell him I called."

After that, I waited.

I waited through dinner, through Spanish homework and algebra sets and reruns on TV and long, excruciating conversations with my mom about the dying tree in the yard. I waited upstairs in my flannel pajamas and the bad feeling just got worse and worse.

It was after ten and I sat in my room, clutching Evan's waterlogged notebook. The pages were wavy and it smelled strange, like dead, wet air and minerals. I crouched on the edge of my bed, turning it over and over. There was a smudge of something dark and chalky on the back, like the fine-textured mud that collected at the bottom of the ditch. It looked like a dirty fingerprint.

Jane is the most badass girl I know of.

Then I put on my boots and found myself a flashlight.

. . .

On the cement slab above the spillway, the smell of the ditch was thick and murky. The flashlight seemed much too tiny to depend on suddenly, throwing a shaky circle of light.

For a long time I stood in the weeds, feeling stupid and disoriented, but under that, there was another feeling. It was the feeling of being in the exact wrong place, and that's how I knew, without any question in my mind, that it was the right one. The ground by the ditch was bumpy and frozen. There was no place else the air hurt so much.

I started down the slope, picking my way through the dead grass. Halfway there I stopped, holding the light in front of me so it sent shadows splashing over the ditch. My breath was puffing out my mouth in wispy clouds.

For one awful second I thought I saw Caleb, lying facedown in his gray jacket, hands floating lifeless in the water. Then the wind blew through the weeds, making the cattails bend and the ditch ripple, I looked away and shivered hard and he was gone.

"Where are you?" I said out loud. My voice shook a little, and I felt stupid for speaking into the dark when no one else was there.

The temptation to leave was strong. It would be so much more sensible to go back to the house, to take off my boots and get in bed and wait for Evan to call, but another part of me whispered that if I did that, I was never going to hear his voice again.

Then, above me, someone moved—the scuffing sound of boots on the concrete, zippers and buckles clanking. She was there, standing at the top of the spillway by the burned-out fire pit, a pale-haired shape in the moonlight.

For a second, neither of us spoke. The sight of her made my heart squeeze like a fist. The air was so cold it hurt.

"What do you want?" she said, and her voice was low and harsh, like the voice of someone used to speaking underwater.

The wind gusted, and I shivered, holding the flashlight tighter. "I need to tell you something."

She stood looking down at me, her hair floating on the air like streamers. "What is there to talk about now? I offered you what I have, and you said no. We have no business with each other anymore."

"You were wrong about the notebook," I said. "You told me it was ugly—that it was full of all this bad, shameful stuff, but you're a liar."

That made her smile into the beam of the flashlight, and her teeth looked sharp and jagged. "Are you saying you don't know how pathetic it is that you let him follow you around like a puppy? How ashamed he was? He told me all about you when he came looking for his book."

"And what did you tell him?"

"Nothing. I just gave it back to him. And maybe I gave him something else. I might have given him a kiss before he left."

The word had a whole mountain range of edges to it, aching in my chest like something icy. "He let you kiss him?"

Her face was a pale oval, glowing like a pearl in the dark. "Don't worry, it wasn't because he loved me. When I kiss a person, it's never about love. They just feel whatever was already there."

"So, sad and guilty?"

She laughed, and it sounded shrill, like a panicked

swimmer screaming a long way out. "And worthless. And hopeless. He was never so sure that his friend's death was his fault as he was when I kissed him. Never so sure that he would end up an abject failure. He had never been so convinced he meant nothing to you. To anyone."

Under the moon, her hair looked white. The buckles on her jacket flashed, and I wondered if, when she drowned Caleb in twelve inches of water, that meant she was really strong, or that he was just really sad. If he went gratefully, willingly, comforted by her tragic face. If misery had a kind of charm.

"Do you get off on hurting people, then?" I said. "On using them? Or is that just the only way anyone will let you near? I bet it is—I bet no one lets you into their heads because they want it, no one *volunteers.* The only reason you picked Caleb is because it was *easy.*"

In the ditch below me, I saw him again, but now he lay faceup. He was smiling, but not like someone smiling because they wanted to. His mouth was blue with cold and drowning.

The girl laughed, like she knew what I was seeing. Then the wind blew harder and the moon came out, reflecting off the sleek, velvety curve of his scalp. Off the steel ring shining at the corner of his mouth, and it wasn't Caleb. It was Evan.

He lay on his back, his face pale in the water. For one electric second I thought that he was dead. Then his chest rose in a huge, shuddering breath, and he gasped, blinking up at the dark sky.

"Evan!" I shouted it, nearly choking on my own voice. I sounded close to tears.

"You can't help him," the green-haired girl said, looking down at me like I was a castaway, miles out to sea. Already so far away. "This is where he belongs now."

For one slow, dismal moment, I knew that she was right. She had to be. No way that anything so terrible, so total, could be changed. There was no fixing the things that were wrong, no taking them back. The world was exactly what it was. It was hopeless.

Then I dropped the flashlight and went splashing down into the water.

It poured into my boots, stinky and freezing, seeping around my toes. My pajama bottoms were heavy, and the flannel stuck to my legs. I flailed across to him, kneeling in the ditch so it sloshed around us, washing over my thighs. Under me, the ground was muddy, soft with silt and rotten leaves.

His eyes were open, empty in the moonlight. It seemed impossible how even with my nose six inches from his, he couldn't see me.

"He won't come back to you," the girl said behind me, and she sounded almost sorry. "It's too late now."

"I read it," I said in a breathless rush. "I read the sad parts and the happy ones and the everyday things and the ugly stuff—all of it, it's all your best parts. Please, you don't have to do this."

"He does," the green-haired girl said, gentle— so gentle. "He'll freeze to death in the creek and everyone will understand. He had to, because he lost his friend and his family ignores him and his teachers think he's not worth their time. When they find his body in the morning, no one will wonder. After all, he left his confession with the girl who was never going to love him back."

Evan lay in the water, blue-lipped and still. I could smell the alcohol on his breath. His eyes were wide, staring past me.

Above me, the green-haired girl was laughing, a damp, desolate sound. "Don't you see? This is my place, and once a person gets here, you're not saving them from anything. He *chose* this."

I didn't answer. She sounded so sure of it, so confident, and it seemed to me that she might be an expert on ugly things, on shame and grief and giving up. But she didn't know me at all.

Maybe it was easy to drown if you were empty and alone, if no one was there to help you. The water would fill you up and then the other things, the bad things, would stop, no room for anything else. But for her to think I would just stand there and watch it was too stupid. With a deep, shuddering breath, like I was about to dive, I reached for Evan.

"Don't," the girl said, and for the first time, her voice was the voice of something awful, coming from everywhere, from the ditch and the leafless trees and the low, empty sky.

I grabbed hold of Evan's jacket, fumbling in the water, feeling around for his hand.

"*Don't*," she shouted. "You had your chance, but this is my place, and now he's mine too!"

The water was rising, pitching and heaving, splashing over Evan's face. With my hands clenched tight on the collar of his jacket, I leaned back and pulled hard against his weight, dragging him toward me through the shallows, his body bumping over the rocks.

"He's not yours anymore!" Now the girl's voice was a broken fan belt, a whirling saw. She screamed it, the sound carving through the night.

Evan lay limp and heavy against my knees, blinking like he was trying to focus as the water roiled and foamed around us. People didn't belong to other people, they just picked who they wanted to stand next to.

I kissed him, and his face between my palms was freezing, but his mouth was warm like his hands had been the day I chose him.

Behind me, the girl was wailing now, howling and shrieking, making a sound like wind around the corners of a house.

I kissed him hard, like I was breathing for him, not minding the sharp, boozy taste or the way our teeth knocked together, only caring that there in the dirty little stream, he was kissing me back, reaching for me with wet, trembling hands, pulling me against him.

Jane is so up-front about everything. She always does exactly what she wants.

He pressed his mouth against my ear, shivering in my arms. My name sounded fierce and choked when he said it, and I had finally stopped waiting for him.

VII. THE LIFEGUARD

Ideas are tricky. They change like a virus or a coastline. They can dominate your thoughts for years, then settle into a corner to gather dust, and when you finally come back to them, they don't always look like themselves. The shape of them can drift away or fall apart, but that doesn't mean they're broken. Ideas don't soften or decay with time, they just grow more complicated.

> Even though the stories I've showed you don't look much like each other, in the jumbled attic of my head they're all still kind of the same thing. I know that realistically, that rationally, they share only a few common elements. Still, they are all stories about sadness and water.

It took so many versions to reach "The Drowning Place." Some I wrote down, and some I only dreamed of. Some were just drifting thoughts that crossed my mind and disappeared again.

I've written a lot of stories, and people sometimes ask if they're about me. They're not.

The stories I write are essentially pretend—math problems, object lessons. They

274

solve puzzles or attempt to answer questions, and while the questions are mine, the stories themselves are purely speculation, told through the lens of someone else.

You don't need to know about the green-haired girl with graceful hands and a face like a mermaid. You only need to know that writing can be a messy, chaotic process. It steals things from real life and then changes them. You don't need to know the truth behind the fiction, but I have this nagging little want to tell you anyway. Sometimes, telling a thing can be a way of proving it's important.

When I was fifteen, I knew a girl with long green hair and a face like a mermaid. She was older than me, and taller, with oval fingernails, pink as seashells, and the clearest, most colorless skin. She had a vintage leather jacket and sang in a punk band, and she was nice.

Once, on a warm, cloudless night in June, I was sitting alone on a stone retaining wall, counting the tiles on a big ceramic planter. She came across the sidewalk to me and tucked a blue jay feather into my hair and said, "This feather is magic. You can use it to fly you away when you're sad. You can use it to escape."

I was a little in awe of her before that, but more after. She was pretty and peculiar-looking, shy and ferocious—a mass of

> For a long time I thought that it was somehow cheating for novelists to write about their own lives. I'm not sure why I was so convinced of this—just that it seemed egomaniacal or lazy, or at least responsible for a lot of interminable books we had to read in school, about English professors who fall in ugly suburban lust with their graduate TAs and have sexy middle-aged adventures of the existential kind and talk about how relentlessly banal everything is. (Okay, that part is probably totally true.)

> She really did say this. Or at least something very close. I was still deep in my phase of documenting everything and this is the way I have it written down.
> I don't think she talked this way all the time, or at least I don't remember it, but she had a strange, precise way of shaping her words, like everything had a tremendous weight, or else like she was from a different planet. The green-haired girl in the story shares this tendency—not out of awkwardness or pretention, but because she really is too far from human to talk any other way.

contradictions. She screamed along to the radio and smoked filterless cigarettes, but she had a beautiful singing voice.

When she offered me the feather, I was slightly bewildered. It surprised me to learn that I was someone who looked sad, or like I needed to escape. At fifteen I was strange, silent and socially disinclined, indifferent to boys or fashion or music that had come out within the last four years, but I read a lot. I knew enough about communication to understand that maybe she was telling me about things that *she* needed.

It was funny to me, a little, that people would think I was sad when I wasn't, but the mistake seemed largely unimportant. It seemed far more important, suddenly, that the same people might think she wasn't sad when she really was.

The feather was streaky blue, flecked with white and gray, and I took it home with me. I sat out on the deck for a long time, turning the feather over and over in my hands. I understood that she had invited me somewhere with her, and also, it was a place I couldn't get to.

It's important to say that she is not the green-haired girl in my story. She was very much the opposite, always kind when she could help it, but she told me once that she wanted to be fierce. To be the kind of girl who thunders.

To me, this is the truest, realest magic of writing—that she could wind up in my story, not as herself, but as something fierce and wicked, at the ending I must have been headed to all along. It's

> I've always been able to escape rather effortlessly by retreating straight into my head.

> The first time I tried to type this, I typed *water* instead.

the place where all my earlier versions—the failed attempts, with their barely explored existential horrors—still show through.

In the most basic terms, the final scenes of "The Drowning Place" and "By Drowning" are about the same—a pair of mirror images, where one story is about alienation, the other about connection. Here, instead of bleak Cora, we have warm, heroic Jane, and instead of the ghost of the unfortunate Adam, we have real, breathing Evan. In the simplest sense, it was always going to come back to drowning.

Even now, there are certain things to remember. Sometimes a drowner doesn't look like they are drowning. They don't splash or struggle. Instead, their eyes slide out of focus. When you're drowning, you go quiet. You sink. Air stops getting to your brain.

I spent so stupid-long trying to figure out this story, when all the time, the one that wanted to be told was simple. I thought I was writing about the boys at my aunt's house, but that story isn't mine. It happened near me, but no matter how I tried to tell it, the words were wrong (not what I meant at all). I had a whole prolific history of my own to draw on. I'd spent years recording, thinking, cataloging, but I was always missing the most crucial detail, which is the day at the pool. My story is the happy one. My story is the lifeguard.

Because water is insidious and sinking is effortless, but in the end, it all comes back to being saved.

If I had to make a list of things that stayed the same between the two stories you just saw, it would look like this:

1) A boy drowns in a creek
2) The narrator finds his body
3) There's a kiss at the end that represents every thematic decision that the story has already been making.

VIII. THE ENDLESS OCEAN

There's a story I've been telling my whole life. It changes in the telling and the retelling, but never actually resolves itself.

When I sit down to write, ideas roll in like a tide, washing over each other. Sometimes it takes a while for them to come into focus. The answers to all my questions and my existential dilemmas are there, but distant—always floating somewhere just beyond the breakers. I've learned to wait.

This is not the last story I'll ever write about drowning.

Here is the thing about ideas: they grow and change. They go racing out into the deepest parts of your subconscious and circle back again. Memory is fluid, and time is a vast, looping thing I still don't really understand. I'm always squinting, trying to see farther. Always trying to wipe a thin film of fog off the mirror.

There are moments in the sea-chamber of my brain that never seem to end, and I know that's not the truth. Time isn't static; it's quantifiable. It moves from minute to minute, but even now, I can't shake the feeling that some part of me is still back where it started, drifting at the bottom of that far-off pool, waiting to surface.

I close my eyes and hold my breath. I fold my hands and sink. And in the long, airless moment before the interruption—before the lifeguard reaches down—time stops. Ideas come in swirling eddies, radiating, making endless rings of possibility. In a moment, the real world will intrude again and I'll rise from the cement depths, blinking in the sunlight.

Until then, I float. I wait. It reminds me of a dream I have sometimes, blue and shadow below, blue and light above.

I'm never scared until I wake up.

DOUBT

Brenna

Sometimes I think I've forgotten how to write. This used to scare me. The thing is, after a while, after I'd written enough stories, forgotten my skill set enough times, I noticed that it always seemed to hit at the exact same point—somewhere in the neighborhood of the second or third draft. Which, when you think about it, makes total sense, because it's exactly the same principle as when you go to organize a closet. First you have to pull everything out and throw it on the floor, and for a while it looks way, way worse than before, and you think you've made a terrible mistake. But actually, you are making progress, and that's why it's important to remember this analogy. It reminds me that the mess is just my process, and once I put away the bolt of upholstery silk and the coyote bones and the weird old medical diagrams, everything will be fine again.

Maggie

I knew ever since I was a tiny, evil child that I wanted to be a professional author, and I knew that learning to write couldn't be much different than learning to play a musical instrument: with enough practice anyone can pull it off eventually.

So I never doubted that I would be an author, even as rejection letters from publishers piled up around me. I was prepared to work for it. That was not where doubt creeps in.

No, doubt creeps in as I write a difficult rough draft, or as I plow through a seemingly endless revision. It's not doubt that I won't be a writer at the end of it all. It's doubt that I can make this particular project look the way I want it to. It's doubt that I can pull it off by my deadline. It's doubt that I can ever write something as good as my last one. It's doubt that it might turn out to be as hard to write as the one before that.

So what helps me through that? Writing more books. As I battle doubt in the first stages of a manuscript, there's nothing like the knowledge that I had a hard time in the exact same place last time I wrote a novel. Experience tells me that even though I feel like it will never come together, it did last time, and the time before that. And when I can't remember when I struggled before, my critique partners are quite able to jog my memory. Really, all kinds of writing problems are solved by this advice: "Great, now do it again."

Tessa

Doubt seems like such a casual word for the crippling melting sensation that occasionally drops me out of my chair and onto the floor. My ego armor is solid enough that little dings and gentle attacks hardly register—I'm doing what I love, and I work hard at it, and I always keep in mind the long game and making sure I write with no regrets.

So the hits that do penetrate are the potentially mortal ones.

Those hits are usually about my ability to communicate this ineffable, swelling story in a way that anybody will not only understand, but connect with emotionally or spiritually or, better yet, both. I write because I want to change the world—affect how people view other people, how they understand themselves and the world. The weight of it crashes onto my shoulders when I'm struggling with a small diction problem or unsure whether to use this or that detail to describe the gender dynamics or if it will be more powerful if they kiss now or if maybe—maybe—I should burn fifty thousand words to the ground and start over with the roughened, ashy pieces. It's a hard, heavy thing, changing the world; even though I chose it, sometimes the responsibility flattens me. All I can do is breathe on the floor, keep my bones intact, and eventually get back up and try again.

WRITE WHAT YOU KNOW

Tessa

I rejected this advice completely when I was a young
writer, partly because it was everywhere and I am a
contrary being, but mostly because it made no sense.
My favorite books were all about dragons and fairies
and witches, so unless the authors lived in way cooler
places than me, they were not writing what they knew,
either. But as I grew and practiced and learned better
how to write stories readers connected with, I came
back around to "write what you know" from a less
rigid, youthful, literal perspective. Now, I think that
despite it maybe being the most *misunderstood* piece of
writing advice, it might also be the *truest*.

I don't think it's about what your brain knows, it's
about what your heart knows.

Write the story only you can tell because of your
unique experiences and your unique dreams and your

unique perspective regarding the human condition. Isn't that what all stories are about in the end: us, our world, our dreams? What do *you* bring to *this* story? *Write that.* What does *your* understanding of how people interact and what people need and how people are good or terrible or impossible bring? That is what you know. *Write that.* Write it with true stories or war stories or stories that are entirely lies or stories about dragons. Go out and have adventures, meet people, learn new skills and new stories, then bring them home and reinvent them in your dreams and *write that.*

Brenna

I do not *actually* remember the first time I heard this—write what you know. I heard it a lot though, starting at about the same time I started actively searching for writing advice.

It can be a difficult rule to feel good about, especially when you're still pretty new to writing. I alternated between being intimidated by it and annoyed by it, because for a long time, I thought I didn't know anything. Instead, when I looked in all the various spaces of my brain where knowing goes, it seemed like I just had a lot of *ideas* about stuff. And if that was true—if I only had untested thoughts and if it was also true that I actually needed to *know* something first—how was I going to be able to write?

I decided, with possibly less trepidation than you'd think, that I would opt not to listen. In fact, I would *only* write about things I knew nothing about!

Characters the exact opposite of me! Worlds that not only didn't, but *couldn't* exist!

Also, as it may have occurred to you by now, I was grossly misunderstanding the underlying purpose of the message. People who tell you to write what you know are not saying (at least, I don't *think* they're saying—individual results may vary) that you can only ever write about things that have personally happened to you. They're really saying, hey, figure out your characters and your story-world, figure out the emotions that make someone act a certain way or choose a certain path. *Understand.* Don't just throw something in there because it seems shallowly self-evident, or it makes the rest of the story easier to write. Empathize. Don't just assume you know enough about something, go learn more. The thing is, sometimes we know things because they happened to us, but sometimes (more times, even?) we know things because we made an actual effort to understand them.

Maggie

"Write what you know" was the most discouraging advice I heard when I was a fourteen-year-old aspiring writer stuck in the middle of nowhere Virginia. I knew a lot about being an animal-crazy bagpipe-playing girl, but that wasn't what I wanted to write about. I wanted to write thrillers and fantasies and novels set in places that weren't my home and all about people who weren't me. I wanted to travel with my fiction. "Write what you know." What did I know about car chases in 1960s Belfast? Nothing, probably.

But "write what you know" isn't really about facts. It's about truth, which is a different thing altogether. "Write what you know" is a bit of advice that is meant to make sure you write as true a story as you can. So that means an isolated country girl could write a compelling story about a person stranded on a moon camp, because that girl would know very well how to write the truth of isolation. A girl with a lot of siblings could write a story about a rock band, because that girl would know the truth of navigating relationships with a lot of people who know you too well. A girl who practiced her bagpipes for four hours a day could write about a girl training to be an Olympic gymnast, because she would know how it felt to sacrifice time to get good at a skill few people understood.

You can research facts. It's much harder to research emotional truths. "Write what you know" means write the emotional dynamics that you've experienced. Write the emotional dynamics that are specific to you. Write something true.

Tessa said writers should have adventures, and I agree. Not to learn facts, but to have as many emotional experiences as you can, so that you can steal them and stuff them in your books. "Write what you know" shouldn't stop you in your tracks. You know enough now.

Get to work.

AFTERWORD

Like the sisters in "Ladylike," I consider myself a
collector of the exotic and the wonderful and the
shocking. And like Viola/Cora/Jane/Brenna, I have
followed faint but persistent patterns of echoes down
many a poorly lit corridor. And, in the course of all
this, I often feel like Rafel, completely captivated and
confused by the strange and magical world I've found
myself in. These are the pleasures of working with
writers: a front-row seat to the sweaty magic of their
work followed by a first look at the seemingly effortless
magic between the covers. These are also the pleasures
I hope we've managed to capture in this book. For
readers and writers alike, we hope this curious anatomy
delights and illuminates. And we hope that more than
a few of you will be inspired to climb the stairs, cross
the desert, and wade into the water with us.

—*Andrew Karre, editor*

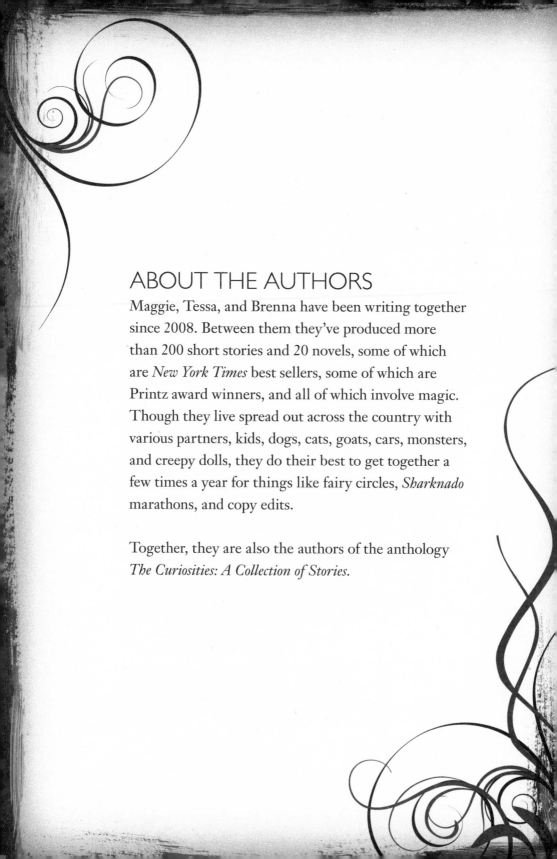

ABOUT THE AUTHORS

Maggie, Tessa, and Brenna have been writing together since 2008. Between them they've produced more than 200 short stories and 20 novels, some of which are *New York Times* best sellers, some of which are Printz award winners, and all of which involve magic. Though they live spread out across the country with various partners, kids, dogs, cats, goats, cars, monsters, and creepy dolls, they do their best to get together a few times a year for things like fairy circles, *Sharknado* marathons, and copy edits.

Together, they are also the authors of the anthology *The Curiosities: A Collection of Stories.*